ALL THAT HAUNTS US

ALL THAT HAUNTS US

SHANNON HATCH

Copyright © 2026 Shannon Hatch

ISBN: 9798904171339
Library of Congress Control Number: 2026908627

First Edition 2026
www.shannonhatch.com

To all of my family and friends who believed in me far more than I ever believed in myself, thank you. I couldn't have done it without you.

Special thanks to my editor, proofreader, and my most complimentary critic (even though she has to say nice things) my mom, Dianna Yadanza.

TABLE OF CONTENTS

DEAD END DRIVE

The fire had burned down to glowing embers by the time someone brought up Dead End Drive. Riley didn't catch who said it first, but soon everyone was sharing what they had heard about it.

"…I'm serious," Jordan was saying. "My brother knew a guy who drove down it in high school and never came back."

"That's every road if you're a bad enough driver," Caleb said.

Riley smiled into her cup, watching a thin curl of steam rise from it. The night had grown colder than she expected, and she shivered against Caleb.

They were gathered in Maddie's backyard, the spot everyone always used for summer bonfires. Someone had strung white fairy lights along the fence, but they did little against the darkness pressing in from the trees beyond the property line.

It was the last party before everyone went back to school for the fall. Nothing wild, just reminiscing around the fire and a few drinks. Riley always thought these last few get-togethers of the summer were sad. She wondered how many more summers they would have before they all grew apart and went off with their own lives.

"So where is it again?" someone asked.

"About twenty minutes out," Jordan said. "Past Moose Hollow, just off Route 20. There's a road off to the right, and they say your phone loses signal the second you turn onto it."

"That happens everywhere out there," Riley said. "There's nothing but farmland and woods."

Jordan shook his head. "No, I mean completely dead. Like your phone shuts off."

"That's not how phones work."

"Tell that to the people who drove down it."

Riley glanced at Caleb. He lifted one shoulder in a small shrug that suggested he didn't really buy into it that much, but wasn't going to waste his breath arguing with them.

"Anyway," Jordan continued, leaning forward, "it's not just the signal thing. People get turned around out there. Roads don't line up with the map, the GPS gets all wonky. One girl swore she drove straight for ten minutes and ended up right back at the same mailbox."

"Maybe she was bad at driving," Caleb said.

"Or maybe," Jordan went on, lowering his voice just enough to invite attention, "the road doesn't always go where you think it does."

Someone tossed another log onto the fire. Sparks climbed briefly into the air before vanishing. Riley pulled her sleeves down over her hands. She wasn't scared, it was obviously an urban legend. She wasn't stupid. Even so, something about the conversation had shifted the mood.

"You know what I heard?" Maddie said. "If you go down it after midnight, the radio starts picking up weird things."

"Like what?"

She hesitated just long enough. "Ghosts," she whispered ominously.

Caleb let out a snort. "Okay, now we're fully in spooky campfire story territory."

"Don't be such a skeptic," Maddie said, winking at Riley.

"I'm not a skeptic," he said. "I just prefer my haunted roads to come with evidence."

Jordan's eyes moved between them. "Well," he said, "there's one way to find out. You two should drive it."

Caleb blinked once. "Excuse me?"

"You heard me. Go tonight, It's basically on your way home."

"It is absolutely not on our way home," Riley said.

Jordan grinned. "Close enough."

A few people murmured their agreement, the harmless, conspiratorial energy of a group that wanted something interesting to happen but didn't want to be the ones doing it.

Caleb looked at Riley and waggled his eyebrows. "What do you think, can we make it down the road without the ghoooosts catching us?"

She laughed and rolled her eyes. She could already tell his mind was made up. If there was an adventure to be had or a dare to accept, Caleb was always game. She both loved and hated that about him.

"Fine, but you owe me a foot massage when we get back to my place."

Maddie clapped excitedly. "Field trip!"

"If we die, I want everyone here to feel extremely guilty," Riley said.

"You won't die," Jordan replied. "At worst, you'll get bored and turn around."

Caleb stood, brushing grass off his jeans. Riley rose next to him, looping her arm around his.

"Well guys, it's been nice knowing you!"

Riley groaned and punched him lightly on the shoulder. "Now, now, no fair jinxing us!"

They grabbed their stuff and walked away from the campfire towards the driveway. Behind him they would hear the fading laughter and chattering of their friends, and it felt to Riley like they were walking away for the last time. She knew it was just the melancholy of the end of the season and pushed the thought down. Caleb must have noticed her mood shift and reached out to give her hand a quick squeeze.

"Come on, let's get you in the car before you freeze."

The road away from Maddie's house was dark and quiet. Riley turned the heat up and rubbed her hands together to warm them.

"Remind me why we agreed to this again?"

"Peer pressure," Caleb said. "A powerful force."

"You volunteered us."

"You didn't say no."

That was true, she was used to giving in to his adventures, and they usually turned out to be fine, if not actually fun.

"You can still turn around," he added.

"And live the rest of my life knowing Jordan thinks I'm a chicken? Absolutely not."

Caleb chuckled and turned the radio on low, settling in for the drive. Dark fields stretched out on either side of the road, silvered by a thin wash of moonlight. It was a clear night, and she watched the stars as they drove.

It always surprised her how desolate the countryside could look at night.

Caleb tapped the dashboard screen, putting in the route for the so-called "Dead End Drive". The navigation software thought for a moment, then displayed a blue line for them to follow, not as far out of their way as Riley had thought. Maybe they would get this over with, and she could get home and get that foot massage started before she got too tired to enjoy it.

"You ever notice," he said, "how most of these local legends and ghost stories always happen around small towns? You never hear about weeping women in white gowns haunting intersections in Pittsburgh or anything."

"Cheaper real estate for ghosts."

"Smart. Low overhead."

She watched the map as the blue line carried them farther out into the country, past the farmland and towards the forests that surrounded the area.

"You don't actually believe any of that stuff, do you?" he asked.

"The disappearing part?"

"Any of it."

Riley considered. "No," she said finally. "But I do think strange things happen, and no one really knows why. I don't think most of what anyone says in the legends is real, but maybe *something* happens. Maybe they just don't know how to explain it, so they assume it's supernatural."

The radio played low in the background, some late-night DJ with a calm voice taking them through a soothing soft rock playlist. It was comforting background noise, the auditory equivalent of leaving a light on.

A green highway sign slid past, announcing that they were 2 miles away from Moose Hollow.

"Guess we're committed now," Caleb said.

"You say that like we can't just go home."

"We can, but then we'd never know."

She looked over at him. "You really want to know?"

"Don't you?"

Riley didn't answer right away. There was something undeniably appealing about brushing up against the edge of the monster under the bed and proving to yourself it was nothing. On the other hand, sometimes you discovered it wasn't.

Riley and Caleb both jumped as the radio was interrupted by a brief burst of static. Caleb looked over at her and laughed nervously.

"I guess that means we're getting close," he said with a nervous laugh.

A minute later, the navigation screen froze. The small arrow that represented their car stopped moving along its blue path and held in place. Caleb tapped the screen a couple of times. Nothing.

"Huh," he finally

"What?"

"It's stuck."

"Like frozen?"

"Yeah."

He zoomed out. The map lagged and then snapped back into place, but now their car icon sat several yards off the road, in the middle of an empty field.

"That's reassuring," Riley said.

"Probably just a glitch." He closed the app and reopened it. For a moment the screen went black, then the map returned. The navigation line was gone, but they were close enough to find it on their own now.

Caleb slowed and peered around as they made their way down the dark road. Just a few minutes later, they saw the wooden sign on the side of the road. It was an old wooden sign, clearly handmade. Someone had stenciled "Dead End Drive" on it with an arrow pointing down the narrow road that branched off to the right of the main road. Neither of them spoke for a moment.

"Well," Riley said. "I think maybe we found it."

Caleb let out a small sound that wasn't quite a laugh. He looked uncharacteristically nervous. "Last chance to back out."

She studied the road. She couldn't tell if it actually looked or felt creepy, or if it was just in her mind from the stories they had been telling.

"And admit we're chickens? We've come this far," she said. "Might as well finish it!"

Shrugging, he turned the wheel and guided the Jeep onto the narrow gravel road. The tires crunched as they left the smooth blacktop. They went slowly, the beams of the headlights seeming to get swallowed up in the darkness of the road ahead.

Suddenly, the radio let out a squealing feedback sound. Caleb jumped in his seat and reached for the volume knob, but just before his fingers touched it, the radio went silent. Before he could say anything, the display flickered and went black, along with all the lights and indicators on his dashboard.

"What the fuck?" he exclaimed, instinctively hitting the brakes and bringing the Jeep to a halt. Even as the words were leaving his mouth, the dashboard and display screen flashed back on, and the radio started back up like nothing had happened.

"I told you to get this thing looked at before it leaves you stranded somewhere," Riley said with a nervous laugh.

"This old thing? She's as solid as they come! Just a little bad reception out here in the sticks."

"I don't think that's how reception works, but sure." Riley glanced around them, trying to make out anything in the darkness, but even the road they had just turned off of seemed to have been swallowed up in the gloom.

"You ever notice," she said, "how roads look completely different at night?"

"They look like roads."

"No, I mean… during the day you can tell where everything is. Fields, houses, fences. At night, it's like the world shrinks to whatever your headlights hit."

Caleb glanced at her. "You're getting poetic on me."

"I'm serious. It makes you realize how much you don't actually see."

He smiled faintly but didn't reply. The trees along the sides of the road seemed to grow closer together as they went down the road, making the road feel more like a tunnel. Riley checked her phone, but she had no service out here. That wasn't completely unusual in these parts, but it did make her nervous. The time read 12:14 a.m. She set it down in the cupholder.

A moment later, the radio let out a loud stream of static. Both of them jumped, and Riley laughed nervously. Caleb tried adjusting the volume, but the hissing static didn't change. He turned the tuning dial, searching for a station, but nothing happened.

"That's weird," Riley said.

"We're in the middle of nowhere."

"Still. Usually you can pick up something."

He tried switching to AM, but it was just more static. Just as he was about to turn it off, a faint voice sounded through the white noise.

"*...don't like this road...*"

Riley felt her breath catch in her chest.

"Did you hear that?"

Caleb nodded, eyes fixed forward. The radio suddenly went quiet again, and for a few moments, there was only the sound of the tires crunching on the gravel. Finally, Riley spoke.

"That sounded like me," she said in a quiet, apprehensive voice.

"I was hoping that was just in my head. What the hell was that?"

Riley didn't answer. A reflective mile marker flashed past on the right shoulder. Mile marker 17. She watched it disappear into the darkness behind them.

"Caleb, how long have we been driving on this road?"

"I don't know, maybe 10 minutes?"

"And we're doing what, like 30 miles an hour?"

"Yeah, I've been going slow. It's super dark out here tonight."

"How the hell did we just pass a mile marker that said 17?"

"You must have read it wrong, the road started where we got on, there's no way we've gone 17 miles already. Maybe 6 or 7, tops."

The road curved gently left, then straightened. A few minutes passed in silence. Suddenly, Riley sat up straighter and grabbed Caleb's arm.

"There, you see it? It's the same one!"

"Riley, I'm pretty sure there are mile markers every mile. It's sort of how they work."

"Well they don't always say 17, do they?"

He checked the rearview mirror instinctively, as if he might somehow see the last one again. "I wasn't paying attention."

"I'm pretty sure it said 17."

"So the last one probably said 16. It's hard to see when we're driving by, they're easy to misread."

"Maybe, but I know what I saw. And how would we be that far down the road, anyway?"

"I don't know, that part is weird. Maybe they changed the road at some point and never updated the markers?"

He slowed a little more now, though neither acknowledged it. The forest thickened, swallowing the Jeep as it rolled slowly down the road. Without warning, the GPS screen flickered back to life. Their car icon sat motionless on the screen. According to the map, they were no longer on a road, just out in the middle of nowhere. Caleb tapped the screen, and the image rolled a few times like an old television screen before stabilizing again. For half a second, the road appeared again, and the map looked normal. Then they were back in the middle of a green expanse of unlabeled land.

"That's not helpful," he muttered. "Maybe it's just losing our signal because of the trees."

"Yeah, maybe," Riley said doubtfully.

He sighed. "Let's give it another minute. If it keeps being weird, we'll turn around."

She nodded, relieved he'd said it first. They approached another turn in the road, sharper than the others. As the headlights swung along the curve, something appeared at the edge of the beam. It was an old mailbox, leaning drunkenly to one side. It looked as if it hadn't been used in decades. There were no numbers on it, at least not anymore. Riley watched it pass. She looked down at the GPS screen, still showing them in an ocean of green space, and looked back up and the road. If she had kept looking down for a few seconds longer, she would have missed it. Leaning crookedly at the side of the road was what looked to be the exact same mailbox she'd seen moments before.

"Okay, what the fuck was that? You saw that, right?"

"I was about to ask you the same thing," Caleb replied, his voice shaky. "It can't be the same mailbox, obviously. Right?"

"I don't know, and I don't really want to wait around to find out. Turn around."

Caleb nodded. He eased off the gas and checked the mirrors, even though they hadn't seen a single car since they turned down this road. He began a careful three-point turn on the narrow stretch of gravel. As they turned around, Riley looked down the road they had just traveled. Her heart sank into her stomach. There was no mailbox behind them. Both sides of the road were lined with unbroken walls of trees.

"Caleb…"

"I know, let's just get the hell out of here." He straightened the wheel and pressed on the gas, piloting the Jeep back down the way they had come. A minute passed, then two. The radio gave another brief burst of static, then both it and the GPS screen died. Up ahead, brightening in the headlights, was a reflective marker with a 17 on it.

Caleb didn't slow down or say anything, but Riley noticed the way his hands tightened on the wheel. Neither of them said what they were both thinking. The road wasn't letting them leave. For the first time since turning onto Dead End Drive, the night no longer felt empty. It felt alive and watchful. Caleb kept driving, the trees sliding past in silent ranks. Riley tried to focus on letting this creepy feeling go and just getting home, but her attention kept drifting back to the marker they had just passed. It didn't make any sense.

"Okay," she said finally. "We missed something."

"Yeah."

"There has to be a side road or a loop we didn't notice."

"There wasn't."

"You don't know that."

"I think I'd remember turning onto a completely different road."

She folded her arms, staring forward. The static returned, softer this time. Riley reached forward to turn it off again and noticed a faint sound underneath it. At first, it was so quiet that she wasn't sure she was hearing it at all. She leaned forward, straining to hear.

"Are you hearing this?"

Caleb didn't look away from the road. "Hearing what, the static?"

"Shh."

They listened. For a moment there was nothing but the crackling white noise, then it resolved into a clear conversation. Riley felt the air leave her lungs as she recognized their own voices.

"*...a loop we didn't notice,*" the radio Riley said.

Caleb's voice answered, *"There wasn't."*

Riley grabbed his arm. "Turn it off."

He stabbed the power button. The display went black, but the voices continued.

"*...I think I'd remember turning onto a completely different road.*" Caleb's voice again. Every word, every inflection was identical to what he had just said minutes before. They listened to themselves finish the conversation they had just had. The speakers clicked loudly, then silence filled the Jeep.

Finally Caleb said carefully, "Okay."

Riley turned to stare at him. "Okay what?"

"Okay, that was weird."

"Weird?" she repeated. "Caleb, it just played us talking."

"There could be an explanation."

"Give me one."

He opened his mouth, then closed it. After a moment, he said, "Maybe it picked up someone else on a different frequency? Like how walkie-talkies and baby monitors do?"

"That was my voice."

"You can't know that."

"You seriously didn't recognize your own voice?"

He didn't answer. The darkness beyond the windshield felt even blacker now, as if the trees had inched closer while they weren't looking.

"Pull over," Riley said.

"Why?"

"Because I want to make sure we're not losing our minds."

He hesitated, then eased the Jeep onto the gravel shoulder. Caleb shifted the transmission into park, and they sat silently. Neither reached for the door.

After a moment, Riley said quietly, "Say something."

"What?"

"Anything."

He frowned, but obliged. "Hello."

They waited. The radio remained silent.

"See? Maybe it was just—" The radio clicked back on, and both of them flinched. Caleb's voice came through the speakers, filling the car.

"Hello."

Riley whipped her head to look at him, just to verify it hadn't come out of his mouth. Caleb looked shaken.

"I didn't say that," he whispered. "What the fuck is going on? Is someone recording us?"

The radio Riley spoke next, a nervous sounding *"Turn it off."*

Neither of them touched the console. Caleb reached out and grabbed her hand as she tried to hold back a sudden, terrified sob.

For a moment, nothing happened. Then, from somewhere behind them on the road, they heard the faint crunch of tires. They both turned at once to see headlights wash across the rear window. Relief hit Riley so fast it almost made her dizzy.

"Okay," she breathed. "Okay, good. At least we're not alone out here now." The car slowed as it neared them, then stopped maybe twenty yards back. Its headlights stayed on, too bright to see past.

"Should we wave them around?" Riley asked.

Caleb was staring into the rearview mirror, his expression tightening. "They're not moving."

"So?"

"Why are they just sitting there?"

"Well maybe they're deciding if we're serial killers," she joked, trying to brush off the increasingly wrong feeling in the car.

He didn't smile. After a long moment, the headlights flicked off. Darkness swallowed the road behind them. Riley leaned closer to the glass, trying to see. The road behind them was invisible in the darkness.

"I don't see it," she whispered. "Where did it go? Is it gone?"

Caleb shifted back into drive. "I don't know," he said. "But I think we should keep moving." He pulled back onto the road, but not before Riley noticed that when the road behind them lit up from his brake lights, it had been empty. There wasn't a car anywhere in sight.

"Caleb…"

"Yeah, I saw."

"Don't pull over again."

He nodded tensely. Neither of noticed the mile marker they passed moments later, marking mile 17 on this endless road. For a while, neither of them spoke. The Jeep rolled forward, headlights carving a narrow tunnel through the trees. Riley tried not to watch the darkness too closely, but it felt heavier now and increasingly ominous. She became aware of how tightly she was gripping the sleeve of her jacket and forced her hands to relax.

"You okay?" Caleb asked.

"Yeah. Well no, but I will be when we get the hell off of this road."

"Hey, you're the one who's already asked me to stop twice," he said with a smile, trying to lighten the mood. "I'm happy to just keep driving!"

Riley gave him a strange look, trying to figure out if he was joking or something.

"What?"

"I think you've been out here too long, we only stopped once. Trust me, I wouldn't ask to stop a second time."

"No, we've definitely stopped twice now. Just now with the car behind us, and before when you got out."

Her stomach clenched. "Caleb… I never got out of the car until just now."

He frowned, looking confused. "You did, I wanted to get out with you, and you told me you just wanted to check something."

"No, I didn't."

"You did," he insisted, starting to sound a little scared. He glanced at her, then back at the road. "You're telling me I imagined you standing outside the car?"

"I'm telling you it didn't happen." She waited for him to laugh, but he didn't.

"You don't remember?" he asked.

"Remember what?"

"You looked down the road for a long time, like you saw something or were looking for something."

A chill slid down her spine. "I never did that."

"You were gone for a couple of minutes."

"I was sitting right here." The panic in her own voice startled her.

"Okay, it's okay. Maybe I was wrong, don't worry. We'll figure this out." Caleb's shoulders relaxed visibly. "Finally. See? We're getting close to civilization again." Up ahead was a dirt driveway leading out to a field with a large barn in it.

"Wait," Riley blurted out suddenly.

"What?"

"That barn wasn't there before."

"Yes, it was."

"No, it wasn't."

"We passed it on the way in."

"I would've remembered, there was nothing on this road but trees and that one weird mailbox."

"You were looking at your phone."

"My phone had no signal."

He exhaled slowly. "Riley… we definitely passed it."

She stared at the barn as it vanished behind them into the night. Something about it bothered her in a way she couldn't quite name. Not the barn itself, but the feeling that it had appeared out of place. It was like a page shuffled into the wrong part of a book. A few minutes later, Caleb spoke again.

"You were crying." Her head snapped toward him.

"What?"

"Earlier, when you got out."

"I did not get out, and I definitely wasn't crying."

"You were wiping your face."

"I have not cried tonight." The firmness in her voice startled him. A tense silence filled the car. Riley stared straight ahead.

"Tell me exactly what you remember," she said.

He hesitated. "You told me you didn't like the road."

"I don't."

"You said it felt wrong."

She felt her pulse quicken. "I said that when we first pulled onto the road."

"No. You said it when you got back into the Jeep."

She shook her head. "No, Caleb."

His grip tightened on the wheel. "You opened the door," he continued. "And I remember thinking you shouldn't, because we didn't know what was out there."

Her mouth had gone dry. "What was I doing?" she asked.

"Just standing there, looking."

"Looking at what?"

"I don't know, Riley. Nothing that I could see." A long silence followed. Branches leaned over the road now, the canopy nearly complete. Riley became acutely aware that she could barely see the sky anymore.

"That didn't happen," she said quietly.

"I know you think that."

"No, I know it didn't."

He nodded, but his expression remained unsettled. They drove on. A minute or two later, Riley noticed something ahead, and her chest tightened.

"Slow down. Caleb, look."

"What?"

She pointed wordlessly at something ahead of the car. On the right shoulder stood a mailbox. Rusty, leaning to one side, exactly like the one from before. Riley felt terrified tears stinging her eyes.

"We turned around," she whispered.

"How? That doesn't make any sense."

"I know, but it was on the right side of the road when we first drove in, it's on the right again here, so we must have changed directions somewhere. Either that, or someone moved the mailbox when we weren't looking."

"Are you sure it's the same one?"

Riley gave him a look that told him she was positive. He didn't respond. They both knew she was right somehow. The Jeep rolled past it, and as it did, the radio gave a loud clicking sound. Caleb hit the brakes, and after several seconds, his own voice emerged from the speakers.

"You left me."

Riley turned toward him. His face had gone pale.

"I didn't say that."

The radio Riley answered, her tone trembling. *"I came back."*

The speakers fell silent again. Neither of them breathed.

Finally, Riley whispered, "Caleb."

"Yeah."

"I think we need to leave. Like, now."

He nodded. "I'm trying, trust me."

He pressed down on the accelerator. The engine responded, but the Jeep felt sluggish moving down the road, like it was driving into some darkness thicker than just the night. After a long moment, Caleb said something so quietly she almost didn't hear it.

"What if we already did leave?"

She didn't ask what he meant, because a worse thought had already begun forming in her own mind. How exactly were they remembering different things? What if they were remembering different versions of the night? The question now wasn't whether this road had something wrong with it, but whether the person beside you could be trusted to see the same thing you saw.

For a while, the only sound was the low hum of the engine. Then, without warning, static started playing from the speakers again. Caleb's voices floated through it, sounding tight with panic.

"We shouldn't have stopped."

Riley's stomach dropped, and she turned to look at him. His mouth was closed.

"I don't remember you saying that," she said quietly.

The radio Riley answered, her voice sharper than he had ever heard it. *"You were the one who wanted to keep going."*

"I never said that," Riley breathed. The argument on the radio continued.

"We're not alone out here."

"Stop saying that."

The words were clearer now, less distorted than before. Riley wrapped her arms around herself, and Caleb reached to try turning the radio off again. She reached out and grabbed his arm.

"Don't," she said. "I feel like maybe we should keep listening to it. Maybe there's something we should be listening for, or something we need to know."

"Are you crazy? You think we should listen to a possessed radio that's making us say things we never said?"

"I don't know, it's just a feeling. Everything out here is crazy."

On the radio, the other Riley spoke again, low and shaken sounding.

"Where did you go?"

Caleb slammed the heel of his hand against the console. The sound cut out instantly, and silence rushed back in. For several seconds, neither spoke.

"Well I guess that decides that," Riley said angrily.

"I'm sorry, I just can't keep hearing us like that, it creeps me out. It feels like a trap or something."

The radio clicked back on again, and they both flinched.

"Riley... where are you?" The other Caleb sounded breathless and scared.

She grabbed his wrist. "Drive faster."

"I am." The speedometer read 45 mph, but it felt like they were only going about 15. As they approached another curve, the beams of the headlights illuminated something between the trees.

"Did you see that?" Riley said, grabbing his arm.

"See what?"

"There was someone out there."

"Probably a deer."

"It wasn't shaped like a deer."

Before he could respond, the radio issued another stream of static before the other Riley's voice cut through it.

"You left me."

Caleb swallowed. "Riley, I would never do that."

"I know." But even as she said it, uncertainty flickered through her chest. The speakers hissed once more, then Caleb's voice came through much louder than before.

"That's not Riley."

Caleb's jaw clenched, and Riley felt sick, a queasy rolling feeling moving through her stomach.

"What does that mean?" she asked.

"I don't know."

But the idea had already taken root. If the radio was playing things they hadn't said, some other version of reality, then somewhere on this road, a moment existed where Caleb believed the person beside him wasn't her. Riley felt her hands start to shake.

"Caleb."

"Yeah."

"If we hear something like that again…"

"Yeah?"

"…don't believe it."

He nodded. "Same goes for you."

A long stretch of road opened up ahead. It looked as if it went straight into a lightless abyss. A second later, Riley noticed something that made her breath catch.

"Caleb, tell me you see that too." Far ahead, barely visible in the gloom, taillights glowed red in the darkness. Relief surged so suddenly it almost made her dizzy.

"Oh, thank God."

As they drew closer to the car ahead of them, they realized it wasn't moving.

"Why would someone stop out here?" she asked.

"We stopped earlier. Maybe they're lost too."

As they got closer, Caleb slowed and brought the Jeep to a stop.

"Don't get out," Riley's voice said from the radio.

Both of them stared at the silent vehicle ahead of them.

Caleb spoke without looking away from it. "I wasn't planning to."

Suddenly the brake lights of the vehicle flashed, and it rolled forward. Caleb followed at a cautious distance.

"Caleb, what are they doing? Do you think they need help or something?"

Caleb's voice responded from the speaker. "Don't follow it."

Riley whispered, "Caleb…"

He was already easing his foot off the accelerator. The other car drifted onward, driving slowly down the dark road. After a long silence, Caleb said something neither of them wanted to hear.

"What if that's us?"

Riley didn't have a response. The taillights of the other car glowed steadily ahead like two red eyes in the dark. For the first time that night, Riley felt something colder than fear settle into her stomach. It was the growing sense that this road wasn't just spooky or haunted, but somehow malevolent. A few minutes later, the car ahead of them went around a sharp bend in the road, and when they came around it themselves a minute later, it was gone. The darkness closed in again. For a long time, the road was empty. There were no more signs or mile markers. Riley became aware that she was counting her breathing without thinking about it, like when she used to run track. In for four, out for four, over and over.

"Are you good?" she asked quietly.

Caleb glanced in the mirror. "Yeah."

The road behind them stretched black and uninterrupted. She nodded and let her head rest against the seat. Despite the fear and panic she felt, she was starting to feel lulled by the gentle movement of the car and the warm, dark quiet between them. Just as she closed her eyes, Caleb nudged her arm, and she jumped, wide awake again.

Something at the side of the road ahead had caught his eye. A shape was standing near the shoulder. At first, it looked like nothing more than a trick of the shadows, a vague suggestion of a person where the trees broke apart. As they got closer, the headlights struck it fully. A man stood beside the road, facing them.

Riley felt her pulse race.

"Caleb…"

"I see him."

The man didn't wave or step forward. He just stood motionless, as still as the trees behind him.

"Maybe his car broke down," Riley whispered.

"Yeah, maybe." He sounded doubtful.

Neither of them believed that. There was something wrong with the posture. He stood too rigidly, his arms down at his sides and head tilted downward at an odd angle. Caleb slowed to a crawl.

"Should we stop?" Riley asked, even though she knew that was the worst possible idea. The question came out automatically, her sympathy overriding her survival instincts. Before Caleb could answer, the man lifted his head, and the light hit his face. Caleb slammed on the brakes and swore. The Jeep lurched to a stop, and Riley grabbed the dashboard.

"Jesus, Caleb, what the hell?" But she already knew before the words were all the way out. She saw exactly what Caleb had. The man looked like Caleb. He was the same height, the same build, and had the same face. He even had the same small crease between his brows. For one impossible second, Riley's brain tried to reconcile the sight of Caleb sitting beside her and Caleb standing in the road. Both of them were real somehow, both of them right in front of her.

The Caleb beside her whispered, "That's not possible. What the hell is that?"

The Caleb by the side of the road didn't react. He stood staring at their car, expressionless. The headlights flickered, plunging them into pitch-blackness for a brief moment. When they came back on, the figure was gone. The space beside the road was empty, with no sign of anyone having been standing there just a second before.

Riley's nails dug into her palms. "Oh my god, what the fuck is happening?"

Caleb didn't hesitate. He stepped hard on the gas, and the Jeep surged forward, tires spinning and kicking up loose gravel.

Neither of them looked back as they took off down the road. Normally Riley would say something about driving that fast on a dark and curvy road, but she just wanted to get the hell out of there and back to safety.

"Did we actually see that?" She finally broke the tense silence.

"Yes."

"You're sure?"

"Yes," he snapped. A beat passed, then she asked the question that mattered.

"Did it look like me to you?"

Caleb turned toward her sharply. "What?"

"If we're seeing things, if we're remembering things differently, I just thought…"

"No," he said. "It was me. Or it looked like me, anyway."

They drove in silence for another minute before Caleb spoke again, quieter this time.

"He was wearing my jacket."

Riley closed her eyes briefly. "That can't be."

"Not just similar, mine."

"You're wearing your jacket."

"I know."

After a moment, Riley whispered, "What if that was… another version of you?" The words sounded crazy the instant they left her mouth. Caleb didn't dismiss it though, and she was secretly hoping he would. Instead, he said something far worse.

"What if we just passed where I get out?"

An icy wave slid down Riley's spine. "What? No, what are you talking about?"

"We heard it on the radio earlier, you asking where I went."

"That doesn't mean—"

"What if we're crossing the same stretch of road more than once, just not at the same time?"

She shook her head hard. "Stop."

He nodded, jaw tight. "Yeah, okay."

Neither of them could unthink that thought now, though. Up ahead, the forest thinned, revealing a stretch of sky. For the first time in miles, Riley could see the moon. It should have been comforting, but instead it made her aware of how long they had been under the strange canopy of trees.

"How long have we been on this road?" she asked. Caleb glanced at her phone in the cupholder. The display on the front read 11:57 pm.

"Almost midnight."

"That's not right. It can't be."

"What time was it when we turned onto the road?"

"It was like a quarter after midnight."

"Riley, look!"

Riley looked up quickly to see a driveway of some type on the right-hand side of the road, about 100 yards away. It was the first driveway they had seen in what seemed like a very long time. The Jeep began slowing down as it approached.

"Don't," Riley said quickly.

"I wasn't going to."

But the Jeep had already dropped to a crawl. Something about the break in the trees lining the road tugged at the eye, making it impossible not to look. As they crept past it, Riley tried to look up the driveway, but it just led off into more darkness. As she turned back to face the road, Caleb's terrified voice blurted out of the car's speakers.

"Riley, don't let me out!"

The speakers fell silent again. Riley turned toward the man sitting beside her. Neither spoke, because without saying it aloud, they both understood something now. Somewhere on this road, somehow, there was a version of the night where Caleb stepped out of the car and never got back in.

The forest swallowed the strange driveway behind them. The road stretched forward, unchanged. They didn't talk about the voice. There was nothing to say that wouldn't make it more real. Caleb kept his eyes on the road, posture rigid now, both hands locked on the wheel. Riley watched the trees slip past and tried to ignore the growing sensation that whatever else happened on this road, their lives might never be the same. She wasn't even sure why, it was just a heavy, final feeling. The engine gave a small, uneven shudder, and Caleb frowned.

"You feel that?"

Before she could answer, it happened again, and the Jeep began to slow down.

"I didn't take my foot off the gas," he said. The speedometer ticked downward anyway. Forty. Thirty-five. Thirty.

"Caleb, we can't stop here, we need to keep going!"

"I know, I'm trying!" He pressed the gas pedal to the floor, and the engine revved, but the Jeep continued to roll forward, coasting to a stop right in the center of the lane before shutting down completely. The night was oppressively quiet without the background noise of the engine.

"Okay," Caleb said. "It's okay, we'll figure it out. Shit."

"Try it again."

He did. The engine turned over smoothly and everything came on as normal, but when he shifted into drive and tapped the gas, the Jeep didn't budge.

"Maybe it's the transmission?"

"Maybe," he said, his voice lacking conviction. He tried reversing, but nothing happened. He exhaled slowly like he was preparing himself for something.

"I'm going to step out."

Riley's head snapped toward him. "No, absolutely not."

"I just want to look under the hood, maybe I can see something."

"We heard it," she said. "The radio, you told me not to let you out."

"That wasn't me, that was something else that sounds like me. That could've meant anything."

"Or it meant exactly this."

He hesitated. The uncertainty flickered across his face, but so did stubbornness.

"We can't just sit here," he said.

"Then I'll go," she said, trying to quell the rising panic.

"No."

"Why not?"

"Because you wouldn't even know what you're looking at. Besides, if something is going to happen, I'd rather it happen to me. I'm not risking you getting out again."

She stared at him.

"That is not comforting." A faint smile touched his mouth and faded quickly into a serious look.

"I'll be right outside," he said. "You'll see me the whole time."

The words did nothing to help her feeling of impending danger. He opened the door, and cold air slipped into the Jeep, carrying the scent of damp leaves and dirt. Riley leaned toward him.

"Caleb… be careful. Stay right by the car. I'm serious."

"I will."

He stepped out, leaving the door ajar so she could hear him. For a moment, he just stood there, one hand resting on the roof, looking up and down the empty road. Riley watched his silhouette in the headlights as he walked slowly in front of the Jeep. The beams stretched his shadow long behind him. She found herself counting his steps without meaning to. One. Two. Three. He crouched near the bumper, running a hand along the underside as if he might discover something.

"What are you looking for?" she called through the open door.

"I don't know yet."

His voice sounded distant, though he was only a few feet away. Riley glanced at her phone. The time display now read 11:59, even though it had been much longer than two minutes since the last time she had checked it. There was still no signal at all. She looked back up and gasped. Caleb was no longer at the front of the Jeep. He stood several yards ahead in the middle of the road, facing away from her.

"Caleb?"

He didn't respond. She opened her own door, shivering as more cold air filled the Jeep.

"Caleb," she called again. This time he turned, and even from a distance, she could see something unsettled in his expression.

"You okay?" she asked.

He hesitated. "Do you hear that?"

She listened. At first she heard nothing, and then faintly she heard an engine approaching. She turned, but the road behind them was empty. No headlights were coming from either direction.

"Where is it coming from?" she called out.

Caleb shook his head. "I don't know, it sounds close."

The noise grew louder for a few seconds, seeming to be right next to them, then stopped completely. The silence that followed rang in her ears. Riley suddenly became aware of how far Caleb was from the Jeep now. He had walked several yards away without her noticing.

"Come back," she said. He didn't move. Instead, he looked down at the pavement and then back at her.

"What is it?" she asked.

"There are tire marks."

"Okay? It's a road, I'm sure they are plenty of tire marks."

"No," he said, crouching. He traced the marks with his finger. "They just… stop."

"Stop?"

"Like a car was here and then wasn't."

A chill ran through her, much colder than the night air coming in through the open doors. "Caleb. Get back in the car."

He straightened, and for a moment, he just looked at her. The distance between them felt wrong now. She hadn't seen him taking any steps, but he kept seeming to be further away from the car. She unbuckled and swung her legs out, stepping onto the gravel road. As she stepped away from the car, his voice exploded from the speakers, loud enough to cause a distorted vibrating sound.

"RILEY, DON'T—"

The sound cut out violently. Riley spun toward the Jeep, and in that tiny, unguarded second she looked away from him. It was just long enough. When she turned back, the road ahead was empty.

"Caleb?" Her voice came out thin and wavering, like a small child's. She took a step forward, then another. "Caleb!"

There was no answer, just silence. Her pulse roared in her ears as she ran to the spot where he had stood. There was nothing. No footsteps, no sounds of him in the trees along the side of the road, just the quiet hum of the engine. Riley stood alone in the center of Dead End Drive, her breath coming too fast, her mind scrambling for something, anything to explain this. Caleb would not just disappear like that, he would never leave her or want to scare her.

Beneath the panic, another realization settled into place. There was a version of the night where she never took her eyes off him, and he was still standing in front of her. For several seconds, Riley didn't move. Her brain refused to process what her eyes were telling it. Caleb had been standing there, not ten feet away. People didn't just vanish.

"Caleb?" The night absorbed the sound of his name without an echo. She took another step forward, scanning the trees. "Caleb!"

Still nothing. No footsteps crashing through the brush, no voice calling back. Her mind scrambled for an explanation. *He's messing with you. He stepped off the road. You just can't see him.*

"Okay," she said loudly, her voice unsteady. "Not funny."

Silence. She forced herself toward the tree line. The leaves beyond the pavement lay undisturbed. She didn't see any broken branches or anything else to suggest that a person had just run through. She turned slowly in a circle. The road stretched empty in both directions.

"Caleb," she called again, louder now. "Seriously, stop."

Behind her, the Jeep idled. She hurried back toward it, not sure what good that would do. The driver's door hung ajar from when he'd stepped out, but her own door was closed now. She leaned in and touched the driver's seat. It was still warm from his body heat.

"Okay," she whispered to herself. "Okay. Think." Maybe he hit his head. Maybe he wandered into the trees, disoriented. The radio turned on again, and static filled the night before her own voice issued from the speakers.

"Caleb?"

Riley swallowed hard. The radio version of her called his name again, sounding as scared as she just had when she was calling for him in the road.

On the radio, she whispered, *"Where did you go?"*

The speakers went dead again. Riley's breath came too fast now, and she backed away from the vehicle, shaking her head.

"No." The word felt useless against the vast darkness surrounding her. She forced herself to inhale slowly. Think. Standing in the middle of the road wasn't helping him, if he was hurt or lost, she needed to move. She climbed into the driver's seat. The interior smelled faintly of Caleb's cologne, and her throat tightened.

"Don't do this," she whispered, though she didn't know if she meant Caleb or the road. She shifted into gear and pressed the gas apprehensively. The Jeep rolled forward, as if nothing had ever been wrong. She drove slowly at first, scanning the shoulders of the road.

"Caleb!" Her voice sounded fragile in the cold air. The headlights swept the trees, illuminating nothing but still, dark woods. She was about to stop when something ahead made her heart skip a beat. There was a reflective mile marker sign on the side of the road with the number 18 on it. They had been driving all this time without ever reaching it before. She finally felt the tears she'd been trying to hold back slip down her cheeks. She knew she needed to drive away and find help, but the thought of leaving him there alone was too much for her to bear.

His voice issued from the radio, sounding heartbroken and scared.

"Riley… you left me."

Her heart ached. "I didn't," she said through her tears. "I tried to find you, I looked for you. Where did you go? Why did you walk away from the car, you knew it was dangerous out there!" The radio had once again fallen silent, as she knew it would. She was just an observer to whatever was going on where those voices were coming from. She wondered if there was another version of this night playing out where they were hearing what she had just said.

The road stretched ahead, dark and straight. Behind her, the trees swallowed the place where he had stood. Without knowing how she knew, she understood that going back to look more for him wasn't an option. He wouldn't be there.

She pressed the accelerator hard, and the Jeep responded. Her speed climbed, and soon she was flying down the road, not caring whether it was safe. A few miles went by before she noticed the trees were starting to thin. She could see the sky fully again, and the moonlight made the surrounding night seem not as dark as it had before. She felt some of the strange weight she had felt in her chest start to lift, and a moment later she saw something she had been starting to think she would never see again. There was a road ahead, stretching from left to right, and she could see a few houses along it. It was over. She started laughing almost hysterically through her tears. Was it this close the whole time? Had Caleb really only been a few miles from safety? Or had the road been waiting to get him before it would let her go?

She pulled up to the stop sign at the intersection that ended the road she had been on. It appeared to be the same place they had turned off Route 20 and onto this road in the first place. She glanced in the rear-view mirror and gasped as she saw what appeared to be a very normal road. There were a few houses behind her that definitely hadn't been there just a moment ago. She jumped in her seat as the radio suddenly began blaring late-night rock music from the station they'd been listening to before this had all started. Her phone lit and chimed with notifications coming in as it reconnected to the mobile network. She checked it, but she knew there wouldn't be anything from Caleb.

She pulled the Jeep out onto the main road and sped off, needing to get somewhere safe where she could find help for him. A few miles down the road she came to a gas station that was open and swung the car into the parking lot and right up to the door, her tires spinning on the gravel. She jumped out and ran to the door, pulling it open and stepping into the warm and well-lit normalcy of a small convenience store. A man behind the counter looked up, startled.

"You okay, miss?"

"There was someone with me," she said, her voice trembling now. "He's still out there. I need you to call for help."

The man frowned and looked past her to the Jeep idling in front of the doors. "Ma'am, I don't see anyone, are you in trouble?"

Her breath caught. "No," she said. "No, we—" She stopped short.

"Miss?" The clerk spoke gently, but his tone was guarded.

"There was someone with me," she repeated. "My boyfriend. He's still out there."

The clerk, a man somewhere in his fifties with silver hair and tired eyes, watched her carefully. "Are you sure, miss? I've been here all night, and it looked like you drove in alone," he said.

"No," she insisted. "We were together. The car stalled, and he got out, and then he was just gone. I think it took him somehow."

The man's expression was starting to look more concerned now. "You want me to call the police?"

"Yes, please call them."

He reached for the phone without hesitation, and she sagged in relief that help could be coming. They could find

Caleb, he had to be out there somewhere. People can't just vanish, whatever happened out there had been their minds playing tricks on them.

Within ten minutes, red and blue lights washed across the gas station windows. The officers were calm, but looked concerned in the same way the store clerk had.

"Start from the beginning," one of them said gently. She took a deep breath and told them everything, starting with the party and the dare, to the voices on the radio and Caleb disappearing. The officer listened without interrupting, his pen moving across the small notebook in his hand.

When she finished, he asked, "What's his last name?" She opened her mouth. And paused. The answer hovered just beyond reach, but for one disorienting second, it wouldn't surface.

"Harper," she said, recovering quickly. "Caleb Harper."

The officer nodded and stepped aside, speaking quietly into his radio. Riley watched him, a thin unease threading through her chest. It took longer than she expected. When he returned, his expression was carefully neutral.

"Ma'am," he said carefully, "dispatch isn't finding anyone by that name and date of birth."

Her pulse stumbled. "What do you mean?"

"I mean, they searched records for anyone living in this state with that information and got no results."

"That doesn't make sense."

"It could just be a glitch in the system," he said calmly. "Let's take a look at the vehicle."

They stepped outside together, the cold air biting after the warmth of the store. The officer angled his flashlight through the passenger window, then opened the door. He swept the beam across the interior. Riley frowned and leaned past him, scanning the floor and the backseats. None of his things were in the car. No scuffed sneakers that he always had in the back, no phone cable trailing from the console, not even his bottle of water from earlier in the day.

"Do you have a photo of him?"

"Yes, of course." Her hands shook as she pulled out her phone and unlocked it. She opened her photos and scrolled, expecting birthday dinners, a hike last fall, Caleb asleep on the couch with a blanket half falling off, all the things that usually documented her everyday life. There were no photos like that. There were images of Riley with friends, family, selfies in various places, but none with Caleb. Her hands shook, and she scrolled faster.

"That's not right," she whispered. "I don't understand."

"Take your time," the officer said. She opened her messages and typed his name into the search bar. No results. The officer remained still beside her.

"Do you live together?" he asked.

"No… but he stays over all the time."

"Address?" She gave it.

He nodded again, making another note. "Is there anyone we can call who might have seen you together tonight?"

"Yes, everyone at the party." Relief flooded her. Maddie would confirm it. The officer dialed and turned away as he spoke quietly into the phone. When he hung up and turned back to her, something inside Riley already knew.

"They said you arrived alone," he told her.

"No," she said, fear creeping in.

"They're certain."

"That's not possible." The officer studied her for a moment, looking concerned.

"Ma'am, when was the last time you spoke to this boyfriend?"

"Tonight."

"And before that?"

She opened her mouth to speak and then closed it. Memories shifted uneasily. Had it been dinner last week? A movie? The certainty she'd always trusted suddenly felt fragile.

"You're sure you didn't come out here by yourself?" he asked.

She let out a short, disbelieving laugh.

"I didn't imagine an entire person."

"No one's saying you did." The officer's radio crackled softly at his shoulder. He listened. Then nodded once.

"Dispatch checked again," he said. "There's no record of a Caleb Harper with even a similar birth date in this state."

The night pressed in around them, vast and indifferent. For a moment, Riley felt the strangest sensation, like standing on a floor that hadn't started falling yet, but might at any second.

"He was with me," she said.

The officer met her eyes. "I believe that you believe that." He wasn't dismissive or unkind, and that made it feel even worse somehow. "Listen, we're sending someone out there to look around. If your friend is out there, we'll find him."

Riley looked past him, toward the dark stretch of highway she'd driven to get here. Dead End Drive lay somewhere beyond it, and a thought surfaced suddenly, cold and inescapable. What if the road hadn't taken Caleb? What if it had instead delivered her somewhere he had never existed? Was she gone in Caleb's new world too?

For the first time since driving away from that road, Riley understood something with terrible clarity. She hadn't just lost him, she had lost the entire reality that had contained him.

The officers suggested she go home after taking her statement, promising they would "look into everything." One of them even offered to follow her back, but she declined without thinking. She wasn't ready to be watched. The drive home passed in a blur of traffic lights and empty streets. Every intersection felt bright after the long, dark stretch of the road.

When she pulled into her apartment complex, she sat in the parked Jeep for several minutes, hands resting loosely on the wheel. She was waiting for something she didn't understand, for something that would snap reality back into alignment. Nothing happened.

Inside, the apartment felt wrong. Not dramatically, just subtle changes. She kicked off her shoes and walked straight to the bedroom. His hoodie wasn't hanging from the hook where he always left it. There was no extra toothbrush in the cup in the bathroom, no phone charger on the side of the bed he slept on when he stayed over.

"There has to be something," she whispered. "You were here, you still exist. This is crazy."

She pulled her laptop onto the bed and opened it. She tried social media first. His name brought up no results, no old messages, no profiles with his photo. She checked her cloud storage to find thousands of photos arranged in tidy rows. Not a single one contained Caleb. Even photos where she knew for a fact he had been in them were of her alone, or with other people. The photos weren't edited, they had simply never been taken here.

Morning crept in gray and slow through the blinds before she realized how long she had been staring at the screen. At nine, she called Maddie. It rang twice before she picked up.

"Hey!" Maddie answered, voice bright with ordinary morning energy. "You disappeared last night, and then I got a weird call from the cops. Everything okay?"

Riley swallowed hard. "Do you remember who I left with?"

"Last night?"

"Yes."

"You left by yourself."

"No," Riley said. "Caleb was with me."

"Caleb? Have I met him?" The question came without hesitation. She didn't sound like she was messing with her, just like she had no idea who she was talking about.

"Caleb," Riley repeated. "My boyfriend. You've met him a million times, he was at the bonfire."

"Riley, is this some kind of prank? You didn't bring anyone."

Her grip tightened on the phone. "Yes, I did."

"You got there alone. You left alone. I remember because Jordan tried to talk you out of going. He feels terrible that he even brought it up in the first place."

"That's not what happened," Riley snapped.

Maddie's voice softened. "Riley, are you okay?" The concern nearly broke her.

"I need you to think," Riley said. "Tall, dark hair, he works at..." She stopped. Her mind snagged. Works at... where? The answer hovered just out of reach. Something with computers? No, that wasn't right. Panic fluttered in her chest.

"You're scaring me a little," Maddie said gently. "Do you want me to come over?"

Riley stared at the opposite wall. "No," she said quietly. "I'm fine."

After they hung up, she sat very still. How could Maddie not remember him either?

Riley stood abruptly and crossed to the hallway mirror. For a moment, she simply looked at herself. She was searching for something different or out of place, but her reflection stared back exactly as it always had. Everything seemed entirely ordinary, except for one thought that slowly dawned on her.

If Caleb never existed... Who was I before last night?

"Say his name," she whispered to her reflection. "Caleb."

The sound of it echoed in the empty apartment. For a moment, she had the strangest sensation that the name itself was fragile, like if she repeated it enough times, it might begin to dissolve.

Three days later, Riley went for a drive. She wasn't going anywhere in particular, just moving. The world looked normal, as if nothing had ever happened. Life continued with a steadiness that now felt almost surreal. She stopped at a red light and caught her reflection in the rearview mirror. For a moment, she studied it the way one might examine a stranger.

"You're still here," she murmured.

The light turned green, and the traffic carried her forward. Almost without noticing, she found herself on a familiar stretch of highway. Up ahead, a green sign appeared reading "MOOSE HOLLOW - 2 MILES". Her breath caught in her chest. She hadn't meant to come this way, had she?

She recognized the turnoff as soon as she got close to it. She slowed down and frowned. This was wrong. There was no old wooden sign declaring the entrance to the fabled "Dead End Drive". It wasn't even a worn-out old road, it was a fairly well-maintained country road, with a bright green sign that labeled it as Ash Lane. She knew this was the spot, it had to be. It wasn't just Caleb who had vanished, the whole reality she was in had changed. She was tempted to drive down the road just to see, but she knew nothing would come of it.

A strange calm settled over her as the miles carried her farther away. For the first time, she finally understood something that had been forming since that night. She would never prove Caleb existed. She would never recover the life that had held him. Somewhere, impossibly close yet unreachable, another version of her might still be driving with him beside her, laughing and arguing about directions. He was alive inside a timeline she could no longer touch. The grief that followed this realization was deep, but no longer sharp. It was more like an ache the body learns to carry.

Weeks passed, and her life reshaped itself around the empty space Caleb had left behind. People stopped asking if she was okay. Work resumed and routines returned, and yet sometimes, in quiet moments, she felt it. There was a subtle sense that reality was less fixed than it appeared.

One evening, unable to sleep, Riley stepped onto her apartment balcony. The night air was cool, carrying the distant sound of passing cars. For a long time, she watched the dark horizon. A thought surfaced, sad but comforting. Caleb existed. Maybe not here, but somewhere. The idea no longer terrified her. Instead, it made the universe feel impossibly vast. Then, not with desperation now, but with something closer to quiet certainty, she whispered into the dark night.

"I remember you."

45

A PERFECT DAY

When John Baker woke up on what would end up being his last morning ever, he mistakenly thought it was going to be a great day. A perfect day, even. John's bedroom was just the right temperature when he woke up, which always put him in a good waking mood. There was nothing worse, in John's opinion, than starting the day uncomfortable. He opened his eyes about five minutes before his alarm went off and felt alert and well-rested. If he had experienced any unpleasant dreams during the night, they had already faded away by the time he sat up and stretched.

As he showered and dressed, he hummed a little tune that had been playing in his head since he woke up. He thought maybe it was from a commercial or something. Maybe a song he had heard in the background of the grocery store the day before. He tapped his fingers to the beat while he waited for his cinnamon raisin bagel to toast.

After a quick but tasty breakfast, John grabbed his car keys, slipped on his sneakers, and pulled the garage door shut behind him. As he sat in his car and waited for the garage door to roll open, he clicked the button to turn the radio on. He wasn't surprised to hear one of his favorite songs playing. It was, after all, going to be a wonderful day.

The drive to the trail where he went every Saturday morning was pleasantly uneventful. There was one other vehicle in the parking lot, but that didn't bother him. As much as he appreciated some solitude on his Saturday morning adventures, running into other people on the trails could always add some excitement to his weekend trips.

John took his hiking bag from the trunk of his car, locked the doors, and set off down the trail into the cool shade of the forest. It was almost silent save for the crunch of his boots on the pine needle-carpeted trail and the occasional trilling of a bird somewhere up in the canopy. He smiled to himself. It really was shaping up to be a fantastic day.

About half a mile down the trail, the broken tree branch he had been watching for appeared. After a glance around to confirm he was still alone on the trail, he stepped off into the underbrush, glad that the ground was still pretty solid after all the rain they had gotten this week. He followed a path he knew from memory, detouring slightly now and then to avoid creating an easily discernible trail. He didn't want other hikers noticing a worn path and deciding to explore it. The officially marked trail was beautiful, but his private route led to his own personal paradise. John didn't need any markers to let him know when he had reached his destination. He knew exactly when he had arrived from the excited fluttering he felt in his stomach.

After glancing around a final time for wayward nature lovers, John kneeled among the damp underbrush and felt around for a moment before locating the edge of a large piece of plywood, camouflaged with a dark green tarp and a thick layer of dead leaves and small tree branches. The tarp slid off the plywood with a dry, rasping sound. His heart raced as he pulled a tiny silver key from under a nearby rock, brushed it off, and unlocked the padlock that secured the handle on the plywood door to the frame that was embedded into the forest floor John lifted the door open, the hinges making a faint. tired squeak. He made a mental note to bring some oil on his next trip out here. He had spent too much time and energy on this little weekend project of his to let it get run down now.

He peered down into the dark space with an excited grin. Shafts of golden light lit up motes of dust in the air and made them sparkle like glitter sifting down below him. It looked like a black hole, thanks to the layers of dark acoustic foam lining the walls and floor.

The girl sat in the corner of the small room, her hair hanging over her face as she stared at the floor. John sighed, slightly irritated at her lack of reaction to him returning This was his fifth trip to visit her, and he thought it would probably be his last The first couple of visits with a new girl were always fun and exciting, but they usually broke by the third or fourth week. He imagined that spending all of that time alone in the woods played a role in that, but it wasn't exactly like he could keep them in his basement. Besides, he left them with food, water, and a flashlight. All things considered, he didn't really think that was so bad.

John was actually surprised that this girl had lasted so long. Maybe it was because she was younger than his usual victims. Most of the time he went for college girls, hanging out later than they should at bars they didn't belong in. It was almost sad how easy it was to slip something into their drink when they weren't paying attention and get them into his car. They were in the soundproof chamber before the drugs wore off, and then they were all his. The room was too deep for them to climb out of, even if it wasn't padlocked. He kept a rope ladder hidden nearby to get in and out.

This girl had been at a bar, like all the others, but when he went through her things and snooped around on her phone, he quickly realized that she had gotten in with a fake ID. She was only a junior in high school and had just turned seventeen a few weeks previously. John watched the girl as he hooked the end of the rope ladder to the hooks just inside the door to his little "weekend retreat" as he thought of it. Something to look forward to during the long, dreary days at work. She remained seated with her head down, motionless except for a slight rocking back and forth. He could see from there that although the water he had left her was nearly gone, the food appeared to be untouched.

His great mood from the morning was starting to wear thin. She had been so feisty the week before, fighting him with a surprising amount of liveliness after four weeks of seclusion. He had hoped that she might last significantly longer, but now it looked like he would spend this beautiful day, which had started off so perfectly, getting rid of the girl's body.

Killing them wasn't actually all that appealing to him. He equated it to taking out the garbage or cleaning the gutters task. It was mundane but necessary. On the plus side, it meant he got to start looking for the next girl. Given that this one had made it over a month, he thought maybe he would change his hunting strategy and find a way to start taking younger girls. At any rate, he still had business to take care of out here today. He thought he might even be able to get her to scream a little before he finished her off.

His mood somewhat restored by the prospect of a new, even younger girl to play with. John gave the rope ladder a last tug to make sure it was secure and lowered his foot to the rung, starting to hum the tune that was still running through his head. The source of it was right on the edge of his memory, and just as he was about to grasp it, he felt his foot slip on the wooden rung. He was falling to the floor of the room before he could fully process what had happened.

He landed on his back with a heavy thud and a sickening cracking sound, like a thick branch snapping. For a terrible second, he couldn't breathe. It felt as if his lungs had been completely deflated by the force of the impact. The world seemed to freeze for a moment, and all he could hear was a faraway ringing in his ears. The sun streaming in the opening above him was blinding.

In a rush, everything flooded back to life. He drew in a deep, tearing breath, and his vision swam back into focus. After a couple of long breaths, he tried to roll over onto his side. Nothing happened. He tried to look down along his prone body to see if maybe he had broken something and was in too much shock to feel the pain yet. Still nothing. He tried harder, panicking now. His body remained motionless. He tried to scream, but nothing came out. Although he was able to breathe just fine, his chest was tightening at the realization of exactly what his situation was. He was trapped in a secret room in the woods that no one else even knew existed. The irony was not lost on him.

It could have been minutes or hours before he finally heard the girl move. This fear and panic made it hard to focus and tell how much time was passing. She was too far out of his field of vision to see her yet, but he could hear small, tentative movements. He strained desperately to turn his head even a little, or make the faintest sound, but he remained silent and motionless. He heard more movement to the side of him, and then she appeared in his peripheral vision. She looked down at him with a mixture of fear, disgust, and distrust.

He saw her leg move suddenly towards his lower body. He assumed she kicked him to see if he was faking, but he didn't feel a thing. He felt an increasing heaviness in his chest, but he couldn't tell if it was due to some internal injury or just sheer panic. He supposed it didn't really matter at this point. His only real hope at this moment was that the girl would run and tell someone where he was. He would end up in prison, sure, but that had to be better than starving to death, paralyzed in a hole in the woods.

Moments later he heard her scrambling up the rope ladder. He heard rustling sounds in the brush around the opening of the underground chamber. He closed his eyes, praying that she would hurry her ass up and get help for him. As he tried to regulate his breathing and ease the awful pressure in his chest, the tune from earlier suddenly snuck back into the forefront of his mind. Out of nowhere, it finally clicked. It had been playing on the radio the night he had driven out here with this most recent girl of his. He tried to smile, but the muscles in his face felt like a mask frozen in place.

For a few moments, the forest was quiet, and he let himself believe that the stupid girl might actually get him rescued. His breathing calmed as the tune from that night played on in his head. Before he got very far into the verse, he registered a shadow falling on his closed eyelids, blocking the warm shaft of sun. He opened them and saw the opening, light blocked out by the figure of a girl holding something large in both hands, almost cradling it. He squinted as she leaned over the opening and dropped what he realized at the last second was a large rock, pulled up from the nearby forest floor.

He didn't even have enough time to be scared, or shocked, or angry before it landed squarely on his head. There was a brief and explosive flash of pain, and then simply nothing. For John Baker, it was an ending not only to what had started out as a perfect day, but to all days after that as well.

WHAT REMAINS

The wind howled outside the old house, and the walls seemed to shudder as the thunder crashed relentlessly. The storm itself felt as if it was full of anger, of fury at something beyond its control. Angela didn't flinch. She sat in the worn leather armchair by the fireplace, as she had for so many long nights, with a cup of tea in her hands that had gone cold an hour ago. She stared calmy into the flames, as if the answers to life's cruelty might reveal themselves in the logs as they crumbled to ash.

Outside, the ocean crashed against the rocks. She could hear the groan of the old wooden dock as it struggled against the force of the waves. This house had once been her sanctuary, her isolation from the outside world. These days it was more of a prison.

Her hand trembled slightly as she reached for a framed photograph on the side table. She and Jacob, standing on the dock the day they had bought this house. They had only been married a couple of months and were still very much in the honeymoon phase. They looked so young and happy in this picture. She tried to remember what everything had felt like back then, but fifty years gave a very deceptive filter to memories. Had she really been as happy as she looked in the picture? Had he really been as warm and kind as she remembered him to be? She wasn't sure if any of it had been real, or if had been a mask all along.

The sound of footsteps in the hallway drew her out of her reverie. She didn't bother to turn and see who was approaching. She already knew. She had called the detective right before she settled into the armchair with her tea to listen to the storm. She knew it was time.

"Detective Raynor, you came."

The detective stood in the hallway, his coat dripping rainwater onto the hardwood floor.

"I knocked, but you didn't answer. The door was unlocked. Are you okay? Your message said it was urgent."

"I'm so sorry, I must not have heard you. You know, my hearing is starting to go these days. Come in, you must be soaked." She stepped aside and waved a hand towards the living room. "Sit anywhere, make yourself comfortable."

Raynor stepped into the living room and stood for a moment in front of the fireplace, the soft warmth doing nothing to soften his features. He was a hard-looking man, and he didn't look pleased to have been called out in this weather in the first place. He was much younger than Angela, maybe in his mid-thirties, but he carried himself like a man twice that age.

He sat on the edge of the couch, laying a manila folder on the coffee table in front of him. He sighed and looked up at her.

"I think you'd better tell me why I'm here, Angela."

She sat back down in her armchair and leaned back. "It's a long story, Detective Raynor. As I'm sure you know. I just thought it was time to lay all the cards on the table. It's time someone knew the whole truth." She leaned forward to the coffee table and poured herself a fresh cup of tea. She didn't bother pouring one for him. "You know, I didn't expect anyone to still be so interested in this."

"Missing persons cases don't just vanish," he said. "Especially not when his family is still looking for him."

She smiled faintly. "Family?"

"Jacob's brother filed another report. Claims you've been refusing to cooperate in the investigation to locate Jacob. He said he believes you know more than what you're letting on." He watched her closely while he talked. She knew he was looking for any sign of guilt, but that was one thing she didn't feel.

"I've told him the same thing I told all the other detectives and reporters. I told him that Jacob had left. Period. He took the car, his clothes, everything. I woke up, and he was gone."

"That's not really the truth, though, is it? I think there's more to it, and it's eating you alive. That's why I'm here, right?" He opened the folder without waiting for her to respond. He slid out photographs and papers that she assumed were his proof of whatever he thought had really happened. "The last signal from his cell phone originated here. His credit cards haven't been used, and no significant amounts of cash were withdrawn in the weeks before he left. There have been no sightings of him or his vehicle."

He didn't ask his next question out loud, but it hung in the air between them all the same. *What really happened to your husband, Mrs. Grant?*

Angela took a long drink of her tea before setting the cup on the table beside her. She folded her hands in her lap to stop them from shaking. When she spoke, her voice was quiet but calm.

"I used to think I was going crazy. He was that good at twisting things. By the end of an argument that he instigated, I would be the one apologizing. He would convince me I was wrong, that he was such a good man, a good husband. He made me wonder if I really was imagining things. Even when there were bruises, I would convince myself that it was something else. That I had bumped into something without noticing. He would say I was overreacting or even doing it to myself. I would find myself apologizing for things I couldn't remember doing or saying because he was so insistent that I had. I thought I was the problem."

Raynor's expression changed little, but something in his eye changed slightly. "Did he hurt you?"

Angela met his eyes defiantly. "Every day. In one way or another, every day."

He slid the papers back into the folder and closed it. "So you weren't exactly heartbroken when he *left*." His voice emphasized the last word, giving it a sly, mocking tone. "Why are you calling me now? What's changed?"

She hesitated. The fire crackled softly, and the rain beat steadily on the roof. She took a deep breath. "Because I think… I think someone needs to hear the whole story. And because I don't want to be alone when it ends."

Raynor tilted his head slightly. "Ends"

Angela stood and walked into the hallway, glancing back only once. "There's something you should see." She walked to the end of the hall, to a door that he assumed led to a broom closet or maybe the basement. She paused with her hand on the knob, then turned it slowly, letting the door creak open.

Beyond the door was darkness, and a smell that Raynor couldn't immediately identify. It was a damp, earthy basement smell, but with something else underneath. A faint scent of sweat, body odor, and rot. He hesitated.

"Angela," he said, his voice wary. "What is this?" She didn't answer, just stepped into the dark room, leaving him with no choice but to follow or walk away. He heard what sounded like a low, rasping cough from deep within the room. He stepped over the threshold, waiting for his eyes to adjust to the darkness. His blood ran cold as he heard a voice that definitely wasn't Angela's.

"Please... please help me. Don't leave me in here..."

He didn't know how long it had been. Weeks, maybe even months. Time was more fluid in the darkness, seconds stretching into hours and hours into eternities. Sometimes she came with food, other times not. The hunger didn't really bother him anymore. He thought starving to death would be merciful. It was bad enough that she had locked him away in here like an animal. The least she could have done was to give him quiet.

Instead, his new existence was constantly filled with the sounds of his own voice. She had recorded him secretly for God only knew how long. His days were a constant replay of everything she wanted him to feel guilty about. From a speaker mounted above the door, he heard his own voice all day and night, even in his sleep. There were recordings of him yelling at her for burning dinner, calling her stupid, and accusing her of cheating when she wore lipstick to the store. Sometimes there were apologies, but only to keep her from leaving. After every playback of his abuse, her voice echoes through the room on a loop: "Still think I was imagining it?"

It was easy enough to ignore at first, the anger and betrayal overwhelming his guilt and fear, and the position she had him in. Eventually it had broken him down, and he had screamed until his throat was raw. It didn't seem to make any difference to her. Now he just sat in the dark, back pressed against the cold, damp concrete, listening to his transgressions like a guilty man in court hearing the litany of charges against him.

He had always been good at control. Even as a child, he had understood the power of words, of pressure. He'd learned it from his father, a man who could make his mother cry without ever raising his voice.

Angela had been so easy at first. She was a sweet, quiet woman who apologized when someone else bumped into her. He hadn't even needed to raise his voice to her in the beginning. Just a look, or a sigh, or a strategically timed cold shoulder.

He thought about their second anniversary. She'd surprised him with his favorite dinner and wore the red dress he had told her was his favorite. When he came home late, reeking of whisky and some other woman's perfume, she had still smiled.

"I waited," she said softly. "I didn't know where you were…"

"You don't need to know where I am every second," he had snapped. "Jesus, Angela, are you that insecure?"

Her smile had faltered, but she nodded. She apologized. Her capacity for self-blame had seemed limitless. Later, when she asked if he had been drinking, he'd made her feel like a paranoid lunatic. He had even laughed and told her she sounded just like her mother. She hadn't dared bring up his drinking again for two whole years.

Somewhere along the way, she had started changing. He couldn't remember exactly when it had happened. Maybe it was after the miscarriage. Maybe it was when she started watching him, no longer with fear but with a kind of patient calculation. She never fought back or even yelled at him. That wasn't her style. Looking back, he thought she had been planning. When she stopped crying at his abuses, that's when he should have started worrying.

The sound of the door opening brought him out of his memories. He squinted his eyes against the sudden flood of light in the room. He heard an unfamiliar voice, not his own or Angela's.

"Angela… what is this?"

Angela stood in the doorway, looking at the man who had wasted so much of her life. The man who had once towered above her, punching holes in drywall or shoving her into doorframes when she spoke too loudly. The man who smashed a wineglass and calmly threatened to slit her throat with it when she asked if they could try therapy. The man who had turned her from a quiet but vibrant woman into a ghost. This same man now lay on the floor, arms and legs seeming impossibly thin. His face was gaunt, and his eyes looked wildly around. She felt no satisfaction in this. What she felt, for once in her life, was in control.

Detective Raynor hadn't moved from the doorway. He seemed frozen by the sight before him. His hand hovered at his belt, but he didn't touch his weapon.

"Angela," he repeated. "What the hell is this?"

"Do you know what it's like," she said finally, "to wake up every day and wonder if today is the day you'll die in your own home?" She took a step into the dark room. "You can't imagine it. You get trained to spot danger. Violence. But this kind…" She gestured toward the man in the corner. "This kind learns to blend in. It took me a long time to realize just how dangerous he really was."

A protest came from Jacob, barely audible. Angela didn't flinch.

"I didn't bring you here to make excuses," she said, still watching Raynor. "Or to ask for help. I just wanted someone to know the truth."

Raynor finally stepped inside. The beam of his flashlight swept the room, catching glimpses: an empty metal plate on the floor, a soiled blanket, a single speaker bolted to the ceiling. He exhaled slowly.

"This is illegal," he said. Not an accusation. Just a fact. "You've been keeping him here… since when?"

She gave a faint, humorless smile. "Since the day he was supposed to leave."

Raynor crouched beside the door, his gaze fixed on Jacob's trembling form. "He looks half-dead."

"Good," she said calmly.

Raynor turned toward her, something in his expression flickering—judgment, pity, something else. "Angela, why not just leave?" he asked. "Why not get out, report him, build a case—"

"He turned this house into a prison," she interrupted. "If I'd run, I'd always be looking over my shoulder. I tried that before. Do you know what he did the last time I left?"

Raynor didn't answer. She stepped closer to him.

"He sent me pictures of our dog. In pieces. Said he'd do the same to my sister." Her voice was steady, but her hands were shaking. "So, no," she said. "Leaving wasn't an option anymore. Plus, I didn't want him gone. I wanted him to understand. To know how it feels to be powerless, to be at someone else's mercy."

"Angela," he said. "What do you expect me to do? Do you really think I can just walk away from this? This in inhumane, criminal. No matter what you say he did, you can't just hold someone captive like this. I understand what you're going through, and I sympathize, but what did you think the outcome would be? Where is this going?"

That was the question, wasn't it? She looked down at Jacob. He wouldn't meet her eyes. She thought maybe he was too weak for anger, and she felt a surprising wave of disgust for the man she had tried so hard to be a good wife for.

"I don't want your pity. It's too late for that." She pulled the door shut behind her and started back down the hallway towards the living room. She returned to her chair, poured more tea, and waited for Raynor to follow her and sit down.

"You haven't answered me, Angela. What are we doing here?"

"Three years ago," she started, "You were in this very same room. Do you remember? I called the station sobbing and told the dispatcher I was afraid for my life. He had thrown me down the stairs, and I was sure that would be the night he finally went too far."

Raynor didn't respond, but she saw his jaw tighten.

"You responded to the call. You must not have been a detective yet. You looked Jacob right in the eye and believed him when he said I was being dramatic." She took a long drink of the tea before setting the cup down again. She was getting tired, but she needed to do this. "My lip was split open, and my wrist was already bruised and swelling. You advised me to try to 'de-escalate' next time. You left me here, bleeding and crying. You shook his hand and told him to have a good night. When you left, he smiled at me and told me he was right all along, that no one gave a damn what happened to me."

Raynor looked away, suddenly unable to hold her gaze. She could feel the weight of his guilt in the air between them.

"He made me stay outside that night, you know. No shoes, no coat, just a nightgown. I sat in the cold on the porch until the sun came up, all because I had the nerve to try to embarrass him in front of a cop."

"Angela," he started.

"No," she snapped, her calm voice cracking for just a second. "You don't get to say my name like that. Like I'm a human to you that deserves basic human dignity. You knew exactly what you were leaving me with that night. You just didn't care. I was just his property to you, a man who had taken an oath to protect and serve. I brought you here because I wanted you to see what you contributed to, to know what you could have prevented. Because people like you ignore people like me every day, and I'm tired of carrying the weight of this alone."

"Angela, don't do this."

She tilted her head slightly. "Do what, Detective? Give you a taste of what you gave me? A locked door, no one listening? No help, no rescue?" She leaned forward in her chair. "Tell me… how long do you think you'd last in that room? I have the feeling there's a woman at home waiting for you, one who could have recordings just like the ones I have of Jacob. Did they sound familiar?"

Raynor started to stand, reaching towards his belt for either his radio or his handcuffs, she wasn't sure which. She was sure he had a gun too, but she wasn't scared of him. She wasn't scared of anyone anymore.

"Sit down, Detective. I have no intention of putting you in that room with him. That's not your punishment." Raynor dropped his hand but remained standing. "I want you to walk back out into that storm. I want you to go back to your job, your desk, your reports. Go back to your wife and family. When you do, I want you to live knowing that you could have helped stop this."

"You think that's justice?"

"No," she said flatly. "I think it's the truth." She picked up her cup and finished the tea, setting it back down with an unsteady clink. "I know how this ends for me. Eventually someone else comes around asking questions. Maybe not tomorrow, maybe not even this year, but someday someone will. It's hard for a man to stay missing forever. I don't plan on answering those questions. I suppose you could arrest me tonight, rescue Jacob, and be the big hero. I do wonder what your sergeant would think about you ignoring the pleas of an obviously battered woman, though."

"That was years ago. It's my word against yours." All pretense of trying to help her had vanished. It was clear that he still sided with Jacob, with the men who think that marriage is a contract allowing them to treat women however they see fit, with no consequences.

"You're absolutely right. Except that I was already planning ahead, even then. I knew that someday I would need evidence. Your whole visit is on tape, thanks to a nanny cam above the fireplace. You can even see you give him a good old boy wink when you shook his hand. You knew damn well what you were doing. If you take me to the station tonight, that recording goes straight not only to your supervisors, but to every reporter in the area. Your career will be finished."

Raynor stared at her, eyes narrowed. Men like him weren't used to being told what to do by women. He stared at her for a long, nerve-wracking minute. For the first time this whole evening, she felt a shiver of familiar fear course through her. Finally, he turned without a word and walked to the front door, shutting it quietly but firmly behind him. She let loose a breath that had been burning in her chest.

The storm raged on outside, a fitting soundtrack to the turmoil that was finally ending inside. She sat back in the armchair by the fire, the same one Jacob used to sit in when he drank late into the night, slurring insults and commands. The fire crackled low, warm against her skin. Her eyes drifted shut for a moment. She felt lighter than she had in years.

She could feel the tea working. She knew it was almost time. She wasn't afraid, she'd made peace with it long ago. She was just glad it was happening on her terms. Jacob would rot in that room. Raynor would live his life knowing that he could have helped stop it and chose not to. And she would finally be free.

She leaned her head against the back of the chair. Her breathing was slowing. Her pulse fluttered, soft and uneven. She had often wondered what would be left after the pain, the betrayal, the fear, the constant noise of what might come next. Once she would free, what would remain? What would she feel?

As her breathing grew even more shallow, and she closed her eyes a final time, she finally had an answer. What remained was silence.

HOME

The rhythmic crunch of ice on the sidewalk was the first thing the woman was aware of. It took a few seconds for her to realize it was her footsteps. A few seconds after that, her vision cleared from black to a bright, hazy mess of colors and settled into a view of a concrete sidewalk along a quiet-looking residential street. She blinked a few times, trying to orient herself. She looked down and saw unfamiliar feet in unfamiliar tennis shoes, laces untied and trailing behind her. They weren't running, but they weren't dawdling either. Was she in a hurry? She didn't know.

The houses on either side of the street looked nice enough, covered in a layer of fresh white snow. It was quiet, and most of the driveways had unbroken snow across them, so she thought it must be early morning. She registered the sound of birds chirping as she continued her journey down the street. Her head hurt, and she felt sick to her stomach. She was confused. Where was she? She remembered nothing before the sound of her own crunching steps.

She thought maybe she should stop, but she didn't know where or why. She had an anxious fluttering in her stomach though, and she thought maybe she was walking away from something. Something bad. She felt the pain in her head growing worse, and the bright winter morning started darkening as if the sun were setting in fast forward. She faintly heard a pause in the icy steps, a rush of air leaving her lungs, then nothing at all. She was gone again.

"Bill? Bill, come here! There's a woman in the driveway!" Edie pushed her feet into a pair of slippers by the door and pulled the screen door open with a creak. The first step onto the porch sank her old slippers deeper into the snow than she planned, but she ignored the cold and plodded down the short driveway to the figure crumpled on the ground. She ignored the yipping of her little dog Tipsy and bent over the woman, brushing the snow away from her face. She was pretty, with fair skin and light brown hair. Her face was peaceful but expressionless. Edie held her hand in front of her face for a moment and felt warm, even breaths.

She turned back to the house, waiting for her husband to come and help her. She was afraid to move the woman, but she didn't want her to freeze either. She patted the woman on the cheek, but her eyes remained shut. Edie studied her face, but it didn't look familiar. After living in this house for nearly 60 years, Edie liked to think she knew just about everyone in the neighborhood. This had been her childhood home, and she and Bill had raised their kids in it. The woman didn't have a purse or bag, and the sweatpants and sweatshirt she was wearing were plain gray, with no brands or decals. She appeared clean and reasonably healthy. She didn't have the sickly look of some women Edie saw down in the city, vacant eyes and hollowed-out cheeks.

The screen door banged open behind her, and she turned to see her husband, Bill, stomping down the driveway in his winter boots, carrying a blanket and his cell phone. Tipsy raced out around him and made a beeline for Edie and the unconscious woman. Before Edie could stop her, Tipsy was in the woman's face, licking her excitedly. The woman's eyes flew open, shocked. Edie rushed to grab the dog and pull it away. The woman blinked a couple of times and peered up at Edie and Bill with pleasant but blank eyes.

"Am I home?"

The woman settled back into the soft couch cushions in the pleasant couple's living room. They had helped her up, led her inside and settled her on the couch with a thick crocheted afghan. The man was in the kitchen, and the lady who called herself Edie was perched on the edge of the couch, watching her with obvious concern. The woman gave her a tentative smile, but it didn't ease the look in the older lady's eyes. She felt clearer than she had outside before she had fallen, but still clueless as to who she was, why she was here, or what was happening. She remembered being outside, but nothing from before that.

The room was warm, and she could hear the faint ticking of a clock somewhere. It tugged at some faraway memory, but the memory was gone again before she could focus on it.

"Honey, can you tell me your name? Is there someone I can call for you?"

The woman shook her head. She had a sad feeling, but she didn't know what she would have been sad about. She tried to think back and remember something about herself, anything. Before she opened her eyes on the sidewalk outside, there was just a blank white wall.

"I'm sorry," she tried to say, but the words came out as a dry croak. She cleared her throat and was going to try again, but Edie put a comforting hand on her knee and shushed her.

"It's okay sweetie, Bill's making you a nice cup of tea. You just sit tight, we'll get this figured out."

The woman nodded gratefully and sat back, taking in the small, cozy room. They seemed like nice people, so she wasn't sure why she kept feeling like she might be in danger.

"Bill, we have to call someone. This poor girl seems lost. I don't know if she's in trouble or got into an accident or something, but I think she needs help."

Bill nodded as he stirred sugar into the cup of tea on the counter. Edie had left the woman in the living room to come help him bring the hot drinks out.

"Let's get her comfortable, and I'll call the police and see if they can send someone out to see her." He set the cups on a tray and turned to Edie. "Has she said anything?"

"No. She looks like she's in a daze or something."

"Well let's get something hot into her, maybe she'll come around."

Edie followed Bill into the living room, and the woman was still sitting in the same position, looking blankly forward. He set the tray down on the coffee table and lifted one of the cups towards her. She reached out and took it, her hands small and thin. Edie caught sight of a small mark on the back of one, maybe a birthmark or a tattoo. Before she could look closer, the woman tugged the sleeves of her sweatshirt down over her hands to hold the hot cup.

"I'm gonna call the police and see if they can help you," says Bill.

The woman took a small sip of the tea and cleared her throat. "Thank you," she says. "This is good. Thank you."

"You're very welcome, honey." Edie smiled warmly at her. The woman smiled back, and Bill left the room to phone the police.

"Do you remember anything at all?"

"I'm not sure," the woman says. "I'm sorry, I remember walking down the street, and then I was here. I think I need to get home. I think someone must be looking for me."

"It's okay, we'll figure it out!" Edie reached out and rubbed the woman's back, feeling how thin and cold she was. "You just sit tight and warm up."

The woman nodded and sipped her tea. Some of her color was coming back, and Edie was pleased to see that she was looking more alert and aware.

Bill came back into the room with a sigh and dropped into his usual recliner.

"Well, the cops said they'll come by when they get a chance, but they didn't seem too concerned. No missing people around here lately. They said to call an ambulance if she needs medical attention." He leaned forward to pick up one of the cups from the table. "You think she needs an ambulance, E?"

"I'm okay," the woman interrupted. "I'm not hurt or anything, I don't want to be a bother."

"Nonsense. You're no bother at all. We just want to make sure you're okay and that we get you home safe." He leaned back in his recliner. "Don't worry, I'm sure something will come back to you. You're probably just in shock or something."

The woman nodded, looking relieved. "I think so, yes. Do you have a restroom I could use?"

"Oh, of course! Here, follow me." Edie reached over and took the woman's cup from her, setting it on the coffee table with a soft clink. She took the woman gently by the arm and helped her to her feet. She showed her down the hall to the small guest bathroom, then returned to the living room.

"Bill, does she look familiar to you? Like anyone we know, or used to know?"

Bill furrowed his brow for a moment in thought. "Not that I can think of. I don't think I've seen her around the neighborhood. Why, do you recognize her from somewhere?"

"No, not exactly. It's just…" She trailed off, reluctant to finish her sentence.

"Just what, E?"

"She just reminds me of someone from a long time ago. I'm sure it's nothing."

*
**

The woman stood in the bathroom, staring into the mirror. She might as well have been staring at a stranger. She knew the information was there, she could feel little tugs of it now. Something familiar about the taste of the tea, the small tattoo on her hand, even the smell of rose pot-pourri in the bathroom. She didn't know what any of it meant, but with every new thing that some deep part of her recognized, a ripple of emotions went through her. Excitement, sadness, wistfulness, joy, all mixed.

More than anything, she felt a sense of urgency. Whatever she needed to do, wherever she needed to go, it needed to be soon. The white wall of blocked memories in her mind was wasting precious time.

She opened the small medicine cabinet and picked up an orange prescription bottle. The name on it was Edith Wright and contained a prescription for blood pressure medication. Edith. Edie, the man had called her. Did she know her? Edie hadn't seemed to recognize her, but that meant nothing. She whispered the name under her breath and felt another one of the tugging sensations in her mind. She closed her eyes and concentrated, but nothing appeared.

Placing the bottle back on the shelf, she closed the cabinet door and turned on the water. She splashed cool water on her face and dried it with a small hand towel on a brass ring. The little wicker basket on the back of the toilet tank caught her eye. She leaned down and breathed in deep, inhaling the scent of the dried and crushed rose potpourri that filled it.

The tugging sensation intensified, and for a second she thought she remembered something. A hint of a memory, sitting in this very bathroom a very long time ago. A lilting voice came from the other side of the door, giggling. She squeezed her eyes shut, desperately searching for the rest of the memory. It was gone before she could grab onto any more of it.

Frustration filled her, and she felt tears burning behind her eyelids. Why was she here? Who was she? What did she need to do?

Bill and Edie were sitting quietly in the living room when the woman returned. She sat back down on the couch and pulled the afghan onto her lap. She looked upset, but when she spoke her voice was soft and childlike.

"I'm sorry. You're both very nice to try to help me, but I can't remember anything. I thought maybe I was starting to, but…" Her voice hitched as it trailed off, and tears filled her eyes.

Edie jumped up and moved to the couch, putting her arm around the young woman's shoulders. "No, don't cry, it's okay! Everything will be okay, I promise. If we can't help you, we'll find someone who can."

The woman nodded through her tears, and Bill leaned forward to offer her a box of tissues from the side table. As she reached out to accept it, Edie started. She covered it up quickly, but Bill saw the surprised look and the color drain from her face. He gave her a quizzical look, but she shook her head at him. The woman dabbed at her tears with a tissue, and Edie looked closely at her, studying her.

"How about something to eat? You must be hungry. I can put together something for you if you want, it's no trouble." When the woman nodded gratefully, Edie rose from the seat next to her.

"Bill? A hand?" He nodded and followed her into the kitchen, where Edie immediately pulled him to the far side of the room, away from the doorway to the living room.

"Did you see her hand?" she whispers. Her face was still pale, but her eyes had a shocked look in them.

"Her hand? No, I guess not. Was something wrong with it?"

"No, not wrong. She has a tattoo on it. A little star tattoo."

"Okay? Does that mean something?"

"Listen, you're going to think I'm cuckoo. Just hear me out before you call the men in the white coats, okay?"

"This whole day has been cuckoo. Try me."

Edie took a deep breath. She knew what she was thinking was insane, but once the thought was in her head, it made too much sense to be a coincidence, even if it were insane and impossible.

"Do you remember the girl I was friends with in high school, who lived a few houses down? The one who went missing right after graduation?"

"Yeah, vaguely. Sally? Sandra?"

"Sarah. Sarah Fineman. She went missing, and no one ever saw her again. The police wrote her off as a runaway, but her family never believed it. Sarah was a wild girl, but she wouldn't just abandon her family or friends like that."

"That's right, I remember her now. Pretty girl, I remember hearing about her getting pretty crazy at parties that last year of school."

Edie laughed, remembering the antics that her old friend had been getting up to instead of studying for their last year of classes. "Yeah, that was her. The whole town searched for her for a few days, and then the interest just died off. She was a party girl, and everyone figured she ran off with some guy. I never believed it."

"What do you think happened? And what does that have to do with anything now?"

Edie leaned closer to Bill, as if whispering would make what she was about to say any less crazy. "She has a tattoo. On her hand."

"Who, the woman?"

"Yes! Both, I mean. Sarah had the exact same tattoo. Like, in the same place. And the more I look at her, the more I think… Bill, she looks just like her. I didn't notice at first because I hadn't seen her in almost 40 years, but now that I picture her… It's crazy, right?"

"So you think what, that she's related to your friend? A granddaughter or something?"

"And they just happened to get the same tattoo? No, I don't think she's related to Sarah. I think maybe she is Sarah."

The woman heard the couple whispering in the kitchen. She knew it was about her. She wanted so badly to help them, to tell them something about herself. She ran her fingers over the small tattoo on her opposite hand, just one more unremembered piece of herself. Like everything else, it tugged at a memory buried too deeply for her to dredge up.

The older woman and her husband came back into the room and sat on either side of her on the couch. She concentrated hard on the woman's face and could remember her name - Edie - but everything else about her was lost. She felt as though she should remember, like it was important.

"Honey, Bill and I were talking in the kitchen, and… well I don't even know how to say this." She reached out and took the younger woman's hand, turning it so the palm was facing down, and the star tattoo was visible. "Do you remember getting this tattoo?"

The woman shook her head, then paused. She looked at the tattoo closely, focusing all her mental energy on it. She heard a voice, two voices. Laughing. She smelled the faint scent of rubbing alcohol and thought maybe she could even taste something faint on her tongue, a bitter, alcoholic taste. She gasped at the unexpected memories, grabbing at them before they could fade away completely.

"I don't know, it's so hard to remember. Just flashes of sensation. What should I remember? Do you know something about me?"

"I don't know. I think maybe I do. It doesn't make any sense, but I don't know what else to think. Listen, do you remember the name Sarah? Sarah Fineman?"

As the words left Edie's lips, a jolt of memory shot through the other woman, making her feel like a lightning bolt. She heard a voice calling out from beyond that white wall… Sarah? Come here, you'll never believe who… and an overwhelming sense of something clicking into place. She squeezed her eyes tight.

She could see something now, a bedroom. It looked like it belonged to a teenage girl. There was giggling, and she remembered sitting on the bed, surrounded by pillows and magazines. The walls were covered in posters of bands, boys, and cute dogs.

"Are you okay? Sweetie?" Edie's voice broke through the intense recollection. She shook her head and started to cry. Edie pulled her close and hugged her.

"Is that me? Am I Sarah? Was I here before?"

"I don't know. I think… I think so. I don't know how, we were the same age. Do you remember anything? Do you know where you've been, what happened?"

The woman - Sarah, she tried to think of herself as, and it seemed to feel right - shook her head, wiping tears from her eyes.

"I remember being in a bedroom, looking at magazines. And something about this house feels like I've been here before."

"I think you have," Edie says. "With me. I grew up here, and you spent so much time here with me. You were like my sister, and then you just disappeared. The police searched for a while, but they decided you must have just run away."

"I don't understand. If you knew me when you were young, then how… I mean, you…" She trailed off uncomfortably.

"I'm old, yeah. It's okay, I don't understand either. You look the same as the last day I saw you, and that was over 50 years ago. You left one evening, late. We had been making plans for our last summer before college started. You were going to walk home, and you just never made it there. There were no leads. It was like you just vanished." Edie was starting to cry now, and Bill stood and retrieved a box of tissues for them from the end table.

"I don't remember much else. Just flashes of things, moments. I think I remember my parents a little, and you. I remember you, Edie. I'm so sorry, I don't know where I've been or what happened. It's all gone. I just want to remember and go home. I'm afraid of something, I don't…" The words tumbled out in a blur, and sobs overtook her before she could finish.

"It's okay, it's okay. You're safe here, we'll figure out what happened. The police will be here soon, and they'll investigate. They can help." Edie rubbed Sarah's back, trying unsuccessfully to hold back her own tears. The women sat together on the couch, holding each other for a few minutes, and then a knock at the front door startled everyone.

Edie laughed nervously. "That must be them now, you just sit tight. Everything's going to be okay now, I promise."

The woman at the front door was tall and elegant-looking. She was wearing a dark blue pantsuit with a long black coat over it. Her blonde hair was pulled back into a slick, no-nonsense bun. She looked very out of place as she stepped into the small, cozy living room.

"Good morning, I'm Agent Claire Carter." She briefly flashed a badge with FBI on it before slipping it back into her pocket. "Edith and William Wright?"

Edie nodded. "That's me, Edie. My husband Bill called this morning. We found this young lady unconscious at the end of the driveway."

Agent Carter nodded and crouched in front of Sarah, still sitting on the couch. "I assume you're the young woman. Do you need any medical attention? I see the Wrights have gotten you inside and warmed up."

"No," Sarah says. "They've been really nice, and I don't think I'm hurt at all. I'm having trouble remembering things, though."

"That's okay, we'll help you figure it out. Do you remember anything at all?"

"My name is Sarah Fineman. Edie said I went missing, but I don't remember any of that. We were friends, which I remember a little of. I don't understand though, if it's been over 40 years since she last saw me-"

"Shh," the agent cut her off gently. "We'll help you sort everything out. We actually received footage from a security camera from early this morning of you walking close to here, and the facial recognition identified you as a missing person from a cold case, Sarah Fineman. That's why they sent me, to figure out what happened and help you." She stood back up and turned to Edie and Bill.

"Thank you for helping her and making sure she was okay. We'll be sending another agent along later to get an official statement from each of you."

"What happens now?" Sarah asked as she stood, folding the afghan and setting it on the couch behind her. "Do you know where my parents are? Do they know I'm here?"

"We already called them, another agent is picking them up as we speak. They're very excited to see you. This is somewhat of a miracle, we rarely have good news for parents after this much time has passed. You'll need to see our medical team as well, just to check you over."

"And then I can go home?"

"Yes," the agent says, smiling finally. "Then you can go home."

Agent Carter thanked them again as she led Sarah down the small walkway to the road, where an unmarked but unmistakably governmental sedan sat. Sarah had hugged Edie tight before leaving the house, promising to contact her as soon as she was home and had more information.

As the sedan pulled away, Edie turned to Bill. "What the hell was that? I didn't want to scare the poor girl, but… Bill, it's like she was frozen in time. She got that tattoo about 2 weeks before she went missing, and it still looked like it was healing. How does that happen?"

Bill shook his head, mystified. "I don't honestly have a clue." He put his arm around her shoulders and led her back inside.

They had just finished putting away the cups from their tea and straightening up the living room when another knock came at the door. Bill left the room to go answer it and called out for Edie a moment later. She went to the door and found two uniformed police officers waiting there.

"They said they're here about the girl I called about," says Bill, frowning.

"They already picked her up," Edie says.

"Who picked her up, ma'am?" The police officer looked both concerned and confused.

"The agent, Agent… Carter, I think was her name? She said they had identified her from security footage and had already notified her parents to come and meet with them."

"Ma'am, we haven't sent anyone at all yet. We've been busy down at the station and this is the first time we've had to come out and look into this. Did you find out what the woman's name was?"

"We think so, but it's strange. Her name is Sarah Fineman. She went missing a long time ago, just after her high school graduation."

The second cop spoke up for the first time. "Wait, Sarah Fineman? Wasn't she the girl who ended up being considered a runaway? What was she doing back here?"

"You remember that?" Edie asks, amazed. No one had seemed to care that much.

"Sure do. I was probably around 10 when it happened. I remember my mom being scared to let me or my sister out of the house for weeks, just in case that girl had been kidnapped. You sure it was her?"

"Pretty sure, but it was weird. She looked exactly the same, like she hadn't aged a day. We were really close back then, and she looks exactly the same now."

The officers exchanged an unreadable look.

"I'm not crazy, Bill saw her too. I might be old, but I'm not senile yet."

"No one is calling you crazy, ma'am. Just trying to figure out what happened. You said an agent came? Did she show you any identification?"

"She had a badge, but I didn't look that closely. She said they had identified her from security footage from earlier this morning and that they had contacted her parents. She was taking her to meet them."

The cop who had remembered Sarah was frowning now.

"Mrs. Wright, are you sure this girl was Sarah Fineman? We pulled footage from all the nearby traffic and store cameras before we came, and we couldn't find anyone out of place."

"I mean, I can't be absolutely certain, but she remembered me, and she had the exact same tattoo on her hand, still healing from back then. I know it sounds crazy, but I'm not making this up!" She looked back at her husband, who was nodding along with her.

"I promise, officers, we're not making this up," he said. "I never met her when we were younger, but if Edie believes she recognizes her, I trust her judgment."

"Mr. and Mrs. Wright, no one contacted any federal agencies about this. I don't know who came and picked her up, but it wasn't anyone we called." The first cop was starting to look annoyed at having been called out here for nothing.

The second cop, the one who was still frowning, spoke up again. "Did you say they called her parents?"

"Yes," Edie says. "Another agent was picking them up, too."

"You must have been away at college when it happened. Mrs. Wright, Sarah Fineman's parents are gone. They both died in a car accident a couple of years after Sarah went missing. I think a deer or something had run out in front of their car, and they tried to swerve. They went off an embankment and were both pronounced dead at the scene."

"Oh my god, that's terrible. I had no idea. But the agent said they talked to them. She said they were going to take her home."

"I'm not sure who you talked to, ma'am, but we never called anyone. In fact, according to the footage we pulled, there's no record that anyone was walking down this street at all today." He pulled a card out of his pocket. "If you need anything else, you can call the department."

"Bill, tell them. You saw her, tell them!"

Bill looked up from his phone, a strange look on his face. "It's fine, officers. We must have been mistaken. Sorry for the confusion."

Edie tried to argue, but Bill gave her a sharp look, and she stopped. The police officers nodded at her and walked back towards their squad car. He pulled her inside and shut the door.

"Bill, what the hell? Were you even paying attention? They didn't believe me at all, they think I'm crazy now!"

Bill didn't answer, just handed her his phone. A news article was open on the screen. The headline at the top simply read, "BODY FOUND IN CHEATHAM STATE FOREST IDENTIFIED". She looked at him, puzzled. He gestured for her to keep reading. She scrolled down the page and gasped. They had found the body of a young woman the day before in a state forest a few hours away. While she had been talking to the officers, a press release had announced that preliminary dental records had confirmed that the deceased was a missing person from 4 decades earlier. Sarah Fineman. There were no details yet on what might have caused her death.

Edie stared at her husband, unbelieving. "What does this mean? Who... Bill, who did we talk to? Someone was here!"

"I think," he replied, "that was your friend Sarah. And I think that agent, whoever she was, was taking her to her parents after all. I think she was taking her home."

MONSTER

Charlie Rhodes was afraid of everything. It was bad enough that he was afraid of all the usual things 10-year-olds were afraid of, stuff like snakes, spiders, clowns, and the dark, but it was worse than that. The ticking of the grandfather clock in the upstairs hallway gave him the chills. He jumped over cracks in the sidewalk in fear of accidentally cursing his mother with a broken back. The kids in his class laughed at him in school one day because he was afraid of the balloons someone brought in for a class birthday.

Charlie was also afraid of being picked on, which was unfortunate because all of his other fears motivated the kids he knew to do just that. They were always daring him to do stupid stuff he shouldn't be scared to do but was. Once they teased him mercilessly to touch a worm out on the playground, and then laughed at him when he threw up after.

It was years of being afraid and being bullied for it that finally pushed Charlie to face one of his biggest fears. He was terrified of the underground parking garage at the mall. His mother insisted on parking down there, and every time they went shopping it was horrible. Charlie couldn't breathe from the moment the mall doors opened to the moment the car door slammed shut behind him. It was ridiculous, of course. There were always stories going around at school about the garage, though. Everyone said that a boy had gone missing from there last year, and that a monster living in the garage ate him. Charlie knew this couldn't be true, since monsters obviously weren't real. It didn't stop him from being terrified though.

Now he stood just inside the doors of the mall, looking out into the half-empty garage. The arc sodium lights cast everything into a strange orange pallor. Three kids from his class stood just behind him, daring him to go to the opposite end of the garage, touch the wall, and come back. For them, it would have been nothing, but for Charlie, it might as well have been across a chasm full of lava.

The teasing and laughing had finally pushed him to the breaking point. He had to do something, and facing the parking garage might as well be it. His mom was busy shopping and had given him a handful of quarters for the arcade. He could feel them clinking in his pocket against the little pocketknife his dad had given him for his last birthday. He said it would keep him safe, but Charlie doubted it would work against a monster. He took a deep breath and pushed the doors open, feeling the stale and slightly mildewy air of the parking garage rush in around him.

The laughter and prodding of the kids faded as the door swung shut behind him. The parking garage was quiet, save for the humming of some hidden machinery somewhere. The lights glared above him, but the areas between them were shadowy and dim. He took a few steps forward, his sneakers barely making a sound on the concrete floor, almost as if the garage were swallowing up his sounds.

Charlie could feel his heart racing already. He knew it was ridiculous, but his body was starting to panic. The garage was about half full, the cars watching silently as he crept down the center aisle. He glanced back at the mall doors and saw the three kids from his class peering through, their laughter clear even if he couldn't hear it anymore. Shame and anger mixed with fear, making his stomach churn.

Turning away, he continued to walk slowly, his fists clenched at his sides. The smell of oil and rubber grew stronger as he made his way deeper into the garage. The orange glow from the lights seemed to intensify, giving the lit areas an otherworldly glow and pushing the shadows in between deeper into darkness. He could feel his heart thumping as he walked, and a trickle of sweat made its way down the middle of his back.

Suddenly he heard a sound from ahead, a muted scrape like someone scuffing their shoe or dragging something along the ground. He froze, ready to bolt back to the safety of the mall. He listened carefully, but couldn't tell if he was hearing faint breathing in the darkness or if it was just his terrified imagination running wild. He didn't bother looking back at the doors, he knew they were still watching him. If he ran now, he'd never live it down.

He smelled something else in the air now, something faintly rotten. He thought of the smell of damp leaves made in the fall and wondered if it was coming through the ventilation system. It wasn't quite that smell, but it was close. Something gone bad, not quite like rotting meat and not quite like body odor, but somewhere in between. Whatever it was turned his stomach and made him want to run as far and as fast as he could.

Charlie shook his head violently, not willing to let his stupid fears ruin his life. He breathed in deep and shouted into the empty garage, a wordless sound of defiance and anger echoing off the walls and cars around him. As his own voice faded away into the depths of the garage, he thought he heard what sounded like a low laugh, a menacing and slow sound. It seemed to come from the very garage itself, seeping out through the damp concrete and metal ductwork.

His heart felt like it stopped in his chest. He could definitely hear breathing now, and it was deep and rasping. He hadn't been imagining it, there was something else in this parking garage with him. He was past most of the cars now, but there were still a few parked here and there. The breathing seemed to come from his left, from behind a large black SUV. Every muscle in his body wanted to run, but it felt like he was made of stone. He strained his eyes to see into the vehicle, but the windows were darkly tinted.

He heard the scuffing sound again, louder and closer than before. He was sure it was coming from the other side of the black SUV now, and his lungs felt like they were deflating. He tried to breathe in, but nothing was happening. The sound continued, and Charlie felt like he was going mad from the terror coursing through him. He begged his body to respond, to turn and run for safety, he didn't care what those kids thought anymore.

As he watched in helpless horror, a figure moved out from behind the vehicle, crouched low to the ground and moving fast. Charlie's muscles finally broke their paralysis as he saw a hard reach out, and he turned and started running. He shrieked in terror and saw the boys behind the mall doors suddenly step back in shock, seeing whatever was behind him.

As the hand snatched at the back of his shirt, he saw them turn and run into the mall, leaving him alone in the garage as he was dragged backward. He tried to scream again, but something covered his mouth. Seconds later, the parking garage was once again silent.

It was nearly six hours later when a passing couple found Charlie walking along the shoulder of the road a mile from the mall. He was missing his shoes and one sock. There was dried blood on his clothes that didn't all belong to him.

When they tried to ask what had happened, Charlie only said that he had fought a monster. After that, he wouldn't speak at all. He just stood there trembling, the small pocketknife clutched so tightly in his hand that the woman later said she was afraid to take it from him.

Police found the body before midnight. The man lay behind a row of dumpsters near the far exit of the parking garage. There were wounds on his hands and throat that suggested a violent struggle. One officer quietly remarked that it must have taken an incredible amount of determination for a child to keep fighting like that. Near the body, they found several items that were later connected to the disappearance of another boy the year before.

Charlie spent two days in the hospital. Aside from dehydration, bruising around his neck, and a handful of shallow cuts, the doctors were surprised by how physically intact he was. His mental recovery was harder to measure.

When the police came to speak with him, Charlie stared past them at the window. They explained that the man who attacked him was dead. Charlie shook his head slowly.

"No," he said. His voice was rough, as if he hadn't used it in a long time. "It wasn't a man."

The officers exchanged a glance but said nothing.

"It was a monster," Charlie continued. "Everyone said I was scared of everything." He swallowed. "But I wasn't scared when it mattered."

One officer gently asked what had happened during the hours he was missing. Charlie looked down at his hands. For a few moments, the room was silent.

"I made sure he stopped moving before I left. The monster won't scare anyone anymore."

That was the last thing Charlie Rhodes ever said about what happened in the parking garage. After that day, no one ever heard him talk about monsters again, and no one ever called him a scaredy-cat.

RESTART

J enny woke up late in the morning, with the sun already streaming through the bedroom curtains. She rolled over to greet her husband, but his side of the bed was vacant. She ran her hand over the wrinkled sheets, feeling the last traces of warmth from his body fading away. She rubbed her eyes and stretched out on the comfortable bed, dreading the moment she had to put her feet on the cold hardwood floor and leave this cozy cocoon.

She could hear Michael banging stuff around in the kitchen and could smell the aroma of coffee wafting up the stairs. She sighed, and with a final groaning stretch, she rolled out of bed and shrugged on a sweater to face the chilly downstairs. It was only the beginning of October, but it looked like it was time to start turning up the heat at night. Luckily, her husband of only five short days was keeping her nice and cozy upstairs. The downstairs looked foreign to her after so many days holed up in the bedroom celebrating their happiness.

She came around the corner into the kitchen to see Michael rummaging through the cupboards and refrigerator, muttering to himself.

"Can I help you find something, dear?"

He jumped at her voice, whirling around sheepishly. He gestured with a hand at their pretty much bare cupboards and pantry.

"I think it might be time to end the honeymoon and go to the grocery store," he responded with a laugh. "Not that I haven't loved the first week of our marriage, but if we're going to keep this up, we need more sustenance than a box of baking soda and half a loaf of stale bread. Unless you were looking for my world-famous baking soda sandwiches, that is. Then you have come to the right place, my dear."

Jenny rolled her eyes and laughed. It had been a whirlwind few days. She hadn't noticed just how empty the kitchen was getting.

"Well, I suppose if this food thing is so important to you..." She stepped into his embrace and breathed in the smell she was becoming so accustomed to.

"It is. But don't worry, your ever faithful and devoted husband will come along to carry the bags. Now the food might be gone, but let's go see if there's a little hot water left to share." He grabbed her up in his arms and carried her squealing over his shoulder back up the stairs to get ready for the day.

The streets were lively as Michael drove the few blocks to the grocery store. They lived in a small town, but there were always plenty of kids running around and families hanging out in the park. It was the kind of town where everyone knew everybody's names, and neighbors were always welcome to stop by for a cup of coffee. Jenny loved the town, but sometimes it just seemed a little too small for her. She loved the idea of being lost in a big city, surrounded by a sea of strangers all caught up in their own lives.

The parking lot at the store was only about half full, which was normal for a Saturday morning. The gleaming row of carts stood ready, and Michael grabbed one and headed into the store. Jenny took a deep breath once inside. She always loved the low buzz of the fluorescent lighting, the faint smell of fruit and cardboard that always seemed to drift about the old market, and the hum of shopping cart tires on the worn linoleum floor. She had been shopping here since she was a kid, and Michael was the boy down the street that she had a major crush on. Years later, he laughed with her over her old diary, and the scribbles of his name decorated with hearts and kisses. They were just meant to be, he said.

"Well, well, if it isn't the happy couple, coming up for air at last!" Jenny and Michael turned to see Mary Holmes waving to them from the opposite end of the pasta aisle. They smiled as they made their way over to her. Mrs. Holmes has been their English teacher in high school. She was a favorite teacher of most kids, and she had been older than dirt even before they had her in freshman year.

"Congratulations, my dears. You look so happy together. What happened, finally ran out of food and had to face the world?"

Jenny blushed. "Yes, actually. We got carried away for a few days."

"Nothing at all wrong with that. It's nice to see such happy newlyweds. I'd better get my shopping finished and get home before Mr. Holmes thinks I got lost out here, but I'm so happy for you two. I wish you both the best!"

Michael and Jenny thanked her and made their way up and down the aisles. Their cart got heavier with every turn, and they finally decided that enough was enough, and they would have more than enough to fill the cupboards back up. Only one register was open, so they took their place in line behind a few other families, and Jenny leaned forward against the cart to wait. Michael stood beside her, lightly rubbing her back. The combination of the warm store and Michael's soft touch was almost putting her to sleep.

Suddenly, all the lights in the store went out. It was bright outside, so light still filtered in through the front windows, but the back of the store was cast into dusty shadows. The silence left from the absence of the fluorescent buzz was filled with worried whispering. Jenny looked up at Michael, who smiled back down at her.

"Just a little power outage. Nothing to worry about. Someone probably hit a pole somewhere, or another squirrel got into a transformer like last year. I'm sure they'll get it back up and running soon."

"I hope so. Although we could always spend a night in front of the fireplace. I guess it wouldn't be the end of the world."

Michael laughed and hugged her.

"That's my girl, always thinking on the bright side."

"Another squirrel, I suppose?" Mrs. Holmes pulled her cart up alongside theirs and squinted towards the big plate-glass windows in the store's front. Michael turned to smile at her.

"I just told Jenny the same thing. I'm sure it's nothing." The hand rubbing Jenny's back slowed to a stop. He had been hoping that this would be a quick trip, followed by a few more hours in bed before they separated themselves again for dinner. He tried unsuccessfully to will the lights on.

The cashier was at a loss momentarily. If the power stayed off much longer, they would have to ring up customers by hand and limit them to the essentials. It had happened before, and Jenny had to stifle a laugh at old Mr. Hodgkins behind them. She saw him tighten his grip imperceptibly on the case of beer in his arms. She was pretty sure he didn't plan on leaving the store without it, working registers or not.

The store murmured with low conversations, everyone quiet with the lack of background music and the ever-present hum of refrigeration units and chiming cash registers gone. None of them were overly concerned with the sudden loss of power until they heard the scream.

Jenny jumped, startled by the sudden sound. It wasn't quite the scream of a woman being torn to shreds or witnessing the horror of an alien invasion, but more of a shock, as if someone had pulled a very ill-timed prank on her. Nevertheless, a couple of the patrons closest to the doors rushed outside to see what was going on.

Michael looked like he wanted to go see what was going on, and Jenny motioned him towards the doors.

"You should go see if they need help. We'll be fine in here, I can't imagine it's anything too bad. Probably that old geezer that hangs out by Sherman Street pulling out his willie again. This will be the third time this year!"

Michael laughed and squeezed her hand. "I'll be back. If you hear me scream, it was definitely the Willie Man."

She laughed as he moved through the crowd and helped the two men already up there pull open the now powerless automatic doors. Jenny turned to Mrs. Holmes and smiled. This was going to be a long afternoon.

Stepping out into the bright sunlight, Michael immediately felt the wrongness in the air. It wasn't obvious what had caused the unknown woman to scream, but you could tell something was off in a big way. He and the other guys from the store stood still for a moment, taking in the scene. A young woman was sitting on a bench in front of the drugstore with her head between her knees. Another man and woman were bending over her, making sure she was okay. A few more people stood around and talked in increasingly loud and worried tones. From the sidewalk in front of the supermarket, Michael couldn't quite make out what they were saying, but they were pointing randomly around the street and towards the park nearby. At first, he didn't get what was wrong. When he finally figured it out, it stopped him dead in his tracks.

Nothing was moving. No tree branches were swaying, not a single leaf fluttered, not even a twitch from any of the flags hanging outside. The air was completely still. This was creepy in and of itself, but it didn't stop with the air. The stream that usually flowed happily through their little town square park appeared to be frozen in place. It was as if the world had been paused. A glance up showed the clouds still and quiet. To his shock, he saw leaves suspended in midair, halted on their voyage to the ground. They had been blown off by the previously breezy day and then stopped by... what?

No one seemed to be hurt or in danger. Birds still soared through the sky, though they appeared to be making wide, slow circles, confused about the sudden lack of wind and air movement. The young woman who had alerted them with her shocked outburst was recovering fine and had seemingly just been frightened by the oddness of the scene.

Michael didn't blame her. He felt a chill run down his spine, even though nothing looked hostile or malicious. He turned back towards the market doors and saw Jenny staring questioningly at him. She must have seen something in his expression because she was headed towards the doors before he could motion for her to wait.

He tried to say something to warn her, but his mouth felt as frozen as the world around him. She glanced around just enough to see no imminent threat, and then turned to him curiously.

"What is it? Why are you all standing out here with your thumbs in your butts? Was it old mister..."

She trailed off as she felt it too. A sense of off-ness everywhere. He watched her eyes widen as she took in the unexplained stillness. She turned to him, not yet panicky, but close.

"What is this? Michael, I don't understand. What's going on out here?"

"I don't know yet, Jen. I just... I don't know. It just stopped. Everything. Like someone pushed pause. The people and animals seem fine, but... did you see the stream?"

She didn't answer, too stunned to think of an appropriate response. Her mind raced with memories of all the science fiction books and movies she had enjoyed her whole life, and in minutes had a whole slew of potential explanations. None of them were very pleasant. Especially not when they heard another loud yell.

This time it came from a large, burly man across the street. He was shouting something unintelligible and pointing up at the sky, where previously only frozen fluffy clouds were scattered across the blue sky. The noise drew more people out of the nearby stores and houses, all rushing outside to stop and stare in shock at the motionless world around them.

Michael and Jenny saw it at the same time, instinctively reaching for each other as they stared at the new development that had set off the yelling. There was a lot of noise and pushing around them. It felt like a violent contrast to their silent and immobile surroundings. Michael pulled Jenny to the side as the crowd of people turned into a more violent swarm of crying and hysterics. He pulled her around the side of the building, away from the shouts about the end of the world, the sins of man, and the imminent takeover of our lives and planet.

Jenny was almost disgusted by how quickly their fellow neighbors and acquaintances fell into despair, horror, and mass hysteria. As she and Michael stood staring up from behind the building, however, she couldn't find any words to describe the hollow and terrified feeling. It felt as dead and silent as the trees and grass. Michael was talking, but she couldn't hear him over the rushing in her ears. She felt tears welling up in her eyes, but she wasn't sure what they were from. It may have been relief or sorrow; it was so hard to tell. Maybe it was just sheer confusion.

The apparition was now solid, having faded in from a hazy, indistinguishable form to a clear, distinct shape. It was a rectangle, slightly less white than the clouds behind it. It took up most of the sky, and the people below had no trouble reading the bold black lettering across it. Jenny's first thought was that this had to be some kind of sick prank. She realized quickly that this had to be real. This was much too elaborate, and frankly impossible, to be a prank.

The application is not responding. The program may respond again if you wait. Do you want to restart this process?

Jenny has seen this message a thousand times on her own computer. The box in the sky was complete with option boxes at the bottom and a white arrow waiting to choose one or the other. The stalled water and leaves frozen mid-fall suddenly made a horrible kind of sense.

Everything the crazy conspiracy theorists had always warned them about was true. This world, this life, their entire existence was just a program or a game on some unfathomably gigantic computer belonging to some other being that we never even dreamed had existed. And who knows, maybe it didn't stop there? Maybe they were nothing more than an even larger, more elaborate game. Maybe it was simulations all the way up.

No matter what the truth was, Jenny couldn't tear her eyes away from the white arrow on the box. Any minute now, that arrow would move and decide their fate. Was this the end? Could everything in her life, in all of their lives, really boil down to this? An error?

Michael stood beside her, equally speechless. He knew he should say something, anything, but there was nothing. He knew they were both thinking the same thing, and the only thing he could do without losing his mind completely was to pull her into his arms and hold her as they watched the sky for any sign of what was to come.

The screaming in the town square, and probably all over the world, sounded muted and distant. The only thing he heard clearly was his pulse pounding in his ears and Jenny's soft breath next to him. He had always thought that when this moment came, he would panic and beg, his life flashing before his eyes. He felt only a kind of quiet emptiness, though.

Together they watched as, almost on cue, the white arrow in the sky started sliding towards the option buttons at the bottom of the terrible error message. It was moving towards the restart button, and as it got close to touching it, the commotion on the streets and across the planet rose in volume and pitch until it seemed like they were drowning in the screams. The panic and fear in the air were suffocating. The sounds and feelings and strangeness of it all came crashing together in a final heart-rending crescendo as the world was shaken by a single, impossibly loud click...

Jenny woke up late in the morning, with the sun already streaming through the bedroom curtains. She rolled over to greet her husband, but his side of the bed was vacant. She ran her hand over the wrinkled sheets, feeling the last traces of warmth from his body fading away.

HERITAGE

Maggie Keller had worked at Halbrook & Payne Consulting for six years, and in that time, she'd walked the same hallway nearly every weekday morning just before 8 a.m.

The sixth floor was always quiet. The office was housed in what used to be a textile mill, a long brick-and-beam structure on the edge of the city's historic district. It had been renovated just enough to pass code, but still had the feel of an ancient structure. The hallways were long and narrow, carpeted in industrial gray, with high windows that never seemed to let in that much light.

Maggie didn't mind the monotony. Most of the time she actually enjoyed it. She kept her head down, earbuds in, coffee in hand. Predictability kept the days neat and manageable, and that was just how she liked it.

There was a painting in the hallway, halfway down the stretch between the elevator and the glass door that led into the main offices. It hung slightly crooked beneath an old, mostly ornamental wall sconce and was framed in thick walnut wood. The canvas showed an old street scene with cobblestones, horse-drawn carriages, and flickering gas lamps. Shops with names painted in spidery gold script lined both sides of the road, though the letters were almost too small to make out clearly.

It was a nice enough painting, she supposed, just boring. She'd barely noticed it the first few years. Just another thing in the background, like the hum of the fluorescents or the sound of her heels on the tile. That all changed last Monday.

That was when she hadn't just glanced at the painting, but really looked at it for the first time. Something about it had caught her eye. A flicker of movement, she had thought, though of course that wasn't possible. Still, she'd stopped in front of it for a moment and looked closer. One of the carriages seemed to be in a different place than she remembered, but she wrote it off as her being overtired and just misremembering the painting. It wasn't like she studied it every morning, it was just a thing she glanced at on her walk in. All the same, she hesitated in front of it a little longer each day.

This morning, she stopped completely. There were two men at the bakery window in the painting. She was absolutely certain that there had only ever been one. He wore a little bowler hat and held a small parcel, hand raised as though greeting someone inside the shop. That's how he'd always looked. Now as she peered closer at the painting, she saw that there were two men. The second man stood just behind the first, with his face turned away from the bakery shop window, angled slightly toward Maggie. He almost seemed to be turning to look at her.

By Thursday, Maggie had stopped pretending she wasn't imagining things. There were three men outside the bakery now. The third man had a dog on a leash, the dog's head turned sharply in her direction, mouth open in what looked like the beginning of a snarl. She was beyond certain that the two new men and the dog hadn't been there the week before. Even the first man, the one with the parcel, was no longer mid-gesture. His hand was lowered now, and the parcel was gone.

That night, after a second glass of wine and a long internal argument with herself, Maggie opened her laptop and typed "painting sixth floor hallway Halbrook and Payne" into the search engine on her laptop. Nothing. She tried artwork, decor, even furnishings, but the only results were PDFs of old office layouts and ads for office furniture. She sat back, frowning.

The next morning, she took a detour on her way in and stopped by the facilities office.

"Hey, sorry to bother you, but I have a weird question," she said, leaning on the counter. "Do you happen to know where that painting in the sixth-floor hallway came from? The one with the carriages and the old street?"

The woman behind the desk gave her a bored look. "Painting?"

"Yeah. In the hallway, just past the elevators. It's been there forever, I think."

The woman clicked her pen, thinking. "Most of the art up there came from the basement when they cleared it out. No one wanted to keep pouring money into the building, so they scavenged what they could find."

"Do you know who painted it? Or how long it's been around?"

The woman shrugged. "Beats me. You could check the back, I guess. Sometimes there's a name or a stamp or something."

That thought hadn't occurred to her, and she felt a little stupid for skipping something so obvious. That evening, after most people had gone home and the hallway was quiet, Maggie slipped out of her office and stood in front of the painting. It still looked the same as it had that morning, as far as she could tell.

She reached up and carefully lifted it off the hook. It was heavier than she expected, and she turned it carefully around, searching for a signature or stamp of any kind. The back was slightly stained and definitely dusty, but there was no writing to be seen. As she went to turn the frame back around, something on the bottom edge caught her eye. She bent down, squinting at the rough wood on the back of the frame. It looked like maybe there were letters carved into it. She pulled out her flashlight and felt her heart stop as she saw what someone had inscribed there. Halberd. It looked like it had been scratched in hastily, not the signature of an artist or framer. She knew exactly what it was, however.

It was her mother's maiden name. What the hell was it doing on the back of an old painting hanging in her office hallway? She stared at it for a long time, the frame growing heavier in her hands. Somewhere down the hall, the building creaked. The painting suddenly felt much too cold against her skin, and she stepped back quickly after turning it back around and rehanging it. She left quickly, without daring to look at the front.

When she got home that night, Maggie immediately called her mother.

"You're sure?" Maggie asked, twisting the phone cord between her fingers. "You've never heard of anyone in the family who painted?"

Her mother laughed lightly on the other end of the line. "Sweetheart, if someone in this family had talent, I promise you we'd have heard about it. Why do you ask?"

Maggie hesitated. "I just… I saw something with our name on it at work. Something that said Halberd, and I thought maybe…" Her voice trailed off, not sure how much to tell her.

"An old file or something?" her mother asked, voice a little more cautious now.

"A painting," Maggie said. "Old, probably early 1900s. I was curious where it came from, and your maiden name was scratched into the back of the frame." There was a long silence on the phone line.

"That's… strange," her mother said finally, but there was something brittle in her tone. "I wouldn't read too much into it. Halberd's not that unusual."

"It kind of is."

"Well, I'm sorry, but I don't know anything about it. Maybe it was someone else's. The name could've gotten there by accident."

Maggie nodded even though her mother couldn't see her. "Yeah, maybe." They said their goodbyes, and she hung up, the call only added to her growing unease.

The next afternoon, Maggie left work early and walked to the central library downtown. She wasn't sure what she was looking for, just that she had to keep looking.

She started with the local history section, then newspapers on microfiche. Eventually she found herself at a long table with a stack of bound city directories, each thicker than her arm. She flipped through pages and pages of old names, addresses, and occupations. Buried in the 1912 directory, she found what she was looking for.

Halberd, Elias - Occupation: Portraitist. Residence: 47 Dalloway Lane.

The name sent a ripple of cold down her spine. She felt as though she had heard the name before, long ago. Judging by the year, maybe a great-uncle?

The address was unfamiliar, and she jotted it down.

Maggie called a cab to take her to the address listed under Elias Halberd's name, more out of impulse than logic. She didn't even know what she expected to find, certainly not the same building, over a hundred years later. The driver stopped at the address and looked over his shoulder at her with a slightly concerned expression.

"You sure this is where you wanna go, lady? You wanna check the address?"

"No, this is it. Thanks." She paid him and climbed out of the cab. He watched her for a moment, then shrugged and drove away.

47 Dalloway Lane was now a narrow patch of weedy grass between two crumbling brick row houses. A rusted fence ran along the back edge. There were no historical plaques, no markers, no evidence that anyone named Elias Halberd had ever lived there at all.

She suddenly had the same nervous, sinking sensation she'd felt the moment she first saw the second man appear in the painting. She stepped off the sidewalk and into what would have been the yard, had the house itself still been standing. Something crunched beneath her shoe, and she looked down and saw the corner of a broken frame, half-buried in dirt. She bent down and brushed it off. It was just a rotted sliver of wood, the glass long gone. She stood up and looked around with an overwhelming feeling of being watched, but the entire street was vacant and silent. She decided to walk back to her apartment to clear her head, and the feeling didn't subside until she was several blocks away from the old property.

That night, Maggie returned to the hallway in her office building. It was just after 10 p.m. and she knew it was insane to come here this late at night, but she couldn't help it. She had sat at home feeling the urge to see the painting again, and before she knew it, she was walking down the street and approaching the building.

She stopped at the painting, already dreading what she was about to see. The scene was quite different now, enough that even a much less observant person would have noticed that it had changed. The bakery was still there, but the men were gone. The gas lamps burned lower, and the shadows had deepened. The shops appeared to be closed.

In the center of the now abandoned street stood a young woman. She had a slim figure and long, dark hair. Maggie realized with a sick certainty that this woman looked quite similar to her. She was facing away from the viewer, towards something just out of the frame, but Maggie was pretty sure that if the figure were to turn around, it would be her own face painted on the canvas. As she peered closer, she saw a dark red shadow on the back of the woman's shoulder, and realized with horror that it appeared to be a bloody handprint. Shaken, she hurried out of the building with the same strange sense of being watched that she had experienced on Dalloway Lane earlier that day.

Maggie couldn't sleep that night, even with the lights on and double-checking that the doors were locked and the windows bolted. The image of herself in the painting with that red, hand-shaped smear on her shoulder was seared into her memory. Seeing a painting change was one thing, but seeing what could very well be herself inserted into it was insane. She felt as if she were losing her mind. She finally drifted off, but her sleep was fitful and full of strange dreams of painting and old vacant lots.

The next morning, Maggie called in sick to work and went down to the city clerk's office. She didn't know exactly what she was looking for, but she knew she had to find some way to explain what was going on. She told the woman at the front desk that she was working on a genealogy project for her family, and the woman led her back to where all the archived records were stored. Luckily, someone had catalogued everything into a database on the computer, so it didn't take her long to find the only record that seemed relevant.

The entry for Elias Halberd was short and simple. He was declared deceased on March 2nd, 1913. The cause of death was presumed smoke inhalation after his residence was destroyed in a fire. He had no surviving spouse or children. There was an accompanying police report that listed the cause of the fire as simply "suspicious and most likely intentional". It also said that his neighbors had been noticing strange behavior from Elias in the weeks leading up to the fire. He had been heard shouting at night and covering the windows of his house. They said he walked around mumbling about a door and needing to stop it before it got too close. The official consensus seemed to be that Elias was a crazy old man who burned his house down and died in the process.

Maggie wondered if her mother knew about this, and why she was hiding it if she did. She thought back to the painting the last time had seen it. Was there something to do with a door? The woman had been looking at something out of the frame. Maggie knew she had to go back and see what was there now, what had changed since the night before. Whatever had happened to Elias wasn't an accident, and he wasn't just a crazy old man. It was happening to her now, and she needed to stop it before something even worse happened.

She waited until she knew everyone at the office would have left for the night, and went back to the building. Her legs were shaking by the time she reached the sixth floor. The hallway was dark, lit only by emergency exit lights at the ends of the hallway. The painting waited for her.

Even in the dim light, the colors looked more vivid than ever. The gas lamps in the street burned with an eerie orange glow, flickering like real fire. And the shadows, deep and foreboding, seemed to move ever so slightly in the corners of her vision.

Maggie stepped closer. The woman was still there, but she had moved again. She was no longer walking down the middle of the street. She had stepped up onto the sidewalk, and her face was turned fully toward the viewer now. Her hand was outstretched, and she was reaching for a doorknob. Just to the right of the bakery, where there had previously been only shadow, was a door. It was made of dark wood, arched at the top, with an ornate brass knob.

Maggie staggered back. That hadn't been there before, she was sure of it. The door wasn't the worst part, however. Just behind her painted self, partially obscured by the shadows, there was someone else. A tall, pale figure, blurred as though caught mid-movement. One hand was raised, not quite touching the girl's back. The figure had no face that Maggie could discern, just a pale smudge under some type of heavy-looking cloak or hood.

She didn't sleep at all that night. She scoured the internet looking for someone, anyone, who might be able to shed some light on what was happening. She wanted to call her mother and demand more answers from her, but she needed to know the right questions to ask first. At 8:00 sharp the following morning, Maggie walked into the local library and headed for the historical reference department with her fingers crossed, hoping for a bit of luck. To her surprise, it had worked.

The woman across from her now was maybe in her seventies, with sharp gray eyes and an encyclopedic memory. Her name was Dr. Theodora Price, and she was a retired professor, self-described "folklore hound," and volunteer archivist. Maggie had found her name online, attached to many articles and papers written about the early 20th-century history of the county.

"Dalloway Lane," Dr. Price said thoughtfully. "Now that's a name I haven't heard in a while."

"You've heard of it?" Maggie asked, breath catching.

"Oh yes. It was a big fire, wiped out half the block. It was a miracle that more people didn't die in the fire, but it happened during the day when most of the residents were at work or school. In fact, there was only one reported fatality."

"Elias Halberd?" Maggie asked.

Dr. Price blinked in surprise. "Yes, that was the name. He was a local painter, if I remember correctly."

Maggie nodded and pulled the copy of the 1913 police report from her bag. Dr. Price lifted it and spent a moment reading it through. Finally, she set the paper down and nodded.

"Yes, that's about what I remembered from the bit of research I did on local tragedies for a book a colleague was writing. It was a strange case, neighbors had been reporting his behavior for weeks before the fire. It's certainly sad, but may I ask what you're looking into it for?"

"His neighbors said that he was talking about a door in a painting. That the painting was moving, and the door was getting closer, and he had to find a way to stop it."

"Yes," Dr. Price said. "Based on some of the toxic materials used in art supplies back then, it was likely that he was suffering from some type of psychosis. It's not unheard of at all."

"That's the thing, though," replied Maggie. "I don't think it had anything to do with psychosis or poisoning from toxic paints. I've seen the painting he was talking about. It didn't get destroyed in the fire. I've seen it, and a few days ago it started moving. Last night I saw the door for the first time, and I have a feeling it will be even closer today."

Maggie took a cab straight to her mother's house from the library. The sky was overcast, low clouds hanging heavy and dark. Her mind was racing with thoughts of faceless figures and magically appearing doors. There had to be more to it than toxic paint.

Her mother opened the door with a furrowed brow and a nervous smile. Before she could speak, Maggie pushed past her and into the house.

"We need to talk," Maggie said. "Inside."

They sat at the kitchen table, the same one Maggie had eaten at as a child. Her mother busied herself putting water on to boil for tea while Maggie sat impatiently. Finally, she blurted it out.

"I know about Elias Halberd." Her mother's eyes darkened, her fingers curling around the edge of the table.

"He was your great-great-uncle. He died in a fire."

"And?" Maggie pressed. "That's all you're going to tell me?"

Her mother looked away uncomfortably. "He didn't just die," she said at last. "Elias went mad, Maggie. That's what they said. He started talking about things that weren't there. He claimed that paintings were watching him, that people were vanishing into them."

Maggie stared at her mother, waiting for more. Her mother finally sighed and sat in the chair next to Maggie's.

"The family tried to help him," her mother went on. "But it was 1913. There wasn't much you could do. My grandparents used to whisper about how he'd scribbled warnings in the margins of his sketchbooks. Claimed he saw people from the past walking in and out of the paintings, even that he saw himself in them."

"And they didn't believe him?" Maggie asked. Her mother shook her head with a small, sad laugh.

"No, of course not. He was sick, Maggie. Today, they'd probably diagnose it as schizophrenia, but back then? He was just 'possessed by his own mind,' as they liked to say. He finally snapped and set that fire. He's just damn lucky he was the only one to die in it."

Maggie stared at her. "I've seen the painting, Mom. It's hanging at my office. Somehow it must have been salvaged from the fire. I saw myself in it. The door he was talking about—"

"Stop looking at it," her mother interrupted sharply.

"I can't. It's like it's pulling me in."

"Then you need to get away from it, Maggie. Far away. These things, madness or whatever they are, they run in the blood. You understand? Don't let what got to Elias get to you. We can get you help, we can figure this out." Her mother sounded pleading now.

Maggie stood up slowly. "I think Elias was telling the truth. I think the painting is trying to show me whatever it was showing him. I'm going to finish what he started."

Her mother started to protest, but Maggie was past listening. She needed to stop whatever was going on. She stood abruptly and walked out, her mother calling out after her, sounding scared.

Back at the office, she went straight to the hallway. It was late by now, and most of her coworkers had gone home. The air felt heavier than usual. She stopped in from of the painting, afraid to see what new development she would find.

The woman, Maggie was now convinced it must be herself, was at the door now. Her hand was on the knob. The tall, faceless figure loomed just behind her, fingertips nearly brushing her hair. Maggie thought she could almost feel the figure behind her in the hallway. Her breath caught in her chest and her vision suddenly swam for a second.

She blinked, and the street was empty. No woman, no faceless figure, no door, just the carriages and the little shops and the bakery, like it had always been. Exactly as it had always been. She blinked again, but nothing changed. Her throat went dry and her pulse roared in her ears.

"No," she whispered, stepping closer. "No, it was there. I saw it." She stared until her eyes stung, heart hammering, willing the image to shift. It didn't. A voice behind her made her jump.

"Maggie?" She turned to see Robin from marketing clutching her laptop bag. "I, um… are you okay? You've been standing here a while."

Maggie opened her mouth, but said nothing. Robin glanced at the painting.

"It's kind of creepy, right? I've never really looked at it."

Maggie looked back at the painting, but that's all it was now. It looked like any other painting of an old-time village.

"Yeah," she muttered. "Kind of creepy." Robin gave her a slightly strange look, then walked off down the hallway towards the stairs. Maggie stood for a long time, staring at the painting and thinking before she finally went home.

Once again, Maggie didn't sleep. She couldn't. Every time she closed her eyes, she saw the door, and every time she blinked, the faceless figure seemed closer. It wasn't just in the painting anymore, it was in her head now. She knew what she had to do. She had to destroy the painting before she went through that door, before the figure followed. She wasn't sure what would happen after that, but she didn't want to take a chance of finding out.

She arrived at the office before anyone else got there the next morning. She didn't want anyone else to get hurt. In her bag was a bottle of lighter fluid and a barbecue lighter. She didn't want to burn the whole building down like Elias had done, but she needed the painting destroyed once and for all.

She gripped the bag tightly, her heart pounding in her chest. She marched down the hallway, the world narrowing around her. The painting was waiting for her. She approached it with grim determination and saw in horror that the scene had changed once again. The woman and the door were back, and the figure was closer than ever. It seemed to be running its fingers through the woman's hair as she prepared to pull the door open.

Maggie cried out and scrambled to pull the bottle of lighter fluid out. As she pulled the cap off and aimed it at the painting, she heard rapid footsteps in the hallway behind her. She whirled around to see her mother rushing down the hallway, an unfamiliar man in a gray jacket beside her.

"Maggie, put it down," her mother said, voice trembling. "Please."

"Why did you follow me?" Maggie hissed. "It's right there! You see it, don't you? You have to see it."

"We do," the man said gently. "But we need to talk. Let's just sit down, okay?"

She stepped back. "Who are you?"

He hesitated. "My name is Dr. Levens. Your mother asked me to come because she's worried about you. We just want to make sure you're safe."

Maggie looked between them, eyes burning. "You think I'm crazy."

"No one's saying that," her mother whispered, crying now. "But Maggie, the painting… it's not changing. It's just not possible. It wasn't changing for Elias, and it's not changing for you. Dr. Levens can help you see that."

Maggie's grip on the axe faltered. "No… no, I saw it. It moved. I saw it myself. There was a door. Elias saw it too, he wasn't mad, he wasn't!" But even as she said it, she began to doubt herself.

She looked at the painting again. A quaint street scene, a man with a parcel outside a bakery. Perfectly normal, just as it should be. Just like maybe it had always been. Maggie suddenly felt exhausted. The lighter fluid slipped from her fingers and dropped to the floor. The silence around her felt deafening.

Her mother moved first, crossing the space between them in a few cautious steps. "Maggie," she whispered, her voice thick with emotion. "Honey. It's okay. You're okay now."

But Maggie didn't look at her. She was still staring at the painting. It was so… ordinary. "I don't understand," she whispered. "It was there, I saw it. Every day it was different. I saw myself, I saw it reaching for me."

Her mother wrapped her arms around her carefully, as if she were afraid Maggie might shatter. "I know. I know you did."

Maggie didn't move. She didn't return the hug. Her arms hung limply at her sides. "I'm not like him," she said quietly, sounding both scared and defeated. Her mother didn't answer right away, just stroked her hands on Maggie's back.

"I didn't want this for you," she finally said. "That's why I didn't tell you the full truth. I thought maybe if I kept it buried, it wouldn't find you."

"But it did," Maggie said. Her voice broke. "It found me."

Dr. Levens stepped forward slowly, keeping his tone gentle. "Maggie, I think you've been under a lot of pressure. Stress can do things to our minds, especially when we have a family history. I'd like to talk with you more about that. Somewhere quiet, somewhere safe."

Maggie closed her eyes. She wanted to argue, to scream, to insist they were wrong, but all she could see was the painting, both the version hanging on the wall and the one in her mind.

"I don't know what's real anymore," she said finally. "I just don't know."

Her mother gripped her tighter. "You're real," she said. "And we're going to get you help, whatever it takes."

Six weeks later, the sixth-floor hallway was quiet again. The painting still hung on the wall, slightly crooked as always. Most people walked past it without a second glance, just another piece of old décor no one had the budget or interest to replace.

Alex was fresh out of college, two weeks into a marketing assistant role, and still learning the rhythms of the building. Walking down the hallway and passing the painting was part of his daily routine. One Monday morning, Alex paused in front of it. Not because he'd heard any stories, he hadn't, just because something felt… different.

He tilted his head. The painting showed a cobblestone street with horse-drawn carriages. There was a bakery and a man in a bowler hat with a parcel. But just barely visible in one corner, near the edge of the frame, was… a girl? She was caught mid-step, her face turned away from the viewer. Alex frowned. Had she always been there?

He glanced around, then stepped a little closer. Her face was just a blur of paint, but for a moment, he thought… No, just his imagination. He gave a nervous little laugh and walked on. Behind him, the girl in the painting took a step forward.

THE BOX

The box hadn't been there when she went to bed, that much Clara was sure of. Her apartment was small, and she had the kind of memory that catalogued everything in meticulous snapshots. A dish left in the sink, the crooked picture frame in the hallway, even a stack of unopened mail on the table. Nothing changed without her noticing.

But now, sitting in the center of her kitchen counter, was a box. It wasn't wrapped or taped shut. It had no seams, no visible lid, no return address, no weight that she could feel when she picked it up. It was about the size of a shoebox, perfectly smooth and matte black. She'd seen enough procedural shows on TV to know she should probably call the police, maybe a bomb squad, and let them take care of it. She didn't do that, though.

She tried to pry at the corners, press different spots on the surface, but nothing happened. Not even a scratch when she ran a kitchen knife across it, searching for hidden seams. It was warm too, as if it had been sitting in the sun. Most disconcertingly, she had noticed it was faintly humming.

Clara set the box back on the counter and took a step back. She lived alone. No one had a key. No one should have been able to get in, but clearly someone had been here, and they'd left her… this.

She glanced at her phone and saw that she was going to be late for work if she didn't hurry. She decided to bring the box with her. Not because she thought it was dangerous, though that thought had occurred to her, but because she needed someone else to see it. She needed to confirm she wasn't losing her mind. Her coworkers might laugh, but at least she'd know she hadn't finally lost the last of her marbles.

Grabbing her purse, she tucked the box under one arm like a package. It was surprisingly light, almost weightless. It was like holding a box made of air. She could feel it humming softly against the side of her body, radiating a faint warmth.

That's when things started to get weird, as if the appearance of a mysterious box in her kitchen hadn't already been strange. As she stepped off the porch and onto the brick path that led to her driveway, she felt the box shift under her arm, and then it was gone.

Not dropped. Gone. Clara froze, too startled to think about being scared at that point. She looked at her arm cradling nothing and looked down at the surrounding ground to confirm that it wasn't lying there somehow. The box was nowhere to be seen.

She spun around in place, her breath catching in her throat. No one was lurking behind her. No one running off, no sound of footsteps, just the city waking up as normal.

Her phone buzzed. Clara pulled it from her coat pocket with numb fingers and stared at the notification.

"Kitchen: Motion detected – 7:58 a.m." Clearly her kitchen should be vacant right now, and she didn't own any pets or robot vacuums that should be setting off a motion alarm.

Knowing this would absolutely make her late for work, she pulled out her keys and went back into the house. Her heart dropped as she entered the kitchen and saw that the box was waiting for her on the counter. It was in the same exact position, as if it had never left.

She tried again. This time she secured it in a reusable fabric grocery bag before exiting the house. She left her front door open so she could see down the short hallway into the kitchen and see the empty counter. She took a deep breath, knowing she was just freaking herself out, and she must have just forgotten to actually pick it up the first time.

As soon as her foot touched the brick path again, the box vanished and the bag dangled limply from her arm. She whirled around, knowing what she would see even as she felt her phone vibrate with a camera notification in her pocket. The box was on the counter, just as it had been last time.

Clara stood in the doorway, trying to steady the spinning in her head. Her fingers were trembling. She walked inside, closed the door, and locked it, although she wasn't sure what she was locking it against.

She stared at the box for a long minute, then picked up her phone and tapped the screen to dial a number.

"Hey, it's me," she said when her friend picked up. "Can you come over? Like… now?"

"Everything okay?" Jordan sounded sleepy. He worked nights, so she rarely called this early.

"I don't know. There's something in my apartment. I mean, it's not doing anything, but… I think you need to see it."

That was all it took. He didn't ask questions, just said he'd be there in twenty. Clara hung up and dialed her office next. Her voice was calm as she left the message, fever, headache, maybe food poisoning, but she felt like her mind was tipping sideways. As soon as she set the phone down, she looked again.

The box hadn't moved. Still no markings. Still warm. Still humming, faintly, like it was waiting. This time, she didn't touch it.

When Jordan arrived, Clara opened the door without a word and stepped aside to let him in. He took one look at her face, and his smirk faded.

"You okay?"

She just pointed toward the kitchen.

The box sat on the counter, unmoved. Unremarkable, plain black, no features, no flourish. But there was something about it that made the hairs on Jordan's arms stand up. He walked toward it, eyebrows raised.

"That's it?" Clara nodded. "What is it?"

"I don't know. I was hoping you could help me figure that out."

He reached out as if he might touch it, then stopped. "Where did it come from?"

"I woke up, and it was just… there."

He turned to her, skeptical. "You sure you didn't—"

"I tried to leave with it. Twice," she interrupted. "As soon as I stepped outside, it disappeared. Then I got a motion alert from the kitchen, and it was back. Same spot."

Jordan frowned, circling the box. "There are no seams."

"I know."

"No label, no markings, no nothing."

"I know."

He leaned in close, listening. "Is it… humming?"

Clara nodded again. "It's strangely warm, too. Warmed than it should be for sitting in a room-temperature kitchen."

He straightened, staring at it as if it might suddenly sprout legs.

"I didn't imagine this, right?"

Jordan shook his head. "No. This is real. But I have no idea what the hell it is."

They stood in silence for a long moment. The air felt heavier, as if the room was holding its breath.

Then Jordan said, "Okay. Let's figure out what's inside."

Clara grabbed her phone.

"If I can't get it out of here," she said, "maybe I can at least record what happens when I try."

Jordan didn't argue. He pulled up a chair while she opened the camera app and set her phone on the edge of the counter, propped against a mug. The box sat square in frame.

She double-checked that the recording was running, then placed the box inside the bag again, not wanting to touch it any longer than necessary, and headed for the door. Jordan followed, watching the screen.

"Okay," she said. "I'm stepping out now."

One step off the porch, and boom. The bag was empty again.

Jordan turned immediately to the phone. "It's gone," he called. "Let's see if it…" His voice trailed off.

Clara rushed back in. "Is it back?"

"Yeah," he said, "but… come look."

On the screen, the box was still there. As Clara watched the video, her jaw dropped, and she felt like she was going to be sick. The video showed Clara approaching and picking up nothing. Her hands pantomimed lifting, her arms wrapping around thin air. The bag bulged awkwardly around nothing, and then she walked out of frame with it. The box stayed right where it was, unmoved.

"That's not what happened," Clara whispered.

"I watched it disappear," Jordan said. They replayed it twice more. Same result. Clara never touched the box. It never vanished.

On camera, the whole thing looked like a bizarre performance, a woman pretending to carry an invisible object while a man looked on, confused.

"I don't understand," she murmured. "I felt it vanish. You saw it."

"I did," Jordan said. "But the camera didn't."

She looked back at the box. It sat innocently in the center of the counter, but now something was different. For the first time since it appeared, there was a marking on the plain black exterior of the box. A thin, vertical line etched onto the top, like a tally mark. They stared at the new marking for a long time.

"It wasn't there before," Clara said.

"No," Jordan agreed. "It wasn't. What does one line mean?"

She didn't answer. She turned and grabbed the box. This time, she didn't bother putting it in the bag. She just lifted it and turned toward the door. Jordan leaned in, watching the live feed.

"Okay," she said. "I'm stepping out again."

She crossed the threshold. Gone. Jordan's stomach turned. On the phone screen, her hands passed through the box as if it had no substance at all, as if it were simply a projection. The box in the video never moved. Her fingers blurred, the way they might if the camera glitched.

He swore under his breath. "Clara…"

She was already coming back, arms empty. "It vanished again. Same as before."

He flipped the phone toward her. "Look."

She watched in silence as her hands phased through the object, her expression unchanged. Like a ghost pretending to carry something real. And then her gaze shifted to the box.

"Oh my God," Clara whispered. "There's another line. What the hell is going on?"

"I think it's counting," Jordan said. "Okay. I've got a friend, Shayla. She's deep into all this weird fringe-science-fiction-paranormal-tech stuff. Like, way deeper than we are. She might know what this is."

"You trust her?" Clara asked, still staring at the two tally marks on the box.

"More than I trust… this," he said, gesturing at it. "She's not going to laugh. She's going to obsess." He airdropped the footage to his phone, typed out a quick message, and hit send.

They sat in silence for a few minutes. Clara got up and paced nervously while Jordan stared at the box anxiously. Ten minutes passed, then his phone finally buzzed.

Shayla: Uhh… Jordan? There's no box in this video.

Jordan frowned. He opened the message and tapped on the attached video. It was their video, alright. Clara reaching toward the counter and then stepping away with a full-looking but impossibly empty bag. But no box.

He pulled up the original file on his phone. The box was there. Black, solid, tauntingly mysterious. He sent a screenshot.

Jordan: It's right there. You seriously don't see it?

Shayla: No, what am I supposed to be looking at? Is this some kind of prank?

He looked at Clara. "You're not gonna believe this."

She leaned in as he showed her the conversation. She grabbed her own phone and opened the video from the original file. The box was sitting on the counter, clear as day. It was right there in the one Jordan had forwarded to his phone, too. Only Shayla's phone apparently showed an empty counter. As they compared videos and Jordan responded to Shayla, Clara's breath caught in her throat.

Three lines. The third tally had appeared, etched beside the others.

"I don't get it," Clara whispered, clutching her phone. "It's the same video. Same file. Why would it show up on yours but not hers?"

Jordan's brow furrowed. He stood and took a few steps toward the door. "What if…"

He walked across the threshold into the hallway, phone still in hand. He stepped across the porch and down onto the walkway. He opened the same video he had just been watching inside. The box was gone.

Jordan's stomach twisted unpleasantly. He stepped back onto the porch, and the box reappeared in the video, as if it had been there all along.

"Okay," he said quietly. "Okay, this is gonna sound insane, but-"

"It only shows up inside the apartment," Clara finished, eyes wide.

Jordan nodded, his face pale. They both looked toward the counter again. Still three marks, still humming quietly to itself.

Clara sat down. "So… it doesn't want to be seen outside of this house. This thing can't possibly know where you're watching a pre-recorded video of it, right? That's insane." Clara turned to him, her voice shaking now. "What if the tally marks… what if they're counting up to something?"

Jordan scrolled through his phone, the screen casting a pale light across his face. Clara sat beside him, the box looming behind them on the counter. He nudged her, almost scaring her out of her chair.

"Shayla thinks she found something," he said, his voice tight. "Actually… a few things."

Clara leaned in. "What kinds of things?"

"Reddit threads, blog posts, weird message boards. Scattered over the last ten years. Different people, different cities. But they're all describing this." He turned the screen so she could see.

"Woke up to a black box on my kitchen table. No seams, no markings, won't open. Warm to the touch. Tried throwing it away, but it always comes back."

Another one: "Thought my roommate was pranking me until she moved out. The box stayed. I've tried everything, but it's still there."

And another: "Can't record it. Tried on four cameras. Only shows up if you're in the same house with it. No one believes me. I'm not crazy."

Clara swallowed hard. "How many of these are there?"

"Dozens. Most get ignored. Some accounts go dark after a few posts. A couple of people say they found tally marks appearing on the surface. One said the marks went up to five before they started hearing things."

She glanced over her shoulder, eyes drawn to the three pale lines carved into the surface of their box.

Jordan kept reading aloud. "Some think it's alien tech. Others think it's some kind of observer or recording device. A few… think it's a countdown."

"To what?" Clara asked, her voice barely above a whisper.

No one online seemed to know, but one post in the screenshot from Shayla caught her attention. It ended with a warning, half-buried in a thread from five years ago.

"DON'T LET IT GET TO SIX."

By the time the fifth tally appeared, Clara truly believed she was losing her mind. She and Jordan had tried everything. More video attempts, thermal imaging, even borrowing an EMF reader from a local ghost hunting club Jordan found on Facebook. Every reading was erratic. The box was invisible to machines outside the apartment but seemed to radiate strange signals inside.

They posted all over the internet and only got one response that seemed to legitimately know what they were talking about.

"We found a black box just like yours," the email said. "My brother tried to take it to the university physics lab. It disappeared in the driveway, just like yours did. The next day, our parents vanished. The box was gone, too. I haven't seen it since. But if your marks get to six—leave the house."

Clara stared at the screen for a long time after reading it. "We should leave," she said.

"We could," Jordan said. "The box will be waiting here when we get back, though."

She didn't argue. Just stared at the five lines now carved into its surface.

That night, they ran a livestream from Clara's apartment using Jordan's laptop. Nothing appeared on the feed. Viewers just saw an empty kitchen with a bare countertop.

In person, the hum had grown louder. It wasn't just the sound anymore; it was a feeling like the apartment had become pressurized. Their skin tingled and static arced across their fingertips when they touched the fridge. The lights buzzed constantly. Something was building.

At 12:04 a.m., the sixth mark appeared. Clara saw it happen in real time. She blinked, and it was just… there. There was no time to decide what to do next. The hum dropped into a lower register. The floor vibrated beneath them. The light over the kitchen sink flickered violently, then burst in a small shower of sparks. The air warped around the box, and with a sound like folded paper tearing underwater, reality buckled. Right above the counter, space twisted open.

It wasn't a dramatic explosion or a flash of light. It was more like a zipper being pulled in the fabric of the world. A swirling hole yawned into existence, six feet tall, its edges flickering with faint, fluid geometry. Inside was movement. A hallway? A tunnel? Stars? It was constantly shifting, and looking at it hurt her eyes. A voice rang out in a calm, robotic monotone:

"Recipient Confirmed. Dimensional Anchor Aligned. Welcome, Designate Zarnak-3."

A tall, insectoid being stepped halfway through the rift, ducking slightly to avoid hitting its translucent crest on the ceiling. It was glowing faintly blue, wearing what looked like a sash made of metal leaves.

It paused, looking around the kitchen. It looked down and Clara and Jordan, who were frozen in shock.

"…This isn't the Azurian Reception Temple." The voice vibrated and seemed to buzz in her ears.

Clara blinked, surprised. "No." Another voice came from within the portal, distant and panicked.

"Zarnak! You input the wrong layer again! That's a Class-3 organic hab-dwelling!" The creature made a sheepish, gurgling cough that might've been a sigh.

"My deepest apologies. Dimensional misalignment. Please disregard the intrusion. You will not be probed."

"Thanks?" Jordan said in a dreamy, not quite believing this was happening tone.

The being stepped backward into the swirling void. With an anticlimactic slurp, the rift stitched itself closed. The box gave a tiny, almost embarrassed ding. The tally marks vanished, and so did the humming. She blinked, and it was gone.

Clara stared at the empty counter for a long moment, then reached into the cabinet and pulled out a bottle of wine.

Jordan sat heavily on a kitchen stool. "So… interdimensional butt dial?"

Clara poured two glasses. "They crossed galaxies just to GPS to the wrong address."

Three weeks later, Clara got a package in the mail. No return address. No postage. Inside was a sleek black object. It was flat and circular, with a glowing green light and a sticky note attached:

SINCERE APOLOGIES FOR THE NAVIGATIONAL ERROR. PLEASE ENJOY THIS TEMPORAL BEVERAGE WARMER. -Z

Clara shrugged and stuck her coffee mug on top of it. There was a quick vibration, and her coffee was almost instantly at the perfect temperature. It never appeared to need any power or recharging, and it stayed on her desk for years to come, always keeping her beverages exactly warm enough. She never saw the box again, and that was just fine with her.

THE THREE WISHES OF BARNABAS CAVANAUGH

Barnabas Cavanaugh was a good man. He was generally kind to others, worked hard, and loved his wife, Patty, devotedly. He didn't expect more than what he was willing to earn and never went out of his way to harm anyone. He had flaws, of course, but overall he was a good, decent man. That's why his wife wasn't at all surprised when he found the magic lamp.

Barn, as he was known to friends and colleagues, had been cleaning out his basement when he found an old-looking cardboard box that he didn't recognize. He'd been spending a lot of his time cleaning and finding old boxes, now that he was freshly retired from the post office, but something about this particular box caught his eye.

It didn't look old and decrepit like the rest of them. Barn had been storing random boxes of unsorted junk down here for quite a while now, hence the gentle prodding from his wife to spend some of his newfound spare time cleaning and organizing. This box, however, didn't have a speck of dust on it. It looked like someone had just plopped it down yesterday.

He pulled it out from behind the other, dustier boxes. It was nondescript, with no labels, stickers, or writing, just blank corrugated cardboard. It was sealed shut with a single strip of clear packing tape. He pulled a small pocketknife from his back pocket and slit the tape open neatly. He pulled back the flaps and stared at the contents, puzzled.

He tipped the box slightly, peering inside. After a few moments, he folded the flaps shut again, returned the knife to his pocket, and headed up the basement stairs, the mysterious box tucked under one arm. This looked like something he felt he should consult his wife about before going much further.

"Patty," he called out. "I think I found a magic lamp." That should get her attention, he thought. Sure enough, she came around the corner a moment later with a bemused look on her face.

"A magic lamp, huh? I know the basement was full of crap, but I wasn't expecting that!"

"You laugh now, Mrs. Cavanaugh, just wait until I show you the box I found." He motioned her over to the kitchen table and set the box in front of her. She lifted the flaps gingerly, as if she were expecting something to jump out at her.

"Wait, are you serious? Barn, this looks just like the kind of magic lamp a genie would live in. Where did you get this? Was it at the church rummage sale?"

"No, it was down in the basement. I just found it."

"You just found a magic lamp in our basement?"

"It appears so."

Patty stepped back from the box and crossed her arms. "Well, I'm not touching it. You found it, you try rubbing it."

Barn laughed. "A little superstitious? I'm sure it's not actually magic. I don't remember this box being down there though, so that's weird." He reached into the box and lifted the lamp, marveling at how heavy it was. It had been cushioned in the box with what looked like straw. If this were a prank, someone had gone all out.

The lamp itself was a deep-burnished bronze color. There were jewels set into an ornate design around the base and handle. It felt warm, as if someone had just been holding it close to their body. Barn held it up over his head, examining the base for a MADE IN CHINA imprint or some kind of artist's signature. Nothing. He looked at Patty.

"It is weird that I'm kind of afraid to rub it? You know, just in case?"

"Yes," she laughed. "It's a little weird that you're concerned about what, an actual magical genie coming out? You know it's not actually a magic lamp, right?"

Barn, always an ardent follower of his wife's usually good judgment, laid his hand along the rounded side of the lamp and rubbed it in a slow circle. When nothing happened, he let out a shaky sigh. Before he could respond to his wife, however, a loud, thunderous boom shook the house. It felt and sounded like a firework going off right in their kitchen. Patty clapped her hands over her ears, and Barn jumped, almost dropping the lamp. A strange, almost spicy smell flooded the house, and they both saw the newcomer at the same time.

Standing in the doorway between the kitchen and the living room was a very tall, very muscled-looking man. He was dressed in what appeared to be the best genie costume Barn had ever seen outside of the movies. His hair was jet black and spilled over his shoulders. Dark eyes watched them with mild amusement.

"Holy shit, Barn. I think you found a magic lamp." No sooner were the words out of her mouth than his lovely wife dropped to the floor in a dead faint.

"Patty? Honey, are you okay?"

Patty's eyes fluttered open, and then widened almost comically when she saw not only her husband but the tall, bemused-looking Middle Eastern man behind him, dressed in flowing robes and tassels.

Barn took her hand reassuringly. "It's okay, hon, he's not going to hurt you. At least I don't think so. I don't think genies do that, right?" He looked back at the man and then realized what he had just said.

"Is that okay to say? Genie, I mean? It's not a slur now, is it? Assuming you are, I mean. Are you? A genie, or whatever?" He was stuttering now, tripping over his words. Barn wasn't usually a self-conscious man, but the strange newcomer made him a little more uneasy than he wanted his wife to know.

"Genie is fine," the man responded in a deep, thickly accented voice. "My name is Alazhar. My kind is referred to as many things, but genie is pretty common. And no, we rarely hurt people. It's sort of against the rules."

"The rules?"

"Yeah, the rules of being a genie. You know, no wishing for extra wishes, no immortality, no murder, that stuff. You've seen genies in movies, right?"

"Well, yeah," Barn replied uncertainly. "I just didn't know… I didn't expect to ever meet one."

"No one does, we're magic. It wouldn't be amazing anymore if genies were everywhere, would it?"

"No," he admitted. "Probably not. So you're going to what, grant me three wishes? You really are an actual magic genie?"

"I came out of that lamp, right? Trust me, that took some magic!"

"You do look like every genie I've seen in the movies. Are you from Arabia?"

"This isn't really what most genies look like, but it's easier for people if they see what they're expecting to see. So let's just say Arabia, yeah."

Barn glanced down at his wife, still sitting on the couch, looking rather stunned. "Well, I'm Barn, and this is my wife, Patty. She's usually a little more outgoing, but I think you scared her a bit. No worries, she'll come around." He reached down and squeezed her shoulder, and she nodded.

"I'm okay, I just wasn't really prepared to see a magic genie today. Barn, you really rubbed him out of that lamp? I didn't imagine that?"

Barn laughed. "Believe it or not, and I'm not yet sure I even believe it."

"Your name is Barn?" asked Alazhar. "Like, as in the building cows live in?"

"Well, it's Barnabas, but everyone just calls me Barn."

The genie looked unimpressed with that answer but shrugged his shoulders and held out his hand.

"Nice to meet you then, Barn. And you, Miss Patty." Patty smiled finally and shook his hand.

"Welcome, Alazhar. Can I get you anything? Water? Do genies even drink?"

"We do, but no thank you. I'm sure this is all quite a shock, but have a seat, and I'll go over the basics. I find this whole thing works better when we have some ground rules and understandings."

Barn and Patty sat obediently on the couch, side by side and holding hands, like a pair of well-mannered schoolchildren waiting for their lesson.

"Okay. First, you can't ever tell anyone about me. If you do, all wishes become null and void, and any benefits from wishes already cast will be removed. Usually, only one person can be aware of a genie's presence, but I'll make an exception for Miss Patty since she saw me by accident."

"Next, you have three wishes. Only three, and you must make all three. Big, small, that's your choice, you can wish for whatever you want within the guidelines. No murder is a big one. I can't simply strike someone dead. That's not to say that deaths haven't occurred in the course of granting wishes, but that can't be the primary wish."

"Love is fair game. The movies got that wrong. Want someone to love you unconditionally for the rest of their life?

You got it. I don't imagine you'll be leaning in that direction though, clearly Miss Patty here did that one all on her own."

"I can't give you anything infinite. I can do pretty much whatever you want, but it has to be a predefined amount. No infinite gold coins or anything."

"You can't take a wish back once it's made. Not all wishes come true in exactly the way you expect. Not like that thing where we go out of our way to twist your wishes against you, just sometimes wishes are tricky. For example, if you wished to be a famous author, it would come true. What you're famous for might not be your writing though. See what I mean? Be specific and clear with your wishes. Some wishes take longer than others, by necessity. We do our best, but even magic can be hard and time-consuming."

"Any questions?"

"Oh gosh," Barn said. "I have no idea. This is all so crazy. What would I even wish for? How do I decide?"

"Do something for yourself, Barn." Patty patted his hand. "You're always so generous and good, do something selfish for once. Wish for something you really want. At least for the first one, treat yourself. You deserve it."

Barn thought for a few minutes, furrowing his brow. "Okay," he finally said. "I'm sure you've gotten this one a million times, but I'd like to wish for money."

"Ah, a classic first wish. And a good one, a smart man can do wonders with even a moderate amount of disposable money. How much do you want? Remember, nothing unlimited, and you only get three wishes total."

"Okay. Here goes. I wish I had ten million dollars. American money, tax-free. And not taken from someone else, fresh money. I'd like it to just show up in my bank account, unquestioned."

"You were paying attention! That's a very well-worded wish, Mr. Barn. And an easy one for me. In fact, it's already done."

"Done? Already?"

"Yes, check and see. You have online banking, do you not? I assume everyone does nowadays."

Barn nodded and pulled his phone from his pocket. He tapped a few times and went pale. He handed the phone to Patty, who gasped and looked dangerously close to passing out again.

"Thank you," he managed. "This is unbelievable, I don't even know what to say. And I can spend this?"

Alazhar laughed, a deep, rich sound in the small room.

"Yes, Mr. Barn. Spend away. I'll give you some time to consider your remaining wishes. When you're ready, you know how to summon me." Before Barn or Patty could respond, the booming thunder from before reappeared, and the tall, mysterious man vanished in an instant.

They looked at each other, stunned. The exotic smell from the man's cologne was already fading, as if they had imagined the whole thing. Except for the bank account balance, that was.

Barn shrugged his shoulders and slid his phone back into his pants pocket. "Shall we go shopping, Mrs. Cavanaugh?"

Six weeks later, Barn and Patty were sitting in the shade on the deck of their new cabin. They hadn't gone crazy with their newfound riches, but they had gone on a few shopping sprees and an amazing three-week trip through Europe before purchasing the modest but beautiful log cabin in the Adirondack Mountains. It was remote and included 30 acres of untouched wild forest for them to explore and relax on. They still had an unbelievable amount of money left and had already started setting up donations to all sorts of charities and foundations.

"This is amazing," sighed Barn. "What else could I ever wish for?"

"Good question. Have you been thinking about it?" His wife hadn't brought it up in a while, because he had seemed worried about what he should use the other wishes for. She knew he wanted to use them to do something good, but it was impossible to choose.

"I have. I think I know what I want to wish for." He filled her in on what he wanted to do, and she couldn't have agreed more. She retrieved the lamp from the mantle over the fireplace, where they had kept it after moving into the cabin.

Barn took the lamp and, with a deep breath, rubbed the palm of his hand over the curved surface. They both remembered what came next from the last time and clapped their hands over their ears just as the thunderous booming crashed through the cabin. A moment later, the tall and mysterious Alazhar stood in the doorway, looking exactly the same as the last time they had seen him.

"Mr. Barn, Miss Patty. I trust your first wish has been working out well for you?"

"Oh yes," Patty burst out. She had overcome her initial wariness of the genie once she realized she wasn't dreaming, concussed, or losing her mind. "They always say that money can't buy happiness, but I think I disagree. Maybe it can't fix everything, but it helps!"

Alazhar chuckled.

"It does look like you two spent it fairly well. I heard you were doing good things with some of the money too, and I commend your generosity."

"You heard? Do genies talk about their… wishers? Or whatever they call us?"

Alazhar shrugged noncommittally. Patty looked over at Bill, who shrugged his shoulders.

"Well, thanks, I guess. I tried to do at least some good with it. Unfortunately, some things just can't be accomplished by money alone. I thought about this a lot, and I know what my second wish is."

"I'm intrigued," replied the genie. "Do tell."

"Well," Bill started, clearing his throat. "I want to wish for a cure for Alzheimer's disease. Not just a cure for the people who can afford it either. I wish that someone would discover a cure and make it accessible to everyone, regardless of their health insurance coverage or bank account. A treatment that not only reverses existing symptoms of the disease but also acts as a vaccine to prevent people from ever developing it."

"That's quite a noble wish, Mr. Barn. I can do it, of course, but it will take some time. Maybe six months, maybe a year. These things can be difficult to predict precisely."

"That's fine, however long it takes will be worth it. My mother passed away from the disease three years ago, and I wouldn't wish it on anyone, ever."

Alazhar nodded, and Patty squeezed Barn's hand. He smiled at her, and they both looked back at the genie.

"As you wish, Mr. Barn."

It was two long months of waiting before they saw any sign of Barn's second wish coming true. It started small, a new article mentioning a small breakthrough at a research facility in Switzerland. It seemed like they had found some kind of switch in the brain that might control a person's chances of not only suffering from Alzheimer's disease but some other forms of dementia as well.

It was a small step, but that's all it took to get the ball rolling. Within weeks, the announcement from the Swiss researchers was international news. Labs across the world were racing to figure out what the implications of this breakthrough were and how they could use this new insight to their advantage in developing treatments.

The first major milestone happened just 4 months after Barn had cast his wish. A laboratory in Germany announced it had isolated an enzyme that could affect that switch in the brain's neurons. Within weeks, they had synthesized the prototype of an entirely new enzyme that immediately and permanently disabled the switch, with no apparent ill side effects. The new enzyme was quickly pushed into human trials, and the effect was immediate. Within days of receiving the enzyme infusion, test subjects experienced a complete reversal of Alzheimer's symptoms.

From there, it was like a movie. Another pharmaceutical company teamed up with the group in Germany and figured out how to condense the enzyme infusion into one single pill. It was safe to be taken at any age, and one dose was effective at reversing current symptoms in people already suffering from the disease. Even better, it was shown in all the simulations and virtual tests to act as a complete and permanent vaccine. One pill and your chances of ever developing Alzheimer's disease were nonexistent.

Just a few months after that, it was approved by all the world's major regulatory groups. A benefactor who wished to remain anonymous had donated enough money to provide everyone living person on the planet with the miracle pill.

Barn and Patty watched this all from their cabin in the mountains. They both cried a lot, both in sorrow for what they had lost and in happiness and relief for the billions of people who would never have to endure what they had. It had been a bittersweet wish.

When it was readily available, they both went down into town and got the enzyme pill at the local pharmacy. That night, they sat out on their deck and toasted Barn's mother, all the researchers who had worked so hard, and of course Alazhar.

They had talked a lot over the past few months about what Barn's final wish should be. These wishes were powerful. The research that cured Alzheimer's was already being used to develop treatments for various cancers and diseases. This last wish needed to be perfect.

Once their champagne glasses were empty, Barn reached out for the magic lamp, which they had brought out onto the deck with them in anticipation of bringing Alazhar back to share in their celebration and construct the last wish. Barn smiled at Patty, and she smiled right back. One ear-splitting crash later, the genie Alazhar stood on their deck, ready for the last wish.

*
* *

"Mr. Barn and Miss Patty, how are you enjoying your second wish?"

"It's perfect," replied Barn. "It's even better than I had hoped for. I never thought I would see a world without Alzheimer's. You literally made a dream come true. Thank you."

"Don't thank me, it was your wish. Genies only facilitate the granting of wishes. You put the thought and desire into it. You're a good man, Barnabas Cavanaugh. Your second wish saved an untold number of lives. Do you have your third wish ready? It's the final one, so be sure."

Barn nodded, suddenly nervous. He knew what he wanted to wish for, it was one of the most common wishes that never seemed to come true in real life. After what Alazhar had made happen from his second wish, though, he thought maybe it wasn't hopeless after all.

"I want my final wish to be for world peace. I know it sounds trite, but we've spent the last few months watching the news of the Alzheimer's research, and I can't help but see all of the terrible things happening in the world at the same time. All of this senseless violence, wars over nothing, it's heartbreaking. I want it all to stop. I wish for there to be no more conflict between humans. No reason to go to war, to kill, to take innocent lives. I want to live in a world where that kind of hate doesn't exist."

The genie listened to Barn, his dark face unreadable. When he was done, the genie was silent for several moments, considering what Barn had wished.

"It will likely take some time to accomplish a wish of this magnitude. I can't guarantee how your vision for world peace will be enacted exactly, as I warned you before. Even genies are just servants of fate. We can start the ball rolling, so to speak, but we don't always know where it ends. We are not all-powerful."

"Mr. Barn, is this your final wish? After this, you will not see me again."

"It is," said Barn. Patty nodded beside him, her hand clasped in his. Alazhar nodded solemnly.

"It has been my great pleasure, Mr. Barn and Miss Patty. I thank you for allowing me to serve you."

Before they could respond, he was gone.

For the next few months, Barn and Patty watched the news every day for signs of the world's conflict dying down, or the local news to have less violence or reports of criminal activity. They started to get discouraged when the wars just seemed to get worse and worse. They were eternally grateful for the results of his first two wishes, but had hoped to see this final one come true as well.

It was maybe 5 months after their last visit with Alazhar that news broke of another virus taking hold. After having lived through the recent COVID-19 pandemic, the news wasn't as scary as it might have been before 2020. Still, the media caught hold of the news, and before long it was overshadowing every else.

The new virus was particularly dangerous. No one seemed to be able to pinpoint how it was spread, or even if it truly was an actual virus. It was attacking all over the world, seemingly at random. The usual models and predictors of disease spread were irrelevant.

The cause of death seemed to be sudden cardiac arrest, unresponsive to intervention. It wasn't just the people more prone to heart disease either. It was random men, women, and children. It seemed to happen in clusters, which is why the scientists researching it assumed it to be some type of contagion.

Things went downhill quickly. Barn looked for any sign of his wish coming true in the news, but it was just getting worse. People were scared, and scared people lash out. Previous peaceful countries were edgy and combative in the media. It seemed like every day there were more threats of civil war and hostile takeovers. He thought maybe he had made his wish too late, that there wasn't a place for peace in a world like this.

Two months into the new pandemic, which people were just calling SUMI (Sudden Unexplained Myocardial Infarction), the President of the United States died. He wasn't the first political leader to die from SUMI, but it did mark a turning point in the virus. Things went from bad to untenable overnight. A group of thugs calling themselves politicians staged a coup and were in the White House within days.

The country was essentially under military lockdown. With control over virtually everything in the country, it was only a matter of weeks before all social media was dismantled, and the only news Barn and Patty got up at the cabin was what the new regime wanted them to. They made a short and nervous trip to town to stock up on what they could, and quarantined themselves off the grid, grateful that they had decided to purchase the out-of-the-way cabin.

Barn and Patty watched what little news was available to them and set about preparing themselves for the coming winter. They filled their cellar with vegetables from their garden, and Barn went hunting almost daily. They chopped wood and kept themselves busy, trying not to think about what was happening to the world around them.

Barn thought more than once that he had wasted that final wish. He should have cured all diseases instead of just Alzheimer's. He should have asked for all children to have enough food, or for a magical talking dog, anything. Even a genie couldn't bring peace to a world as damaged as the one they were now living in.

It was a Thursday when it happened. Barn had a calendar in the kitchen and still paid attention to what day of the week it was, so he could pretend anything about this life was still normal. He was washing dishes and thinking about how to apologize to Patty when she came back in from gathering the last of the vegetables from the little garden they had tended all summer.

Barn and Patty didn't argue often. They were both levelheaded, rational people. Most of the time, even minor tiffs were easily and quickly settled. They were scared and stressed out, though. Their world was crumbling, and they had no idea if the people they loved were even still alive. They were suffering from some cabin fever too, as anyone would.

When Barn said he would do the dishes later instead of right after breakfast, Patty snapped at him. She said she didn't understand why he needed to wait, it wasn't like they had a lot else to do. He rolled his eyes, and she called him a rare curse word before stomping out to the garden. He decided to stay inside and do the damn dishes to give her a chance to cool off. Afterward, he would apologize to her. Right or wrong, she was his wife. Her happiness was one of his only priorities anymore.

Barn found her lying between the rows of tomato plants. Her face was calm, as if she had died before she even knew what was happening. He supposed he should be grateful for small blessings, but he wasn't. He cried and screamed at the forest, at the sky, at the cabin. He screamed until his voice gave out and cried until he was afraid he might never stop. When he was done, he buried her. It was the only thing he could do.

Barn spent the next couple of weeks watching the world disintegrate on television. Even the censored propaganda that passed for news couldn't hide how bad things were. Countries were collapsing, and infrastructures around the world were crumbling. Barn didn't care anymore.

One morning he turned on the television, and all of the stations were off the air. The radio was just static too. He drove the 2 hours into the nearest town, and the devastation was beyond anything he could have imagined. It looked like a scene from a zombie apocalypse movie. Cars were all over the roads, buildings had been looted and then burned, but worst of all was the silence. No motors, no voices, nothing at all. He drove around town, stopping and checking out random buildings, but he didn't find a single living person.

He drove back to the cabin slowly. He walked up the steps onto the deck and sat heavily in one of the wooden chairs he and Patty had spent so much time in. He stared out into the forest. He couldn't remember feeling such profound emptiness before. Seeing the fallen and empty world had drained the last bit of energy he'd had. Finding Patty dead in the garden had left him grieving, but alive. This… he just didn't know.

Barn gradually became aware of the tall, imposing man standing next to his chair. He looked up at Alazhar blankly.

"I thought you weren't coming back? Not that there's anything to come back to."

"I wasn't supposed to." He stood silently for a few more minutes, then sat in the empty chair next to Barn's. "Genies don't normally follow up with their masters once the final wish has been cast. Once I saw how yours turned out though, I felt I had to."

"How mine turned out? It didn't turn out at all. There was fighting right until the end, until that damn virus killed every last one of them. My Patty included." He choked on the last words, trying not to cry.

"It did though, Mr. Barn. You wished to see a world with no conflict, to live in a world without senseless hate and violence." He gestured broadly with his hands. "Here it is. That virus everyone was so scared of? It was spread through conflict. Every time conflict arose, SUMI, as you called it, eradicated it. As it spread, the world panicked. That only sped up the process."

"I don't understand. What are you saying, that I wished for this? That I caused this? That I wanted my wife to die?"

"No, of course not. I wish it hadn't turned out that way. You wished for a world without conflict, though, and that's what you got. Fate doesn't always perform the way we want or expect. Conflict is human nature. It's essential. As long as there's more than one person, there is the potential for conflict."

"You could have warned me. You could have told me what could happen."

"We're not omniscient, Mr. Barn. And we don't influence wishes. We just do what we do."

"Well it's shitty. It's a scam. I wanted a better world, not a mass extinction event. I'm responsible for this." Barn was openly crying now, no longer caring if Alazhar saw. Alazhar rested a hand on Barn's shoulder.

"You're human. You weren't the first, and you certainly won't be the last. You're only responsible for yourself, and you did the best you could do. Sometimes fate has her own plans. I have to go now, Mr. Barn."

Barn sat alone on the deck long after the genie had gone. Finally, as the first rays of sun began to peek over the edge of the trees and the birds started to greet another day, he stood and wiped his eyes. He took a last look at the cabin he and Patty had spent the end of the world in and walked away from it into the woods. Not long after, Barn's final wish was completed. The world was finally free from the conflict and hate of the humans who had once lived there.

TRUE LOVE

5/14/2016 - I saw an angel today. I don't think she saw me, or at least I hope she didn't, but I saw her. She was gorgeous, ethereal. I didn't believe in love at first sight until today. I was in a coffee shop just minding my own business when she walked in. It must have been fate that I went to that location today instead of my usual one. My ex works at my usual one and I just couldn't face her today.

5/16/2016 - She was there again today. She got an iced mocha latte with oat milk. I was right the other day, it's definitely love. I couldn't bring myself to talk to her, but I smiled at her from across the shop and she smiled back! Is this what a meet-cute is? She had a book with her, but I couldn't see what the title was. She was on the phone while ordering, which I don't normally approve of, but I can make an exception for her.

5/17/2016 - I looked for my angel today, but she must have had other plans. I waited and read my book for 3 hours at that coffee shop, hoping she would come in. I know that sounds pathetic, but I really feel like we're meant to at least meet officially.

5/20/2016 - I've been at this coffee shop every day for the past couple of days, and she hasn't come. I know she doesn't know I'm here waiting, but it's frustrating to be so close to that level of beauty just to have it torn away before I even get a chance to speak to her. If she doesn't come tomorrow, I might have to resign myself to this just being a fleeting heartache.

5/22/2016 - I almost didn't believe it when I saw her today. She was even more beautiful than the first two times I saw her. She floated into the coffee shop on a breeze of vanilla-scented body spray that I could just barely catch a whiff of from the table I was sitting at by the door. My heart almost stopped when she glanced my way. She was still carrying the book, but I could only see the back cover. She ordered another iced coffee, and I watched as she read the book while she waited for her drink to be prepared. I was just getting up to finally introduce myself when her phone rang. She tucked her book under her arm and answered the phone as she grabbed her cup from the counter. She was gone before I could do anything, chattering away to whoever had interrupted what was possibly my last chance to meet her. I felt sick and threw away the rest of my coffee and croissant before leaving.

5/24/2016 - I don't believe it. I saw her today, and not at that coffee shop she likes so much. I was sitting in the park across the street from my apartment, and there she was. She was reading her book, sitting on a bench with a coffee. Had she been enjoying her drinks right across from his door this whole time? How had I not known? How had I now felt her there? I couldn't let another chance slip away. I went over to the bench she was sitting on and sat down beside her. When she didn't immediately look up, I cleared my throat a little, just enough to catch her attention. She looked startled, and I apologized and introduced myself finally. I told her how I'd seen her in the coffee shop and how beautiful she was. She said her name was Angela. What are the chances that my angel is actually named Angela? It's got to be a sign. I suggested dinner at a nearby Italian place that I've always liked, and that's when she told me she was married. Married! How could someone as young and perfect as her already be tied down to some jerk who probably didn't appreciate her? I tried to give her my number in case she changed her mind, but she said her husband wouldn't be happy about that. She looked sad as she said it though, and I wonder just how controlling this guy is.

5/25/2016 - Angela was at the park across the street again today, on a different bench. It didn't look like her husband was with her, so I walked over and chatted with her for a bit. She's so amazing. She's smart, funny, gorgeous… I get butterflies in my stomach just thinking about her. I never thought I would get involved with a married woman, but something about her is irresistible. I think she feels something towards me too. She didn't come out and say it, but I'm pretty good at reading body language.

5/28/2016 - I'm starting to get worried about Angela. It's been a couple of days since I've seen her at the park, and she hasn't been to her coffee shop either. I've been hoping to have another chat with her, but maybe her husband stopped letting her go out. He sounded like kind of a jerk when she talked about him.

5/29/2016 - Something crazy happened today. I still can't believe it, it's like something out of a movie. I was getting ready to go out for coffee and a walk, and she knocked on my door. Angela! It was raining outside, and she was wet and shivering. I invited her in, of course, and she told me that she was in trouble and needed help. She said she didn't know anyone else in the area, but she remembered that I lived across from the park. Once she got inside, I realized she had a split lip and her eye was turning black and blue. Her husband. I still wish I could have gone after that son of a bitch, but she didn't want me to. She said he could be dangerous, and she just needed a place to crash for a night. I wish I knew where he lived.

5/30/2016 - I still can't believe that the woman I love spent the night in my apartment! She slept on the couch, of course. I offered to sleep there and let her have the bed, but she said she'd be more comfortable on the couch. We spent a long time talking today about her situation. She wants to leave her husband, but she's scared of him. I can't believe any man would hit an angel like her. I invited her to stay as long as she wanted to.

6/1/2016 - I think she's going to leave him. She's been at my apartment for 3 nights now, and we've made a real connection in that time. Not puppy love, like when I saw her at the coffee shop. Real love. True love. She feels it too, but she's afraid to admit it. I'm helping her make plans to start a new life on her own, away from him.

6/2/2016 - Things are amazing. This woman is everything I ever dreamed of, and she wants to be here with me. She moved into my room last night and... well, I don't even have to write it down, it's a memory that will never leave me. It's like my life changed overnight. I spend all day at home with her, and it's glorious. I'll never let that asshole hurt her again. I went out and bought her some new clothes today since she left everything at home with him. She looks beautiful in everything. I can't believe how lucky I am.

6/6/2016 - Angela wants to leave town. She said she's scared of her husband and wants to get as far away from him as possible. I told her to get a restraining order and a divorce, but she said she doesn't want any communication with him at all. I don't blame her. I'll find a way. I can work anywhere, and I'll take her somewhere he can never find her. She deserves that and more. I know it's quick, but I feel like I've known her my whole life. She's a part of me. I'll do whatever I need to do to keep her safe and happy.

6/10/2016 - It took a lot of planning, but it's done. Angela and I leave tonight. He'll never be able to find us, and we can have a life of our own. My dreams are finally coming true. After tonight, it's just the two of us. Fate brought us together, and true love will keep us together.

From the Warwick Town Herald, 6/25/2016

Officers from the Warwick police department responded to a call for a welfare check Friday evening after neighbors of the apartment at 32 Bradford Lane reported an odor coming from the apartment. Police entered the residence after not being able to contact the tenant, Jeffrey Thompson. Mr. Thompson was found deceased in his bedroom from an apparent suicide. A handwritten journal was found near his body, although the contents have not been released.

A second body was found in the residence as well, and preliminary reports from the medical examiner indicate that the individual had been deceased for approximately four to six weeks. Police are waiting for the final identification of the victim, but the initial details match a recent missing persons case: 24-year-old Angela McKinney.

McKinney was reported missing by her husband on May 29th after she failed to return home from running errands. He reported that she had told him about a couple of encounters with a stranger recently that had made her uncomfortable.

Police reported that the second body recovered from the apartment appeared to have been moved around frequently post-mortem, and multiple items of women's clothing were found on the scene. The medical examiner has listed her cause of death as blunt force trauma to the head. Interviews with neighbors mention how quiet Mr. Thompson was, and describe him… (cont. on pg 8)

SOMNUS EXCHANGE

Mark Mercer woke before his alarm because the radiator in his apartment had started knocking again. He lay still for a few seconds, staring at the water stain on the ceiling while he tried to remember what day it was. Wednesday? Or maybe Thursday? It didn't matter much. Every day had begun to feel the same.

He rolled onto his side and reached for his phone, then winced as his shoulder protested the movement. He had slept badly again. His mattress was old and cheap, and so worn out in the middle that no matter how he positioned himself, he always woke up in some variety of pain.

His phone's lock screen was full of notifications. Three payment reminders, two promotional emails, and a final notice from the electric company that had been flagged as urgent. He read that one, then set the phone face down on the nightstand, as if that could make the emails not exist.

He had turned the heat down last week to save money, and now he shivered in the cold apartment. Somewhere upstairs, he could hear a television through the thin floorboards. Someone laughed at something, sounding muffled and distant.

Mark swung his legs over the side of the bed and sat there for a moment with his elbows on his knees. He tried to do the math in his head again, and he came up with the same answer he always did. He was behind on rent, he was behind on utilities, and his credit card balance had reached a number he was afraid to even think about.

He dressed in yesterday's jeans and a sweatshirt that had begun to fray at the cuffs. In the kitchen, he stirred the last of the instant coffee into a chipped mug, popped it in the microwave, and drank it standing up. The bitterness made his stomach tighten, but it also made him feel briefly alert, and he clung to that sensation to get him moving through another day.

Outside, the morning air cut through his clothes as he walked toward the bus stop. Traffic hissed along wet pavement, and people moved past him with the practiced focus of commuters who had learned not to look at one another. He was fine with that, he preferred to go unnoticed anyway.

His job at the fulfillment warehouse required little thought. He scanned packages, stacked crates, and followed the steady rhythm of conveyor belts that never slowed down. By midmorning his lower back had begun to ache, and by lunchtime he could feel the familiar exhaustion settling into his muscles. It was the best-paying job he could find, but it was barely keeping him afloat. It didn't feel worth it lately.

He was sitting in the break room contemplating a vending machine sandwich when Kyle dropped into the chair across from him.

"You look like hell," Kyle said cheerfully, and began unwrapping a protein bar.

"Thanks," Mark replied. "You always know what to say."

Kyle grinned. He was younger, energetic, and possessed the irritating optimism of someone who believed all problems were only temporary. He chewed for a moment, then leaned forward conspiratorially.

"You ever hear of Somnus Exchange?"

Mark shook his head and took a reluctant bite of the sad-looking sandwich, already regretting his choice.

"It's this new thing," Kyle continued. "You rent out your body while you sleep. Rich people pay to experience stuff without actually doing it themselves. You just lie there, and the money shows up."

Mark swallowed. "You're kidding."

"I am not," Kyle said. "My cousin signed up last month. He cleared two grand in one weekend."

"There has to be a catch," he said.

"Everything has a catch," Kyle replied. "But this is legit. They monitor everything, no sex, no drugs. Rock and roll is probably allowed, though. It's mostly rich old people who want to feel young again for a day, and famous people who want to do shit without everyone knowing."

Mark snorted, but he didn't argue. He finished the sandwich without tasting it and spent the rest of his shift watching packages slide past while he thought about what Kyle had said.

That night, back in his apartment, he sat on his bed and opened his laptop. He typed the name of the company into the search bar. Somnus Exchange. The website loaded with smooth animations and warm colors. Smiling people floated across the screen in slow motion, hiking through forests, floating in hot air balloons, and laughing in crowded clubs. A banner near the top displayed a simple message in bold, reassuring letters.

Earn while you sleep.

Mark scrolled down to the payment estimates, and his jaw dropped. He read the numbers again, then again more carefully, as if they might vanish if he blinked. Rich people really had nothing else to do with their money. For the first time in months, he thought there might be a light at the end of his tunnel. He stared at the sign-up button for a long time before he finally clicked it.

The Somnus Exchange office occupied the upper floors of a glass building downtown that Mark had passed a hundred times without noticing. Up close, the place felt much more elite than he had expected. The lobby was decorated in a way that made everything appear both futuristic and welcoming. A woman at the reception desk smiled as he approached and gave her his name.

"We've been expecting you, Mr. Mercer," she said in a soft, melodic voice. "You can follow me."

They moved down a hallway lined with abstract artwork and frosted glass doors. The air smelled of citrus, with something antiseptic underneath. Based on the look of the office, Mark assumed this must be a very lucrative business.

The orientation room contained about a dozen chairs arranged in a semicircle to face a large screen. A few people sat scattered among them, all wearing the same cautious expression Mark suspected he had on his own face. After a few minutes, a man in a tailored suit entered and introduced himself as Daniel Rourke, Client Experience Director. His handshake was firm, and his smile appeared practiced enough to inspire confidence.

"Thank you all for coming," Rourke began. "Somnus Exchange exists to create opportunities. Our donors earn significant income, and our clients gain access to experiences they might otherwise never have. It is a mutually beneficial relationship built on safety, consent, and groundbreaking neuroscience."

The screen behind him came to life with smooth, elegant graphics. Diagrams of the human brain rotated slowly while lines of data flowed across them in calm blue pulses. Rourke spoke about neural synchronization, biometric monitoring, and adaptive safety protocols. He explained that each session was overseen by advanced systems designed to prevent harm, and he emphasized that the company had an impeccable record.

"Our violence inhibition layer prevents clients from initiating harmful or potentially lethal activities," he said. "If stress indicators exceed safe thresholds, the session is immediately terminated. You remain protected at all times."

Several people nodded, and Mark found himself nodding too. The presentation continued with testimonials from smiling donors who described paying off debts, traveling, and learning to live without the anxiety of financial struggles. A woman on the screen laughed as she recounted waking up to discover she had apparently gone surfing while she was "asleep". A client who had been confined to a wheelchair for most of his life was able to use a donor body to walk his daughter down the aisle at her wedding. While most client activities were private and confidential, there were a few cases where they chose to share their experiences with their donors.

When the lights came back up, tablets were distributed so contracts could be reviewed and signed digitally. The document scrolled for what felt like miles, dense paragraphs of legal language blending together until Mark's vision began to blur.

He skimmed enough to recognize familiar words. Liability, consent, behavioral variance. He would be signing a contract for 90 days, with a minimum of one exchange session required per week, although he was allowed to complete up to four if he wanted to. There was even a section that explained that certain more "explicit" rentals could be arranged with additional consent and contracts. He told himself he would read the rest later, when he had more time and a clearer head. He pressed his thumb to the screen and watched the confirmation message appear.

A technician led him into a medical suite where sleek white pods stood in a neat row. Each one resembled a cross between a tanning bed and a hospital device, and the sight of them made his stomach tighten despite all the reassurances he had just heard.

"First time is always the strangest," the technician said, fastening small sensors along Mark's temples and wrists. "Most donors wake up feeling like they had a very active dream. This one is just setting things up, it will be a staff member who will act as a client while we fine-tune the setting for you individually."

Another staff member, a nurse with kind eyes and steady hands, checked the readouts and adjusted a dial.

"Some clients prefer physically intense experiences," she said in the same calm tone one might use to discuss the weather. "You may notice residual soreness, but it will pass. Think of it as a free workout!"

Mark lay his head back as the pod hummed around him, and for a brief second he considered sitting up and walking out, then he thought about the overdue notices on his nightstand and the number he didn't want to think about on his credit card statement.

The interior lights dimmed to a soft blue glow.

"Just relax," the nurse said. "We'll take it from here."

A low hum filled his ears, steady and soothing. His muscles loosened despite himself, and the last thing he saw before his eyes closed was his own faint reflection in the curved surface above him, staring back with an expression he didn't quite recognize.

Mark resurfaced slowly, as if he were rising through deep water. At first, there was only warmth and weight. His limbs felt heavy and distant, and his thoughts moved with the same sluggish resistance. A soft tone pulsed somewhere nearby, repeating at calm, regular intervals. He lay still and listened to it for a moment before realizing the sound was meant for him. He opened his eyes and saw the nurse from before standing next to the pod, waiting for him to wake up.

"It's okay, Mr. Mercer. There's no rush, you will probably feel a little groggy. You were only out for a couple of hours, but you're not used go it yet. We induce a REM cycle before and after the donor accesses you, it helps to offset the mental fatigue that can accompany the "sleep" state you're in during an exchange. It also gives us a window to get clients in and out privately."

"So is this what it will feel like every time?" Mark actually felt a little rested, like he had taken a good nap, even though his body had been active.

"It varies a little, depending on how long the rental period was, how physically active the client was, factors like that. In general, though, yes."

Mark nodded. He had been expecting the disorientation that sometimes came with anesthesia or heavy medication, but he actually felt fine after a few minutes of letting himself wake up.

"Okay, then. When do I start?"

Two days later, Mark had his first real Somnus experience. It was a client who had requested a daytime experience, so he had come in on his day off from the fulfillment center. He was curious to know what this anonymous client would do with his body while he slept, but he knew most of the time the donors never found out.

He arrived back at the Somnus office and was escorted into a private room with a pod just like the one he had done his trial experience in. Just as before, the staff were pleasant and efficient, and before he knew it, he was drifting off to sleep. Although Somnus didn't use any type of medicinal sleep aids because of the side effects while the client was in control of the donor, the pods were equipped with some proprietary hardware that helped induce a quick and deep sleep. Within minutes his eyes were closed, and the exchange had begun.

For several seconds, he didn't move. He was aware of a powerful fatigue in his muscles, the kind that followed long physical exertion. His calves throbbed like he had run a marathon while he was unconscious. His shoulders ached, and even his hands felt sore somehow, as though he had been gripping something for hours.

"Welcome back, Mr. Mercer," the technician said. Her voice sounded very far away.

He sat up too quickly and felt the room tilt. A wave of dizziness passed through him, sharp enough to make him grab the edge of the pod until his vision steadied. The medical suite looked exactly as he remembered it, sterile, orderly, and softly lit, but for a few minutes it had the strange, impermanent feeling of a dream world.

"How long has it been?" he asked.

"Eight hours," the technician replied, checking a screen. "Your vitals remained well within acceptable parameters."

Mark swung his legs over the side of the pod and stood carefully. He glanced down and noticed dried mud along the sides of his sneaker, flaking off onto the polished floor.

"That's normal," the nurse said before he could ask. "Some clients choose outdoor excursions. You may feel residual soreness for a few hours, but it will pass."

Someone handed him his phone. A notification banner stretched across the screen, informing him that the session had been successful and his compensation had been deposited into his bank account. The number beneath it was larger than any single deposit he had ever received.

Relief flooded him, swift and overwhelming. He let out a deep breath, and a laugh escaped him before he could stop it.

"See?" the technician said with an easy smile. "Most donors are surprised by how much they accomplish while they rest."

Mark nodded, his body still humming with a faint, unsettled energy, like the aftershock of an adrenaline rush. Somewhere at the edge of his awareness lingered the sensation of movement, of wind against his face and hard pavement rushing beneath his feet. When he tried to focus on it, the feeling dissolved into nothing like a fading dream.

He dressed and signed a final discharge form, then stepped out into the afternoon sunlight. By the time he reached the bus stop, the worst of the dizziness had faded. He checked his bank account again just to be certain the transfer was real. The numbers remained what they had been when he had left the Somnus office.

For the first time in years, he allowed himself to imagine what it might feel like not to worry about money every hour of the day. That night, he set his alarm later than usual and slept more deeply than he had in weeks.

When he woke in the morning, his muscles still ached, but the decision that followed the discomfort was simple and immediate. He opened the Somnus app and scheduled another session.

The second session felt easier. This time he didn't hesitate before closing his eyes. When he woke, the soreness was worse. It ached deep in his ribs and across his shoulders, a dull pressure that made breathing feel heavier than it should have.

He sat up slowly, expecting the dizziness now, and waited for the room to steady itself before standing.

"High-intensity sessions can involve physical strain," the technician explained. "Don't worry, your metrics remained within safe limits."

The payment was larger, and that made the decision easier. He scheduled two more rentals that week. He began to organize his schedule at the fulfillment center around his sessions. He worked shorter shifts at the warehouse so he would be available more. The numbers in his bank account continued to climb, and overdue notices stopped arriving in the mail.

About a month into his Somnus contract, he noticed the split skin across his knuckles. He stood in the bathroom, turning his hands under the harsh light, studying the shallow cuts and purple swelling. He wondered what he had been doing and assumed maybe his client that day had been doing some type of boxing or martial arts. The muscle soreness certainly supported that theory.

Instead of worrying too much, he found himself calculating how many more months he would need before he could finally breathe easy again. Getting out of immediate debt was great, but he wanted to set himself up for a successful future as well. He never wanted to worry about getting his lights shut off or going hungry again.

Residual sensations began to follow him into waking hours. They arrived without warning and disappeared just as quickly. The distant wail of sirens while he stacked crates at work, the sudden impression of running at full speed while he waited in line at a grocery store. Once, he even became convinced he could smell metal, sharp and unmistakable, even though there was nothing around him except his own bedroom.

He contacted Somnus support through the app, and a representative responded within minutes. They reminded him that mild sensory carryover was a known side effect of immersive sessions, no action required. The message included a smiling emoji. He accepted the explanation because it was easy work, and it was making a huge difference in his life. So what if he had some weird sensations now and then? It was nothing he couldn't handle.

He didn't know if he always had the same client, but whoever was renting his body was certainly putting some mileage on it. Once he had awoken with a bruise blooming along his side, gravel embedded in the heels of his shoes, even dirt beneath his fingernails. Each time he woke, he performed the same quiet inspection of his body, then reassured himself that everything could be explained.

His bank account grew steadily larger. By the end of the second month, he had cleared enough debt to see a future he had almost stopped believing in. He began to think of the sessions not as something strange or temporary, but as a practical solution, a system designed to help people like him survive and to let other people live in a way they, for whatever reason, were unable to in their own physical bodies.

One evening, after another rental, he rode the bus home with his head resting against the window. City lights slid across the glass in blurred ribbons, and fatigue pressed down on him with a now familiar weight. Somewhere between one stop and the next, a sliver of something surfaced in his mind. A narrow alley, echoing footsteps, someone shouting something he couldn't understand.

Mark bolted upright, and the sensation vanished. He told himself it had only been particularly strong sensory carryover. They had warned him that this could happen, and that it was no more harmful that remembering a fragment of a dream the next morning.

The knock on Mark's door came just after sunrise. He had been awake for less than ten minutes and was still standing in the kitchen holding a mug of coffee when the sound reached him, followed by a murmur of voices in the hallway.

For a moment he considered not answering. For once, he wasn't late on any bills, and the rent had already been paid, so he couldn't imagine it was anything too important.

There was a second knock, much louder than the first, and he set the mug down and crossed the room to open the door. Two men stood outside, both looking obviously like plainclothes detectives. One of them held up a badge before Mark could speak.

"Mr. Mark Mercer?" the taller one asked.

"Yes?"

"We'd like to ask you a few questions." They didn't wait for an invitation. The shorter detective stepped inside first, his eyes moving quickly across the apartment. The other remained near the doorway, watching Mark with polite focus.

"This won't take long," he said. "We're following up on an incident that occurred yesterday afternoon."

Mark felt something tighten in his stomach. He tried to keep his voice steady.

"What kind of incident?"

"A man was assaulted behind a bar on Fulton Street," the taller detective replied. "He was hurt pretty badly, he's in the hospital."

"That's terrible, but I'm not sure what that has to do with me."

"I think you do, Mr. Mercer. We ran the prints on the beer bottle the assailant used to smash the poor guy's face in with, and they came right back to you. You were in the system for an assault about 10 years ago, does that sound familiar?"

Mark closed his eyes, feeling sick. "Yeah, I got into a bar fight. It was no big deal. I didn't touch anyone yesterday, though. There must be some kind of mistake."

The detectives exchanged glances.

"It wasn't me," Mark repeated. "I was… working."

"That's interesting, because your boss told us you had the day off yesterday."

The taller detective reached into his coat and removed a tablet. He tapped the screen once, then turned it toward Mark. Grainy security footage filled the display. The image showed a narrow stretch of sidewalk and a figure moving past the camera.

The figure was unmistakably him. Mark watched himself glance over one shoulder before disappearing out of frame, and a strange detachment settled over him as if he were observing a stranger.

"Do you want to rethink your story, Mr. Mercer?"

Mark swallowed.

"I was at work," he said. "Not at the warehouse, I was in a Somnus session. I started donating my time there a couple of months ago."

The detectives stared at him.

"The body rental program," he continued quickly. "They take neural control while the donor sleeps. It's monitored, there are safeguards."

The shorter detective frowned slightly, as if trying to decide whether Mark was joking.

"You're saying someone else was using your body," he said.

"Yes."

"And you don't know who?"

"No, the clients are anonymous."

The taller man studied him for a long moment. His expression didn't change, but something behind his eyes seemed to harden.

"Mr. Mercer," he said, "we're not charging you with anything at this time. We just need you to understand that we have evidence that you were physically present at the scene of a violent crime."

Mark nodded, feeling overwhelmed and disconnected.

"I understand," he said.

"Good. If you remember anything at all, we expect you to contact us."

They handed him a card and moved toward the door. Just before leaving, the shorter detective paused.

"You might want to reconsider whatever arrangement you've made with this company," he said. "Sounds like maybe their safeguards aren't so safe."

The door closed behind them, and Mark stood in the center of the apartment for several minutes without moving. The radiator continued its slow knocking, and somewhere outside a siren rose and fell like a distant warning. He turned back toward the kitchen and noticed, for the first time, the dark smudge along the cuff of his sleeve. When he rubbed at it with his thumb, dried blood flaked away.

Mark didn't go to work that day. He sat at the small table beside his bed with his laptop open and the Somnus contract filling the screen. He had already skimmed through the document once before, but now he forced himself to read every line. The language was precise and undeniable.

Donors retained full legal responsibility for all physical actions undertaken by their bodies during active rental sessions. Somnus Exchange assumed no liability for outcomes resulting from client use. Client identities were protected under strict confidentiality agreements. Neural session data couldn't be disclosed without court order.

He scrolled further. Early termination of participation was prohibited until completion of the assigned service cycle.

Mark leaned back in his chair and sighed. He had signed all of it. He could see the image of his thumbprint on the digital signature line. There would be no arguing that.

He opened the Somnus app and tapped through the menus until he found the support portal. He clicked the button to request a cycle suspension or cancellation and explained the conversation with the detectives in the comment box.

The response came quickly.

"Your concern has been logged. All sessions are conducted within approved safety parameters. You remain scheduled for participation through the end of your current cycle."

He stared at the message until the words began to blur. Another notification followed almost immediately.

"Reminder: Breach of contractual obligations may result in financial penalties and legal action."

Mark closed the laptop and pressed the heels of his hands against his eyes. The apartment felt small and airless, as though the walls had shifted inward while he wasn't looking. He tried to think logically. The company had insisted that the safeguards were functioning. There had to be an explanation that would explain why his prints were on a weapon, when the client shouldn't have been able to carry out an assault like that.

He stood and began pacing the length of the room. Every few steps he caught sight of himself reflected in the dark screen of the television or the narrow bathroom mirror. Each time, the image startled him slightly. He had the unsettling impression that his body belonged to someone else now, and that he was the one borrowing it while the real owner was away.

He checked the calendar in the app again. Four weeks remained in his service cycle. His bank balance made the situation worse, not better. The money had erased immediate panic about rent and utilities, but it had also tied him more firmly to the program. He had begun to rely on it and build plans around it. Walking away now would mean giving up the first stable ground he had felt in years.

The knock from that morning echoed faintly in his memory. He imagined the detectives returning with handcuffs instead of questions. He imagined trying to explain again that he had been asleep, and hearing the doubt in their voices grow stronger each time.

Mark opened the app and selected his next scheduled session. For a long moment, he hovered over the confirmation button. If he canceled, he risked penalties he couldn't afford. If he continued, he wondered if he was risking something even worse.

He pressed confirm, and then stared at the screen until it dimmed and his reflection surfaced faintly in the glass. He looked haunted.

The next session felt different even before it began. Mark noticed it in the waiting room while he sat with his hands clasped together, staring at the muted television mounted on the far wall. A news anchor's lips moved silently above scrolling headlines, and he had the strange sensation that he needed to be somewhere else, anywhere else.

A technician called his name. The routine unfolded as it had before. Sensors were placed along his temples, the low hum began as he laid back and tried to relax. He tried to focus on his breathing, but tension coiled through his muscles despite the relaxing properties of the session.

He didn't remember falling asleep. He woke with a violent jolt. His entire body felt as though it had been struck by a passing vehicle. Pain flared along his ribs and down his spine, sharp enough to force a gasp from his throat. For several seconds he lay there struggling to orient himself, convinced he had been injured in some accident he couldn't recall.

"Welcome back," the technician said. Her voice had the same mildly pleasant tone as usual.

Mark sat up, and the room tilted hard to one side before righting itself. The technician glanced at the screen and nodded once.

"Your session remained within safe parameters," he said.

Mark laughed, a short and brittle sound that startled even him. He wondered who exactly those parameters were keeping safe.

On the ride home, he noticed something dark under a couple of his fingernails and prayed that it was just dirt, and not the blood he suspected it was. His arms and hands ached like he had been holding tightly to something. He had already logged into the Somnus app again and requested an appeal to his case, asking again for his contract to be at least suspended while they looked into it, but the response had been the same as before. He gazed at his reflection in the bus window, a man who appeared exhausted and afraid, as though he had just woken from a nightmare he couldn't describe.

Two days later, the nightmare came true, and he saw the first news reports. A woman had been found dead in a parking structure downtown. The anchor spoke in grave tones about the brutality of the attack and the lack of an apparent motive. Surveillance footage showed a figure entering the structure shortly before the estimated time of death. The image was blurred, but the height and build were unmistakable.

Mark turned off the television and sat in silence. He wasn't a violent person. He had gotten into one stupid bar fight years ago and had stopped drinking because of it. There was no way someone could use him to do this, could they? The possibility made him sick, and he found himself retching and running to the bathroom to throw up his dinner.

More reports followed. There was another victim in a different neighborhood, then a third. Each killing was described as methodical and disturbingly controlled. Witnesses mentioned a man who moved with calm purpose, who didn't appear to be in a hurry even as he left the scene.

Mark checked the timestamps, and every incident aligned perfectly with a rental session. That afternoon, he stood in line at a convenience store and saw his own face as a police sketch staring back from a newspaper rack, under the headline "Police Search For Serial Attacker".

For a long moment, he couldn't breathe. He reached out and touched the surface of the page as if confirming it was real. The clerk watched him carefully.

"You know that guy?" she asked.

Mark withdrew his hand.

"No," he said, and left the store without buying anything.

Mark decided he would find a way to stay awake. If they wouldn't let him stop, and the murders were happening during the sessions, then remaining conscious might allow him to interrupt whatever was being done through his body. He didn't know how the neural transfer worked in detail, but he understood enough to believe that awareness might give him leverage.

He bought energy drinks and over-the-counter stimulants on the way to the Somnus office. His hands trembled as he paid, and he caught the cashier studying his face with a flicker of recognition that made his pulse quicken.

By the time he reached the building, his heart was already beating too fast. The waiting room looked as it always had. Mark sat rigidly in the chair and focused on keeping his hands from shaking.

When the technician called him, he stood immediately. He allowed the sensors to be attached and lay back inside the pod.

The interior light glowed the same calm blue, and the familiar hum started to vibrate through his skull. He clenched his jaw and forced himself to focus.

He felt the pod begin to work, spreading warmth through his limbs and dulling the edges of his thoughts. He fought it by counting backward, by flexing his fingers, by concentrating on the faint ticking sound that seemed to echo from somewhere deep inside the machinery.

For a while, it worked. His awareness narrowed but didn't disappear completely. He remained suspended in a strange half-state, neither fully awake nor entirely gone. He couldn't fully see, but he sensed flashes of light and shadow. The sensation of movement crept into his muscles without his permission.

Panic surged through him as he felt his body moving. He tried to force the limbs to remain still, but they weren't responding to his commands. It felt like he was being used as a puppet, which he supposed was exactly what was happening.

The next thing he was aware of was hearing footsteps. Time must have passed, although he had no idea how much. He was standing, moving forward at a steady pace. The world around him existed only in fragments of light and motion. Streetlamps blurred into long white streaks. Cold air struck his face. His heart pounded against his ribs, but the rhythm didn't feel entirely his.

He fought the movement of his body, but his legs kept moving. He was watching everything as if through a faraway screen, blurry and distorted. A shape appeared ahead, and he strained to make it out. As it got closer, he saw it was a person, possibly a woman. They turned to look at him, and he saw his hand reach out. He yelled out inside his own head, and for a second, Mark thought felt another presence beside his own. They were calm, focused, unconcerned with the possibility of Mark sensing them.

Before he could process all of this, everything went dark. He woke up lying on rough concrete, with rain soaking through his clothes. The sky above him was unfamiliar, and he could hear traffic somewhere nearby. Pain radiated from his shoulder and down his side, making it difficult to sit up.

He checked his phone with shaking fingers. The session had ended hours earlier. He had no recollection of waking up in the Somnus pod or how he had gotten out here on the street. His last memory was that moment of shared control, and the sense of being watched from inside his own head had not entirely faded.

When he finally stood, his reflection stared back at him from the dark window of a parked car, and he had the eerie feeling that someone else was looking back at him.

Mark called Somnus Exchange the moment he got home. He didn't bother changing out of his damp clothes. Rainwater dripped on his floor while he paced the length of the apartment, his phone pressed to his ear. He was just about to hang up when the line finally clicked and a recorded voice welcomed him with practiced warmth.

"All representatives are currently assisting other clients. Please remain on the line."

He remained on the line. After ten minutes, the message repeated. After twenty minutes, the call disconnected without explanation.

He tried again, but the same result followed. By the third attempt, his hands were shaking badly enough that he had to put the call on speakerphone and set it down while he braced himself against the kitchen counter. The radiator knocked in slow, hollow bursts behind him, and the sound made his nerves feel stretched too thin.

When someone finally answered, the voice that greeted him was unfamiliar.

"This is Legal Liaison Services. How may I direct your inquiry?"

"I need to speak with support," Mark said. "There's something wrong with my sessions. I stayed conscious this time. I could feel—"

"Mr. Mercer," the voice interrupted gently. "Your account has been flagged for formal review. All communication must now proceed through designated legal channels."

"I'm telling you someone is committing murders using my body," he said. "Your safeguards aren't working."

A pause followed. He imagined the person on the other end glancing at a screen, scanning a summary of his situation.

"Somnus Exchange maintains the highest safety standards in the industry," the voice replied. "Our systems indicate full compliance during your recent sessions."

"That's impossible."

"We understand that this situation may be distressing," the representative continued, still calm. "However, public statements or unauthorized disclosures regarding proprietary technology may constitute a breach of your contract."

Mark stared at the wall while this settled in.

"You're threatening me," he said quietly.

"We are reminding you of your obligations."

The call disconnected. He stood motionless for several seconds. Outside, a siren passed somewhere in the distance.

His phone vibrated, and a notification from the Somnus app appeared on the screen.

"Reminder: Failure to attend scheduled sessions may result in financial and/or legal penalties."

Mark let out a breath and sank into the chair by the table. The apartment felt colder than usual, and he pulled his sleeves down over his hands and tried to think.

If the company would not help him, he would find someone else who understood what was happening. He opened his laptop and began searching for donor forums, support groups, anything that might connect him to people with similar experiences.

Several links appeared, but clicking on them returned error messages or redirected him back to the Somnus homepage. Threads he had skimmed days earlier no longer existed. Mark was finally understanding that the program was not designed to protect donors at all. It was designed exclusively to protect itself and its clients.

The next knock on the door came three days later. This time there were four officers instead of two, and they didn't ask permission before entering. One of them handed Mark a folded document while another began moving methodically through the apartment, opening drawers and cabinets.

"Search warrant," the taller detective said. "We need you to sit down."

Mark sat numbly on the edge of his bed. The room seemed to tilt slightly as adrenaline flooded his system, and he had the sudden urge to run despite knowing there was nowhere to go.

"I already told you," he said. "I was in a Somnus session during those times."

"We're aware," the detective replied.

He watched them dismantle his life piece by piece. Items were lifted, examined, and placed into evidence bags with gloved hands. His laptop, his phone, his jacket, even the shoes with dried mud still caked on the soles.

The shorter detective emerged from the bedroom, holding something wrapped in a clear plastic sleeve.

"Pretty sure we found the murder weapon," he said with a smirk.

Mark stared at the knife without comprehension. The blade and handle were stained deep maroon with what could only be dried blood. He didn't recognize it.

"That's not mine," he said. "I don't know where that came from."

"It was found beneath your mattress."

Another officer called from the kitchen. "There's more, you guys might wanna come look at this."

They had uncovered a small box tucked behind the radiator. Inside were objects Mark had never seen before. A bracelet, a keycard to a hotel, a torn strip of fabric. Each item was labeled and sealed away.

"Trophies," the detective said.

The word seemed to echo inside Mark's head.

"This is insane," he whispered. "Someone put those there."

"I'm willing to bet your DNA is on all of them," the shorter detective replied. "Along with your fingerprints."

Mark felt his world seem to drop out from beneath him. He tried to reconstruct the past few weeks, to locate any moment when he might have brought strangers into his apartment or hidden evidence without realizing it. Every memory dissolved into the same blank wall he encountered whenever he thought about the sessions. It didn't make any sense. Even if someone had used his body during the sessions to commit a crime, the anonymity was supposed to go both ways. The client shouldn't have had any idea who he really was, where he lived, or anything like that.

Outside his apartment, voices had begun to gather. Someone had seen the police vehicles, and the other tenants were already talking. It made sense after all. He was quiet, he lived alone and kept to himself, he was the perfect fall guy for something like this.

"We have surveillance placing you near all four crime scenes," one detective was saying. "We have eyewitnesses who identify you. We have forensic evidence tying you directly to the victims, not to mention everything we just found here."

"I was asleep," Mark said again.

The words sounded small now, stripped of conviction.

"Mr. Mercer," the taller detective replied, "you need to start thinking about what comes next."

Mark lowered his head into his hands. For the first time, the possibility that no one would believe him was real. Who was going to stick up for him, a couple of guys at work that he barely spoke to? Certainly not the company that had allowed this to happen. He was alone in this.

They arrested him at work, in front of everyone. Mark had considered not going in that morning, but routine had become the only thing holding him together. The warehouse lights hummed overhead while conveyor belts rattled steadily, and for a few hours he managed to lose himself in the mechanical rhythm of scanning and stacking.

He almost didn't notice when it got suddenly quiet. Conversations trailed off, and he heard someone near the loading dock call his name. When Mark turned, he saw uniformed police officers walking toward him. They moved in quickly, although it's not like there was anywhere Mark could run from here.

"Mark Mercer," the taller detective said. "You're under arrest for multiple counts of murder. Go ahead and turn around, hands behind your back."

For a moment he couldn't make his body respond. The faces of his coworkers blurred together in expressions of shock and revulsion. Kyle stood near the break room doorway, his protein bar forgotten in his hand.

"This is a mistake," Mark said. "I told you, I was in Somnus sessions during those times. Someone else—"

"Turn around," the officer said again.

Hands gripped his arms. Cold metal closed around his wrists. The sound of the cuffs locking into place seemed louder than anything he had ever heard. They led him across the warehouse floor while people stepped aside to make room. Some stared openly, while others avoided his eyes. He saw a phone appear in someone's hand, recording the whole thing.

Outside, flashing lights painted the pavement red and blue. A small crowd had gathered near the entrance. Mark heard his name again, this time shouted by strangers. A woman raised her voice above the noise.

"How many did you kill?"

He tried to answer, but the words tangled together in his throat.

"I didn't," he said finally. "I was asleep."

The officer guided him toward the back seat of the cruiser.

"You chose to give up control," he said quietly. "That doesn't make you innocent."

The car door slammed shut. Through the window, Mark watched the warehouse shrink into the distance as the vehicle pulled away. Sirens cleared a path through the traffic. Buildings slid past in distorted reflections, and his own face hovered in the glass beside them, pale and unfamiliar. Somewhere in the city, a television was already showing his photograph.

The trial began three months later. By then, Mark had learned the rhythms of confinement. He woke when the lights snapped on, he ate when food was placed in front of him, and he slept only when exhaustion forced him into it. Time no longer moved forward so much as it accumulated, like layers of paint.

The courtroom was larger than he had expected. High ceilings amplified every sound, from the scrape of chairs to the quiet rustle of paper. Rows of spectators filled the benches behind him. Some were reporters, some were strangers drawn by curiosity. The worst were the families of the victims, people who had lost someone and were waiting for an explanation that would never be enough. Mark kept his eyes forward.

The prosecution had a devastatingly solid case. Surveillance footage broadcast his crimes across large screens, showing him entering parking structures, walking down dim corridors, and disappearing into shadows where bodies would later be found. Expert witnesses testified to every type of evidence imaginable. DNA evidence, fiber transfers, digital timestamps, fingerprints, each one ironclad.

The victims had been chosen at random, the prosecutor explained. The only thing the crimes had in common was the slow, unhurried assault and the complete lack of concealment of any evidence at the scene. As they described it, the murderer had no worries at all about leaving behind copious clues that would lead directly back to him.

Each time Mark heard the description of one of the murders, he searched his own memory. He didn't believe there was a way his brain could so completely block out experiences that traumatic.

His defense attorney spoke about Somnus Exchange and about neural transfer technology and the safeguards that were supposed to prevent misuse. She called specialists who discussed theoretical vulnerabilities and rare cases of sensory bleed-through. She argued that the presence of Mark's body at the crime scenes didn't prove conscious intent.

The prosecution responded by calling representatives from Somnus.

"Our systems have never permitted violence of any sort, let alone lethal violence, during a session," one executive said. "Any claim to the contrary indicates deliberate fabrication. Simply put, it's just not possible. This is a completely safe system."

The jury listened. They saw a man on video committing heinous acts with seemingly no remorse. They heard experts insist that the technology was reliable. They heard a defendant who couldn't explain his own actions except by saying he had been asleep.

During a recess, Mark sat at the defense table and tried not to look at the families of the victims. One woman clutched a photograph to her chest as if afraid it might be taken away. A teenage boy stared with open hatred that made Mark want to apologize for something he still didn't understand.

His attorney leaned toward him.

"We only need one juror," she whispered. "Just one."

He nodded, although hope had begun to feel like a dangerous indulgence. Closing arguments arrived faster than he expected. The prosecutor spoke about responsibility, choice, about the folly of believing that choosing to surrender control would absolve a person of consequences. He described the murders again in language that allowed the horror to seep slowly into every corner of the room.

The jury filed out to deliberate, and was gone for almost three hours. Mark had assumed it would take days, if not longer. When they returned, their faces told him everything he needed to know before the verdict was read. He stood because the judge instructed him to stand. He listened because there was nothing else left to do.

"On the charge of first-degree murder," the foreperson said, "we find the defendant guilty." Mark listened in horror as the list of charges was read off, each one ending in a proclamation of "guilty". He knew there was always the chance to appeal, to demand a retrial, but would it matter? He couldn't fight a company like Somnus.

Sentencing took place the following morning. Mark had not slept. He sat at the defense table, still not believing that this was all happening. Part of him still thought maybe he was in a Somnus session, dreaming away while someone took his body out for a kayaking trip or a ball game.

The judge spoke for a long time. Words like gravity, irreparable harm, and societal protection filled the room, but Mark barely heard any of it. Victim impact statements followed. One by one, people stood and described lives that had ended violently and without warning. They spoke about birthdays that would never come again and empty chairs at dinner tables.

Mark listened closely to those. He searched himself for some reaction that might confirm what everyone else already believed. Maybe he had experienced some kind of psychotic break and really had done everything he was accused of. There was nothing there though, no recollection at all. Someone had committed these horrible crimes, but it hadn't been him, no matter whose fingerprints were on the murder weapons.

When they reached the end, the judge read out his sentence. Life imprisonment without the possibility of parole. He closed his eyes and tried not to pass out as his world spun around him. Faint sounds moved through the gallery, and someone began to cry.

The judge turned to him. "You may make a final statement."

Mark rose slowly. He had imagined this moment many times during the past months. He had rehearsed explanations and denials, arguments about technology and responsibility.

Now that he was standing there, none of those words seemed to matter.

He looked at the jurors, at the families, and finally down at his own hands. They appeared ordinary, just as they always had. It was impossible to reconcile them with the images that had filled the courtroom screens.

"I don't remember," he said. His voice sounded calm, much calmer than he felt inside. "I'm so sorry, I don't remember any of it."

Silence followed, and the judge gave a small, almost imperceptible nod.

"Then there is nothing further," he said. The gavel fell.

As the officers moved to escort him away, Mark felt a final, terrible thought settle into place. His body had committed the crimes and he would do the time, but someone else had gotten away with murder, and probably not for the first or last time.

WHAT'S DONE IN DREAMS

Julia found the book at a yard sale one day. She was on her way to work when she saw the tables lined up in a driveway and figured she might as well stop and see if there was anything good. She was a few minutes early for work anyway, and God knows she didn't want to spend any more time there than necessary.

She browsed the tables of someone else's junk, piles of old clothes, cracked and mismatched dishes, the usual tacky garage sale fare. She had just about given up when she spotted the box of books at the end. Always up for a good read, she crouched down and flipped through them. Most of them looked old and boring, but the book she found at the bottom looked like it might have some promise.

Controlling Your Reality: The Art of Lucid Dreaming. She had always had a weakness for stuff like that, so she dug a quarter out of her purse and gave it to the dour woman sitting behind a metal cashbox. The woman barely glanced at her as she dropped the quarter into the box, the clang echoing out into the still morning air.

Julia tossed the book in the backseat of her car and sped away towards the office. She had spent too long looking at the books and was now in danger of being late. She dreaded being late, and the yelling and bitching it would bring from her boss, Ms. Griffin.

The Griffin, as they called her, was a grumpy old spinster who ran their department like a boarding school for delinquent teens. Even their lunch choices were scrutinized and ridiculed by her if she was in a mood. Everyone kept secretly waiting for her to kick the bucket, but it didn't seem to be happening anytime soon.

She made it to her desk with a minute to spare and breathed a sigh of relief as she started up her computer and settled into a long, monotonous day of underwriting. She basically took what other people wrote and made it sound like it was written by someone with half a brain and a couple of years of college. It sucked, but it paid the bills.

The end of the day could not come soon enough, and she practically ran out of the building to her car. The Griffin had been in fine form today, ripping into her for every minor infraction she could think of, real or imaginary. Nothing she did was good enough, and there was a reason she was still single and working at an entry-level job. Screw her, Julia fumed. She should take a good, long look in the mirror. She sighed as she navigated her car back to her little one-bedroom apartment. Her boss was a decrepit old bitch, but she knew how to hit where it hurt. Julia trudged up the stairs to her apartment, wondering why exactly it was that she was still single. She was reasonably pretty, had a steady job, a sense of humor... she seemed good on paper, but when it came to real life, she just couldn't seem to win.

She tossed her coat and purse on the couch and carried the dream book to the small kitchen with her. As she waited for her microwave dinner to cook, she flipped through the old book, amused by the idea that she could improve her life by controlling her dreams. She wondered if it were really possible to attain consciousness while in a dream, and fly around the world or hang out with movie stars in dreamland. If so, she may never want to wake up again.

She read as she ate, getting more excited about it with every page she finished. Lucid dreaming could be fun if she could figure out how to do it. The books had tips and tricks to realize that you're in a dream, and from that point, it was a piece of cake. Just do whatever you want, and wake up with no consequences. It sounded too good to be true.

That night, Julia left the book on her nightstand, hoping that maybe its presence would inspire her to figure out this lucid dreaming thing. She settled down in bed, determined to be as comfortable and optimistic as possible. She certainly didn't want to wake up in a nightmare. She thought pleasant thoughts as she drifted off to sleep.

Julia woke up disappointed, but not that surprised. She knew it would take longer than one night for it to work, if it even worked at all. She dragged herself through another boring day, typing mindlessly on her computer and trying to ignore the harassment from her evil boss. She daydreamed about what she would do if she managed to lucid dream. She thought about all the things she would come in and say to her dream boss, without worrying about losing her job, or worse.

The next few nights passed uneventfully, and Julia had almost given up on the whole idea. She got to work on Wednesday morning, desperately wishing it could be Friday already. She sat down at her desk, just like every other morning. It wasn't until she powered on her computer that she realized something was different. The screen looked the same, but instead of the familiar words across the screen, it was just random symbols. None of it made any sense to her. She clicked a file on the desktop and stared in confusion as weird symbols and blurry characters filled her screen.

Suddenly, she remembered the tips in the book. One way they mentioned recognizing that you're in a dream is that most people can't read in dreams. Letters and numbers just appear as gibberish, although when you're dreaming, you don't notice it. If you do notice, you can become aware that you're dreaming without actually waking up.

She sat up straight in her chair. This was it! She had done it! She pulled up the sleeve of her jacket to look at her watch, and sure enough, it was just squiggly lines. The hands spun around in meaningless circles, and she almost cried with happiness.

Jumping out of her chair, she made her way to the back of the office and slipped out into the hallway. Even if this were a dream, she didn't want to spend it being berated by her boss. She had better things to do. She got in her car and thought about what she wanted to do. She assumed that she only had a limited amount of time before she woke up, but if she did it once, she should be able to do it again.

With the Griffin's constant ridicule about her dismally single personal life running through her head, she decided that her first order of business would be a good, old-fashioned fantasy. She headed back to her apartment to pick out the sexiest outfit she owned. It might be broad daylight in dreamland, but she was going to have a one-night stand.

30 minutes later, armed with an alarmingly short black skirt, a see-through blouse with no coverage underneath, and the highest heels she owned, she headed straight for the sleazier part of town. The bars there opened early, and she figured if she was going to have a one-night stand, she would do it with a rough biker guy, the kind of guy that would drink this early. The kind of guy she would never go for in real life.

She felt like a cheap hooker as she walked into the dim bar, and she knew she looked like one, but knowing that this was all in her head was exhilarating. She could do or say just about anything, and yet here was walking into a shit-hole bar at ten in the morning looking to get screwed by a stranger. She felt a thrill of anticipation run down her spine.

She made a beeline for the guy sitting at the end of the bar. He looked just like the guy she had in mind. Sure enough, after a few minutes of flirting that she never could have managed in reality, he followed her to the bathroom at the back of the bar. As he pulled her roughly into the dingy room and pushed her up against the wall, she felt both disgusted and incredibly turned on. She didn't know who this wanton woman was in her skin, but she was glad to give her control of things for a while.

When she walked out of the bar a little later, it was with a sore but satisfied spring in her step. With one thing crossed off her list, she was ready to take a quick break and get out of the hooker outfit. She also felt like she badly needed a shower after that encounter, but wasn't sure she wanted to waste her time doing such mundane things as bathing. When she got back to her place, she noticed it was already getting darker outside. Time was flying by, as it usually does in dreams.

With her baser instincts taken care of, there was something else she was itching to do. She was finally going to confront the Griffin, even if it was only in her dreams. She knew where the old bat lived since she and her coworkers were required to attend a terribly uncomfortable Christmas party there every year. Throwing on jeans and a clean t-shirt, she grabbed her car keys and headed out for one final dreamland fantasy.

It was almost full dark by the time she pulled up in front of her boss's house. The lights were on inside, and she could see a sitcom playing on the TV through the window. She was probably sitting on her fat ass, right in front of it. Maybe having a snack, or petting the numerous cats that prowled the house. They seemed to be the only creatures that could stand her.

Parking in front of the house, Julia started walking towards the front door before having a better idea. A smile growing on her face, she snuck around the side of the house. Just as she had hoped, she found the back door unlocked. She opened it quietly and walked slowly through the kitchen. She could see the old woman through the doorway, watching TV just as she had imagined. As she thought about what she would say, a darker idea crept into her head. Maybe she didn't need to say anything. This was a dream, after all. No repercussions.

Julia was part horrified and part excited by the idea. She would never do such a horrible thing in real life, but who didn't dream about it now and then? Nothing wrong with a little fantasy. She retreated a few steps into the kitchen and looked around. She spotted a heavy silver candlestick on the dining room table. Taking a deep breath, she grabbed it and snuck up behind the couch as quietly as she could.

The Griffin must have heard something because she started to turn and look just as Julia swung the candlestick. The look on the face was a glorious thing. Her mean, piggy eyes widened at the last second as she saw the weapon rushing towards her. The candlestick hit her face with a very satisfying thud. Julie was surprised at how much it knocked the Griffin back, but it didn't knock her out. She rose from the floor, blood running down her face from a gash above her eye. Her expression was full of bewilderment and rage.

"This is for everyone you fuck with, you miserable bitch," shouted Julia as she raised the bloodied candlestick like an axe, and releasing all the repressed rage that had built up over years under her command, she swung.

This time she heard a much louder crunch on impact, and her boss went down hard. Julia leaned over her, but it was obvious that the Griffin was gone. Her eyes were rolled back in her head, and blood was pooling under her ruined head.

Julia felt momentarily sick until she remembered that this was only a dream. It was no different from watching it in a movie. Sure, she wanted the woman dead, but she would never do something like this in real life. This lucid dreaming seemed to be a great way to handle aggression and anger without hurting anyone.

She was still uneasy, though, and decided it would be best to get back home and find a way to wake up. It felt like this dream had lasted way too long, and she didn't want to oversleep and catch hell from the real Ms. Griffin in the morning. Pulling the back door shut behind her, she sped home, ignoring red lights and basking in the exhilaration of acting on her wildest impulses.

When she got back home, she was more than ready to fall into her nice, soft bed. Dreaming was tiring business, and she hoped she wasn't too worn out the next day. Her arm hurt from swinging the weapon, and she still had a faint ache between her legs from her morning encounter. They were both pleasant pains though, and before she knew it, she was fast asleep again.

Morning came quickly, and the first thing she noticed was how sore she was. She stretched for a minute, and the night before came flooding back into her memory. She must have tossed and turned a lot during her dream because she ached. Pushing herself up and out of bed, she marveled at how calm she felt, as if all her anxiety and anger had been drained away. Whoever discovered this lucid dreaming business was a genius.

She showered, dressed, and drove to work in a glorious mood. For once, she didn't dread walking into the office. She could just sit back and picture the look on Ms. Griffin's face in her dream last night and have the last laugh. She sat down at her desk and powered up her computer. Remembering what had happened last night, she checked her watch. The familiar numbers circled around, and the hand pointed steadily at 8:56. Looks like this was the real deal.

She started her work and didn't realize how much time had passed until her co-worker, Brian, came up to her cubicle.

"Hey, you haven't heard anything about Ms. Griffin, have you?" She didn't know Brian very well, but she knew he was a suck-up whose lips were lost without the Griffin's ass to stick them to.

"No, I haven't. I assumed she was in her office. Is she not here?"

Brian shook his head. "No one's heard from her all morning. She's not answering at home either. It's not like her."

"Hmm. Well, I'll let you know if I hear anything. She's probably just stuck in traffic or something."

Brian nodded and wandered back off toward his own cubicle. Julia started to panic. She had always heard that if you die in a dream, you die in real life. That didn't count if it was in someone else's dream though, did it? It couldn't. She was just being silly. She busied herself rewriting an insurance document and tried to ignore the guilty feeling she had for being so horrible in her dream.

She had almost forgotten about it when she heard talking and jingling over by the door to the hallway. She glanced up and felt her heart jump into her throat. Two uniformed cops were standing there, along with a man in a long trench coat. He looked like a detective on television. They were talking to the Griffin's boss and looking around the room at people. Julia felt her palms starting to sweat, and before she even knew what she was doing, she grabbed her purse and slipped out of her seat. She tried to look casual as she made her way around to the other exit.

She was almost there when Brian stepped out in front of her. She cursed silently and tried to put on a relaxed, non-guilty expression.

"What's going on, Brian? I saw the cops, did someone finally get caught stealing paperclips from the supply closet?" She tried a weak laugh, but it died away as she saw the look on Brian's face.

"Uh, no. It's Ms. Griffin. They're asking about her. I guess someone went to her house to check on her when she never showed up here, and... oh my god. I can't believe it."

"What is it? What happened?" Julia was in full panic mode now, desperate to hear any other explanation in the world come out of his mouth. She knew what she was thinking was impossible, but she still felt her stomach clenching in fear.

Brian was pale as he sputtered out the news overheard from the officers.

"She's dead. Someone... someone beat her to death. They just walked in and killed her. Nothing was missing, no note or anything. Just killed her."

Julie struggled not to throw up as she responded.

"Oh no. That's horrible... Uh, listen, I have to go make a call, but I'll be right back. Do they want to talk to us or something?"

"Yeah, I think they're going to have a meeting in the conference room in a few minutes. I hope they catch the sonofabitch that did this."

Julie nodded in agreement. She suddenly felt as if she were suffocating. She edged past him and escaped into the hallway. It was empty at the moment, everyone was busy going over the news in hushed whispers at their desks. She went down the back stairwell and outside to her car. She didn't know where she was going, but she knew she had to get out of that building.

A couple of blocks away, the reality finally set in. She pulled into a parking lot, shaking so badly she thought she was going into shock. It had just been a dream. How could something like this have happened? Was it some freak coincidence? Something worse?

As a fresh wave of horror hit, she scrambled to get her door open and barely gotten her head out before she lost her breakfast all over the pavement. She knew people were probably watching, but she didn't care. She wiped her mouth on her sleeve and leaned back into the car. She didn't know what to do, but she knew she couldn't sit there all day. She didn't want to go home either, in case this was real and they came looking for her.

She finally settled on driving around for a while as she calmed down and tried to convince herself that she was hallucinating or just overreacting to a very strange coincidence. She wasn't usually much of a drinker, but right now she felt the need to get lost in the numbing haze of alcohol and the dim shadows of a quiet bar. She drove around some more until she realized she was close to the bar she had gone to in her dream.

Feeling a strange pull, she drove into the parking lot and turned off her car. If the dream really had been true, then this would have been true as well. She could just walk in here, reassure herself that she had done nothing wrong last night, and be on her way.

She felt a strong sense of déjà vu as she pushed open the heavy wooden door and was greeted by the musty, slightly sour smell of the bar. A few patrons were seated at the counter, but it was still relatively quiet this early. She sat down on a stool at the end of the bar and waited for the bartender to make his way down there.

She was starting to feel a little better. Although the bar seemed familiar, all bars did after a while. She had been in bars like this one a hundred times. She knew herself, and there was no way she had banged a guy in the bathroom in this sleazy place. Just like there was no way she had murdered her boss in cold blood.

"Hey there, pretty lady. Back for some more?" Julia jumped as the rough voice spoke in her ear. Her blood ran cold as she turned and saw him. The man from her dream was smiling at her, a dark and dangerous smile. She started to feel sick again and struggled to her feet.

"Uh, excuse me... I have to go."

"What's the problem, sweetheart? Not up for some fun today? You really made my day yesterday. Thought about it all night." He was leering at her, almost menacingly. She panicked and pushed herself away from the bar, running out onto the sidewalk.

Julia locked herself in her car, shaking. The whole thing was true. She hadn't been dreaming, she really had done everything. She had screwed a stranger in a bar. She had murdered an innocent woman. She tried to choke back the tears as she put her head down on the steering wheel.

Through the shock and disgust, she realized one very important thing. Since she thought she was dreaming, she had taken no precautions at all. Her fingerprints were all over Ms. Griffin's house, and on the murder weapon itself. Julia started hyperventilating. She was going to prison as soon as they figured it out. She was torn between running for her life and turning herself in. The guilt about what she had done was threatening to drown her.

She jumped and screamed when her phone rang on the seat next to her. It was the office number. She took a deep breath and tried to steady herself.

"Hello?"

"Julie, it's Brian. The cops are asking when you're going to be back. They don't want to talk to us until everyone is here. Where are you?"

"I just had to run a quick errand, that's all. Tell them I'll be back as soon as I can."

"This isn't going to be like yesterday, is it? Tom said you stopped in for a few minutes in the morning and then you were gone the whole rest of the day. Without an excuse, I might add. You won't get sick pay for that, you know."

Julia struggled to contain the maniacal laughter threatening to burst out. She was way beyond worrying about getting paid for yesterday. She was about to pay for it for the rest of her life.

"Yeah, I know. Something came up. No, I'll be there soon. Just stall them for a few more minutes while I get there."

Brian huffed into the phone and hung up. Her mind raced, trying to come up with a plan. She was pretty sure that thinking she was dreaming wasn't going to be a very good defense in court. They were going to lock her up and throw away the key. She tried to imagine what it would be like to sit in a cell every day for the rest of for life, trapped with her own guilt.

Julie knew she couldn't let that happen. She had done the most horrific thing possible, and she was headed straight to hell for that. This was a no-win situation already. Luckily, she was single, a loner, and had no family left. No one would miss her too much if she were gone. Just one less drain on the judicial system. She couldn't believe that she had gone from shopping at garage sales to contemplating suicide this quickly, but here she was. She had nothing to look forward to.

Even if by some miracle she didn't spend her life in prison, there was no way she could ever overcome this terrible weight of guilt pressing down on her. She already felt as if she were drowning. Julia made up her mind and chose the only viable option she saw left. She got out of her car and circled the building to the back door.

There was a fire escape leading up the side, all the way to the roof. She climbed over a chain warning trespassers away and ascended the fire escape. It was hard, but she tried to keep her mind as blank as possible. Every thought led to an image of the look on the Griffin's face when she pulled back the candlestick for a second swing.

Reaching the top, she looked over the edge, the pavement a dizzying six stories below her. Knowing there was no point in waiting, she sent up a quick prayer for forgiveness. She knew it was too late for that, but it never hurt. She took one last deep breath, smelling and tasting the city around her. She closed her eyes and jumped.

Keeping her eyes squeezed shut, she felt an exhilarating feeling of weightlessness, like she were floating in a bubble instead of plummeting to her death. She felt the wind in her hair and a strange buzzing in her ears. She waited for the final impact and...

She sat bolt upright in bed. Her breath was still trapped in her lungs. Her heart stopped for a beat before resuming its quick and unsteady pace. She looked around her bedroom, speechless. Her breath exploded out of her, and she started feeling tears run down her face. She was lost in a confusion of guilt, fear, and relief. Her stomach twisting, she grabbed her cell phone off the nightstand, thumbing the screen on to check the date. It was Wednesday morning again. None of it had happened at all. She fell back against the pillows, struggling to make sense of it in her mind. As with dreams, parts of it were already fading from her memory. It had all just been a horribly vivid dream.

Julia calmed down a little and looked down at the floor to find the book that she had knocked off her nightstand in her sleep. She stared at the cover for a few minutes before deciding. She threw it in the dumpster outside on her way to her car that morning. She never tried lucid dreaming again. In fact, she tried not to dream at all.

218

A MURDER OF ONE

rthur Bell looked up as the young lady approached him, armed with a notebook and a messenger bag.

"Hi Mr. Bell, my name is Tara Hanson. I'm sure they already told you this, but I'm here working on a history of Auburn, and some of the more unusual stories from the area. I came to talk to you about the Delaney murder, I was told you would be the best person to tell me what really happened."

Arthur Bell leaned forward slightly in his wheelchair, arranging a blanket over his legs. He had originally told the nurses he wanted nothing to do with any reporters or journalists, or whatever this Tara girl was, but nursing home life got awfully boring sometimes. After the third request came in, he figured he didn't have that much else to do.

"Yeah, they told me you wouldn't stop until you got to talk to me. You know it's all public record."

"I know, I've read the police report and news articles. I want to hear it from someone who was actually there, though. I've heard stories about the case, but I want to know what really happened. I was told you were the Delaney's neighbor at the time?"

"Yeah, that's right. I didn't know them real well, but they both seemed nice enough. Never had a problem with either of them. You're not really here to talk about them though, are you Miss... what was it again?"

"You can call me Tara. And no, I guess you know that's not really the story I'm talking about. Is it okay if I record this? It's just for me to play back later, so I can make sure I quote you correctly and all that." She pulled a small digital recorder from her bag and set it on the table between them. Arthur shrugged, and she pressed a button on it before settling back into her chair."

"This is Tara Hanson, and I'm speaking with Arthur Bell about the rumors surrounding the Delaney murder case of 1987. Arthur, thank you for talking to me today, I really do appreciate it. It's important for my book that I get the true stories of the area, and not just the ones cleaned up and polished for the news."

Arthur gave a wheezing, slightly unpleasant laugh. "Oh, I'll give you the true story all right. Whether or not you believe it is up to you."

"Oh believe me, Mr. Bell. I've heard some strange things since I started this project. I'm here with an open mind. Why don't you tell me a little about yourself and how you're connected to the Delaneys?"

"I've lived in Auburn my whole life. The Delaneys weren't from here, I think they were from somewhere a couple of counties over. By the time they moved in next to me, their kids had grown up and moved out. I saw them from time to time on the weekends, but most of the time it was just Margaret and John. Other than maybe a word or two when we crossed paths at the mailboxes, I didn't have any connection to them at all. I just happened to live next door, and that gave me a front-row seat to everything that happened that October.

"They were a normal couple. Margaret was a teacher, and John worked on a dairy farm. They were quiet, kept a tidy yard. Honestly, I never even thought about them that much. What happened was a tragedy for sure, but also not all that shocking. We'll get to that, but I don't think the Delaneys are really what you want to hear about, are they? You're here about the crows."

"Well that's definitely the part of the story that stood out, yes." Tara smiled at him encouragingly and gestured towards the recorder. "I'll try not to interrupt you, just tell as much as you can remember."

"I remember it all, young lady. It wasn't the sort of thing you forget about, and I'm not that decrepit that my mind is gone yet. Everyone knows about the crows around here. No one knows exactly why Auburn is such a popular roosting spot for them, but I've heard it has something to do with the fields around the city. They forage during the day, then get drawn to the lights and warmth of the city at night. Crows are very smart, once they find a good place to roost, they keep coming back. Some people find them to be a nuisance, but I never really minded them.

"What I'm getting at is that the crazy part wasn't the presence of the crows, Auburn is known for them. It's a weird phenomenon, but not unheard of in places either. What was weird was what the crows did that fall. Crows are smart, everyone knows that. What happened with Margaret Delaney… I've never seen that before, or since. I guess the real story starts in late October 1987.

"Like I said, I didn't really know the Delaneys personally. I did have the opportunity to overhear them quite often, though. Our houses were close, and a privacy fence doesn't do much to stop sounds. I wouldn't say there was a lot of true fighting, really. John wasn't abusive or anything, not at all. He would never raise a hand to her. Unfortunately, the other thing he would never do is shut up.

"That man complained about everything. The mail was delivered later than usual, the traffic was slow on his way home, he couldn't find his glasses, anything that John Delaney could possibly say something about, he did. Often over and over, until Margaret would finally snap at him to just shut the hell up. I didn't blame that woman one bit. John was a nice guy, I don't mean to make him sound like he wasn't, but he was a handful for sure. She was a saint for putting up with him for as long as she did.

"The day it happened was unusually warm, and they were standing outside in their backyard, semi-arguing about something or other. It wasn't that unusual, so I really wasn't paying that much attention. I just remember trying to enjoy one of the last nice days of the year, thinking that if he didn't shut up soon, I'd be saying something to him myself. Margaret must have been getting close to the edge too, because she yelled at him all of a sudden, and it was a lot louder and a whole lot madder than she usually sounded. I remember thinking, 'Good for her, it's about damn time.' A second later I heard him cry out, and then a thump and a sort of cracking sound. I still didn't think much of it. What wife hasn't thrown a dish or two in an argument before? None of my business. Old John had finally shut up, and that was enough for me.

"I mentioned we had a privacy fence between the yards. It was a prime spot for squirrels and birds to perch, and that day was no exception. As I was getting up to go back inside, a crow sitting on the top of that fence gave a big old squawk. I didn't pay much mind to it, but Margaret wasn't in the mood for backtalk from a bird, apparently, and shouted at it to get lost. I think the phrase, 'Mind your own fucking business,' was close to what she yelled. I had to bite my tongue pretty quick to keep from laughing out loud, and the bird took her advice and flew off. I went inside, and didn't think again about any of it until about a week later."

"So you didn't know at the time what had happened?" Tara was leaning forward now, listening intently. She had written a few notes down in her journal, but was mostly just listening to him talk.

Arthur appreciated that. At his age, most people just ignored him, so it was kind of nice to have a captive audience, as it were. Especially one that was open to hearing about his experience all those years ago.

"Nope, just assumed she was done yelling at him. Which I guess she was, in a way. It wasn't unusual for me to go a few weeks or longer without seeing them, so I didn't think anything at all when I didn't see him again. The first thing I noticed was the crows.

"Like I said before, and I'm sure you know very well, it's not exactly unusual for there to be a lot of crows around. It would be stranger if we didn't see any. About a week after the day I overheard them fighting in the backyard, though, I started noticing that there were way more crows than usual, always sitting right on that fence and always facing the Delaney yard. They were noisy too, just cawing non-stop. I thought maybe they had gotten a dog or a cat or something, some birds will sit right up there and taunt pets like that. I tried to shoo them off a few times, but it seemed like there were more of them every day.

"Margaret must have noticed too, because I heard her out there a few times trying to scare them off. After a couple of days of trying to ignore the cawing and screeching next door, I went to run to the store and saw the damndest thing. Margaret Delaney's car was covered in crows. They were perched on the bumpers, across the hood, everywhere. Not a single one on John's car. I've never seen crows do anything like that before.

"Now you've gotta understand that most of this story is pieced together from what Margaret said later and what people around town saw and heard. I can't swear to you that any of it's true, but I saw enough with my own eyes that I believe what everyone else says. If you're gonna start in with the naysaying and tell me you don't believe any of my nonsense, I won't go any further. There's a reason I don't normally talk about this anymore, and it's because of people too stubborn to open their minds a little bit and believe in things they don't understand."

"No, Mr. Bell," Tara assured him. "I'm open to the truth, I want to know what happened that fall and what led to what happened with Mrs. Delanay in the end. I've read the reports, I want to hear what really happened."

"Okay then. Keep that recorder on, because this may well be the last time I tell this story." Arthur cleared his throat with a wet, phlegmy sound and took a long drink of his water. "A couple of days after the incident with the car, and the crows just roosting all over it, I was sitting outside the library over on Genesee Street with Moira Johnson. Her husband died a few years after my wife did, and we used to sit and talk sometimes, just to pass the time. That doesn't matter, what matters is what she told me about Margaret. She said she had been at the grocery store the day before and saw Margaret pushing a cart of groceries out to her car. She said she'd never seen anything like it, but there was a group of crows following her. They were swooping down at her and landing on the sides of the cart, cawing at her. Moira said a couple of them looked like they were trying to peck at her hands and arms. A young man ran over and tried to help shoo them away from her, but they were all over her car too.

"Over the next week or so, I heard similar stories from other people around town. Someone saw a crow dive down and knock her hat right off outside the Harriet Tubman house one day. Someone else said they saw her running from a couple of crows right downtown. I would have said that was the craziest thing I'd ever seen a flock of birds do in my life, if it wasn't for what happened next.

"They started dropping stuff on her. Nothing heavy, not like that, but in a way it was worse. There were people around town saying they saw the crows dive at her and drop buttons, scraps of fabric, bits of paper, even a shoelace. It was weird as hell, but these crows really seemed to have it out for poor Margaret. If she went to a store, she would come out to her car being littered with scraps of all sorts of stuff, not to mention copious amounts of bird shit, pardon my French. Within a week or so, it got to where she wasn't leaving her house anymore. No one knew what to make of it at the time, but of course now we know.

"Now, at this point, no one had thought much about John Delaney. It had only been a couple of weeks after all, and he hadn't missed anything important enough that anyone would notice. The first time anyone suspected something might be going on with him was when his driver's license was found on the front steps of the police station. The officer who found it assumed that he must have dropped it somewhere and that a good Samaritan had left it at the station. He went by the Delaney house to drop it off, and Margaret told him that John had gone to bed early with a headache.

"There was no reason for the officer to doubt that, especially since Margaret and John were known around town as being good, decent people. It turns out that officer was one of the few people in Auburn who hadn't heard the strange stories about Margaret and her war with the crows yet. Maybe if he'd known, he would have had a few more questions that day. Not that it would have made any difference."

"Was he dead already? Mr. Delaney, I mean?" Tara blurted out, then blushed. "Sorry, I know you said no interruptions, but was he, do you think?"

Arthur nodded. "I believe so, yes. No one knew yet, other than Margaret, but it was about to come out that the day she had snapped at the crow in the backyard, the last day I heard them arguing, she really had snapped. I don't think she meant to kill him, goodness no. From what she told the police later on, she just couldn't take one more word out of his mouth, and she shoved him. He fell back and hit his head on the picnic table they had on the back porch, and that was it.

"I'm getting ahead of myself, though. No one knew it at the time, but after Margaret stopped leaving her house, the crows decided to bring the fight to her. I don't know how they got inside, but everyone said later that when the police finally went into the house, there were feathers all over the place, and the birds had clearly been crowding into the house. They say there were even scratches from their beaks and talons on the outside of her bedroom door from them trying to get in there. No one knows for sure what went on in that house during the last week she was there, but people sure have some theories.

"The day it all came to a head was a Saturday, about 3 weeks from the day they got into the fight. I woke up to screaming next door. It wasn't angry screaming, like they were fighting again, this was mindless shrieking. I'd never heard anything quite like it before, and I never have since. I called the police right away, but I didn't dare go over there. I sat on my front porch and waited for them to get there. She was still screaming when they showed up just a couple of minutes later. Maybe I was chicken for not going over to see if I could help her before they got there, but there was something about the screaming…

"I'm sure what they found in there was in the official police report. It's the how that was never officially determined, but most everyone around town was pretty sure they knew. The officers knew as soon as they walked into that house that something had gone horribly wrong. It wasn't just the feathers, or the scratches in the door, or the fact that the place seemed trashed. No, the real shock was when they got to the dining room and found John Delaney. Or more precisely, John Delaney's head.

"It was sitting in the middle of the table, the neck ragged and torn apart. Or, maybe more accurately, torn away from the rest of his body, which the officers found in the backyard covered up with a vinyl swimming pool cover. Now, this is the part you won't find in any official reports, but what we all knew to be true back then, as crazy as it sounds.

"It was them crows that did it. There is absolutely no doubt in my mind that the crows went to work pecking that poor dead man's head off and dropped it right smack in the middle of her breakfast. The paramedics sedated her before they took her from the house and to the hospital, but everyone within a block had heard her screaming about the birds, how the birds had done this to her, the birds had ruined everything, just rambling on. I think she was absolutely right, too.

"Everyone knows crows are smart, and they remember people. Now, those crows wouldn't have given two hoots about her husband. She could have butchered him right there in the yard, and they wouldn't have paid her any mind. Her mistake was telling the one crow that witnessed the fight to mind its own fucking business. That crow, and all its buddies, decided they would very much not mind their own fucking business at all.

"Margaret told the police that she crows had been sent to drive her mad, promised to plead guilty, anything she had to do so they would leave her alone. Despite everything that happened, she really didn't mean for anything to happen to her husband. I think it was the guilt that ate her up more than the crows. They were just there to egg it on and punish her for insulting them.

"It turned out it didn't really matter whether she pled guilty or not. They did an autopsy, and it turned out old John Delaney died of a heart attack, what they call a 'widow-maker'. The poor guy was probably dead before he even hit the ground. Oh sure, she was in some trouble for not reporting it and covering his body up in the backyard, but she wasn't going to do any time in prison or anything. She was a retired teacher with a spotless record, not some hardened criminal.

"Now I don't know if this was what the crows were going for or not, I don't think they usually get quite this involved in human drama, but they had pushed this poor woman right to the very edge. We'll never know everything that went on during those couple of weeks between the day her husband died and the day they dropped his head on her plate, but I can only assume it must have been traumatizing. Honestly, I think she started losing her mind the moment she realized he was dead. Either way, she had decided she wasn't going to be tormented by those crows anymore, one way or another.

"They let her know they would be releasing her on bail the next day, and that was the last straw for Margaret Delaney. When they went to gather her in the morning, they found her hanging in her cell. Whatever happened in that house with those crows, she must have thought it would be worse than death to go back to it."

"Oh my God," Tara whispered. "I knew she had passed away shortly after the arrest, but that's not in the report anywhere."

"No," Arthur replied. "I don't imagine it would be. I think they put it down as a death due to natural causes, and buried her right in the plot next to her husband over in Fort Hill Cemetery. I don't think they wanted any more sensational rumors going around. Especially after it got out that the officer who found her body had gone home to tell his wife that the weirdest part had been the crow feather, stuck right into the knot on the bedsheet she had hung herself with."

"You're not saying…"

"No, I'm not saying anything. Like I said at the beginning, I'm just telling you everything I heard, I don't know for sure what's truth and what's speculation. All I know is that whenever I see a crow around these days, whether I'm behaving myself or not, I make damn sure not to piss it off."

THE TRUNK

The rain drummed a steady beat on the roof of the Harrison house. In his bedroom on the second floor, Teddy Harrison sat on his bed watching the storm. The cowboy curtains he had begged his mom to take down already (too babyish for a 10-year-old) were pulled open, and the old oak tree outside the window swayed and groaned with the force of the wind. Teddy was idly watching the shadows of his action figures (not babyish at all) fight strange and disjointed battles with every blinding flash of lightning.

He was trying unsuccessfully to ignore the sound of another fight going on down the hall. The elder Harrisons were having their own war, and Teddy had once again been drawn into it against his will.

He leaned back against the pillows on his bed, rubbing his still stinging cheek absentmindedly. He supposed it was his fault for speaking up, but they just got so loud sometimes, and all he wanted to do was watch the end of America's Funniest Home Videos and escape to his room. He would have excused himself sooner, but he was afraid that they might take it as a sign that he didn't want to be around them.

He wished he could be older like his brother and have his own car so he could drive off to exciting faraway places when the fighting started. Joey had his own place too, although their parents still kept his room looking the same as it had the day he moved out. There was a lot of yelling that day, too. Teddy was only 7 when Joey left, but he still remembered his older brother leaning in close as he left and whispering to him. Wish you could come with me, buddy. Just call me if things get too bad. Teddy didn't know what counted as too bad, but it sure felt like it was getting close.

Snatches of furious conversation seeped under Teddy's door, as if they were rain leaking in with the storm. This is your fault, it never would have happened if… Blame me? You… I wish this could all be… If you would quit being such a… He's just a kid, you can't… Better off not…

Teddy got up and opened his window a crack, hoping that the sound of the thunder would drown out the anger coming from the other room. It worked for a few minutes before the dripping and trickling sounds of water running through the gutter above his window had a predictable effect on Teddy's bladder. He squirmed on the bed for a few minutes, hoping it would go away, but it didn't. Sighing, he moved his cat, Sprocket, to the side and slid off the bed into his slippers, hoping to make as little noise as possible creeping down the hall. He really didn't want them to hear him leaving his room. He wouldn't be in trouble for that alone, he just didn't want to see either of them again tonight.

Teddy loved his parents, and for the most part they were okay to him, but they really seemed to hate each other. Nothing ever happened in this house without a fight about it later. If his dad took him out for ice cream, his mom spent the night crying because he was trying to buy their son's affection. If his mom helped him with his homework, his dad felt accused of being too stupid to figure out simple math. Sometimes Teddy felt like the real grown-up in the house and wished he could send them to their room for a time-out.

He creaked his door open, listening carefully for a change in the voices from the other room. As usual, they were oblivious to anything other than their own problems. He padded down the hall, avoiding the notoriously creaky spot in the middle. That's how he knew to shove his comic books under the bed when his mom or dad came down to check on him after bedtime.

Upon reaching the bathroom, he swung the door almost shut behind him, but not enough to set off the click of the door handle settling into place. He shrugged down his pajamas and relieved himself quickly. He winced at the sound of the toilet flushing. He had considered not flushing at all, but he thought the aftermath of that would be worse than them hearing him out and about.

He pulled the bathroom door back open and almost screamed as he saw a dark shape moving toward him from the other end of the hall. He stifled it as he realized it was his dad, trudging down the hallway and carrying his pillow and blanket.

"Can't sleep, son?" His voice sounded rough from hours (years) of arguing and fighting.

"Uh, the rain made me have to go. I'm sorry." Teddy started edging backwards towards the door to his room, where his comic books and action figures waited for him to make a safe and quick return.

"You're fine. Listen, bud, I'm sorry about earlier. I don't know what happened. How about we go do something tomorrow, just the two of us?" His dad looks sincerely sorry, and Teddy started to feel bad for all the horrible things he had thought about him after the slap.

"Yeah, okay. That sounds good."

His dad nodded and turned towards the stairs. Teddy spoke up one more time on a sudden impulse.

"Hey dad? Good night."

"Good night, son. Sleep tight." Teddy watched his dad's larger-than-life shadow descend the stairs towards the couch he often ended up sleeping on. Not for the first time, Teddy wished his parents were like his friends' parents, who loved and hugged each other. Maybe like Mikey's dad, who would come up behind his mom in the kitchen and pinch her bottom, making her squeal and playfully hit him with a dishtowel. He couldn't remember the last time he saw his parents hug, or even hold hands.

Back in his room, he crawled under his covers and tried to fall asleep. His cat circled his head a few times before plopping down next to him and purring loudly in his ear. He thought again about how nice it would be if they would stop fighting once in a while. It took a long time for sleep to come.

The next morning, Teddy woke up to silence in the house. He strained his ears for the sound of his dad banging around in the kitchen or his mom on the phone, but there was nothing.

He pulled on his clothes and tiptoed down the hall to peek into their room. His mom was still asleep in bed, with the covers tangled around her. Teddy wanted her to get up and make breakfast, but he was always nervous to wake her up. He stood and watched the blankets rise and fall with her breathing for a minute before quietly easing the door shut and going downstairs.

The couch where his dad had slept was empty, and the pillow and blanket were stacked neatly on the chair next to it. Teddy went around the corner into the kitchen to find a note from him on the fridge. Got called into work for the morning. Should be home after lunch. Teddy pulled the note out from under the Ricky's Pizza magnet and crumpled it up.

After tossing it in the trash, he climbed up on a stool to get cereal and a bowl out of the cupboard. It looked like he was on his own for the morning, since his mom probably wouldn't wake until later.

Teddy was halfway through his second bowl of Star Crunch (which his mom would not have approved of) when he heard music drifting down the stairs. Oh, my love… every day with you… all my love… every night it's true… It didn't sound like anything his mom usually listened to, and he assumed it must be coming from the neighbor's house.

He ate a few more bites of sugary cereal before realizing that the music did, in fact, seem to be coming from up above him somewhere. He rinsed his bowl in the sink and started back up the stairs. Sprocket twisted through his legs with every step, nearly tripping him on the way up. He padded down the hall towards his mother's room, but all he heard was her gentle snoring and the tick of the grandfather clock in the corner.

Sprocket nosed her door open and went in to accompany her for a catnap. Teddy continued down the hallway, still looking for the source of the music.

He followed the faint sound all the way to the other end of the hallway until he hit the door to the attic. Normally he wasn't allowed to go up there, but since his mom was fast asleep and his dad was gone for the morning, he figured what they didn't know wouldn't hurt them.

The attic door creaked as it opened, and Teddy froze, waiting for his mom to wake up and catch him in the act. No one came out yelling at him, and after waiting a minute to make sure he was undetected, he started climbing the steep stairs into the dusty darkness.

The light switch was at the top of the stairs, but even that did little to banish the shadows lurking in the corners of the room. Even though Teddy had been up there a few times with his dad, the attic still creeped him out. He was right about one thing, though. The music was definitely louder up here. He could still only catch bits and pieces of it, but it was clearer. He wandered around the edges of the room, careful of the weak spots in the floor. As he got to the far end, he realized where the music was coming from.

There was an old wooden steamer trunk in the corner. He guessed he had seen it before, but he didn't remember ever paying much attention to it. He wondered what could make music inside of it, and ghost stories from the pulp comics under his bed flashed through his mind. Stop, that's nonsense, he told himself. Only a baby would be afraid of ghosts.

Taking a deep breath, he leaned over and grabbed the lid of the trunk, raising it slowly in case, God forbid, there really was something monstrous in there. The only thing that jumped out at him was a puff of dust and the smell of old wood. The music got louder instantly, though. He leaned over to look in the trunk, wishing that he had brought a flashlight up with him. He would make sure he was better prepared next time.

He couldn't see anything except blackness in the trunk. The darkness was so thick that it hid even the bottom of the trunk from inspection. The music was soothing, though, and as the song drew to a close and another one took its place, he did something that only an innocent and curious young boy would do. He stepped one foot into the trunk, and then the other.

Settling down on his butt, he found he had just enough room to lower the lid and still sit comfortably. He sat in complete darkness, letting the gentle music swirl around him and breathing in the old scent of varnished oak. He let his eyes close, imagining he was in a prehistoric forest with unseen woodland creatures playing songs just for him. For a minute, the worry about his parents fighting so much slipped away, and he relaxed. The sounds and smells of the old trunk had started to lull him into a light doze when he heard a voice calling for him.

"Teddy? Teddy, where are you? Breakfast is ready!"

Teddy sat up so fast that he banged his head on the lid of the trunk. He breathed out a curse word he would surely get paddled for if his dad were to hear him, even though he had heard it from his dad in the first place.

Teddy scrambled out of the trunk, brushing the dust and cobwebs off his shirt. He could smell bacon frying down in the kitchen. He wondered how long he had been asleep in the trunk. He sighed with relief, knowing his mom must have woken up in a pretty good mood if she was cooking a good bacon and egg breakfast for him.

He hurried down the attic stairs, being sure to latch the door behind him. The last thing he wanted when she was in a good mood was to get in trouble for snooping around up there.

His mom was standing in the kitchen when he got there, her back turned to him as she tended to breakfast on the stove. He noticed right away that something was different. For one thing, the music he heard coming from the trunk was playing on a radio in the kitchen. His mom liked more modern music, and even then she rarely played music in the house. The kitchen looked pretty much the same, but it seemed brighter. It took him a minute before he realized that the heavy blinds that usually covered the windows had been replaced with gauzy white curtains that were swaying in the breeze. He tried hard to remember if they had been that way this morning, but like a typical boy, he paid little attention to those kinds of things. It wasn't until his mom turned around that he realized the full extent of the weirdness.

She looked younger. Her hair was a lighter shade and cut in a shorter, carefree style, not the heavy braid that she usually had. The other major difference was her smile. His mom always had a smile that looked frozen and painful, at least on the mornings when she smiled at all. The woman in front of him had a real, genuine smile. She seemed happy, and as she saw him, her face seemed to light up even more.

"Well, there you are! I've been calling you. Where were you?" she sounded the same as his mom, but not as tired.

"I was upstairs playing with sprocket. Sorry, I didn't hear you the first time."

"Sprocket? Oh, one of your action figures? You know I can't keep them all straight."

Teddy started as he realized she didn't even remember their own cat. This was starting to feel like some strange dream, and he wondered if he was still asleep in the steamer trunk. If so, he didn't want to make the mistake of waking up now. This was a pretty good dream, especially if the breakfast tasted as good as it smelled.

"Um, yeah. He's a robot cat. fights evil dogs, that sort of thing."

She smiled at him and seemed to accept this as a perfectly reasonable explanation.

"Well, hurry up and eat. Your dad will be home in a little bit, and I thought we would do something fun today. Get out of the house for a while."

"That sounds great, Mom. Really great." Teddy leaned back in his chair and decided that as far as dreams went, this was the best one he had, except maybe for the one where he himself had become a superhero and ruled the world from a castle in the sky. That dream hadn't included bacon though.

He started in on breakfast and decided to enjoy this dream as long as he could. He tried to ignore the voice in the back of his head that insisted that if you knew you were dreaming, you woke up automatically. Who made up the rules for dreaming, anyway?

After breakfast, these warm and happy versions of his parents walked down to the park with him, something his real parents rarely did. His dad threw a ball around with him while his mom settled in under a tree to read a book in the shade. At one point they walked over to the pavilion and got sodas to bring back and drink with his mom. No arguing or fighting, no snotty looks or snide comments. They were just nice to each other, and to Teddy it felt foreign.

As much fun as he was having, that little voice in his head got louder and louder, and he finally had to admit to himself that there was no way he was having a dream this real, or this long, for that matter. And if it wasn't a dream, his real-life mom would be getting really pissed pretty soon when she couldn't find him.

"Hey Dad, do you think we could go back home for a little while? I'm getting kinda hungry." He felt bad about interrupting the fun, but he had to get back up to the attic and check out the trunk. He had to know what was really going on. His dream dad nodded and called to his dream mom to grab their stuff from the bench. They all trotted home together, tired from playing.

"You know, kiddo, I had a great time with you this morning. You've been pretty quiet lately. It's nice to know that you still want to have some fun with your dear old dad."

Teddy almost tripped, startled. He hadn't ever stopped to think about whether there was another version of himself running around somewhere. If these parents hadn't noticed the difference, could Other Teddy be running around at his house? And would his real mom realize that something was off? He guessed she wouldn't. She didn't even notice him half the time.

Teddy walked a little faster, a chill running down his spine as he thought about what Other Teddy might be doing in his life while he was busy playing at the park.

When they got home, he excused himself to the bathroom and ran up the familiar stairs to the attic door. He didn't know if Other Teddy was forbidden to go in the attic here too, but he eased the door open quietly just in case.

Just like everything else in the house, the attic looked pretty much the same, except for a few minor differences. His dad had an old model train set in their attic, but when he looked over in the corner here, he saw a mannequin, the kind women used to make clothes on. Luckily, the trunk looked just the same as it had in his own attic. He listened next to it for a minute, but only heard faint scuffling noises, not the calm music that had drawn him to it before.

Taking a deep breath, he climbed in and shut the top behind him, just as he had done before. He closed his eyes and breathed in the same dusty, woodsy scent. He got the same sleepy feeling for a few minutes, and just as he thought he was going to fall asleep, he caught himself and threw open the lid of the trunk. He scrambled out, not sure what to expect.

Remembering the mannequin and the train set, he whirled around to the side to see which was there. His breath caught in his throat as his eyes registered the sight of his dad's old train set peeking out from under the yellowed sheet that covered it. He could see the tail end of the caboose, its bright red paint dulled by layers of dust. The train set used to be in the spare bedroom, but his mom got sick of cleaning around it and banished it to the attic.

Teddy just stood for a minute, trying to absorb this. It could still be a dream, he supposed. A really elaborate and detailed dream, but they say that's what happens when you read too many comic books, especially before bed. Teddy had never had such a realistic dream before, though, especially not during the day.

He listened at the top of the attic stairs and could hear his mom moving around downstairs. He climbed down and latched the door shut behind him. He had to find out whether or not this was a dream.

He made a beeline for his bedroom and had his answer as soon as he opened the door. Toys were strewn all across the room, tossed around as if a tornado had blown through. The sheets and blankets were torn off the bed, and his comic books were pulled out of their hiding place and crumpled up on the floor. Teddy started to panic. If his mom saw his bedroom this way, she would flip! He couldn't very well blame it on a mysterious "Other Teddy", but it was, wasn't it? While you were over there enjoying his nice, happy parents, he got to have a whack at your life too. Teddy shook his head, silencing the pesky, but often right, inner voice.

He hurriedly started picking up the toys and tossing them into the big toy box at the end of his bed. He felt anger growing as he tried to straighten out the comics that he had saved all of his allowance money to buy. He piled the blankets back up on the bed, figuring that it was the least of the damage, and an unmade bed was often overlooked, anyway. He was grabbing the last few toys when he noticed something odd on the edge of an old toy fire truck that he had kept, even though it was clearly for little boys. It had been a Christmas present from his grandmother before she passed away, and he couldn't bring himself to part with it yet.

He turned the faded red truck over in his hands to see what was stuck to it. A tuft of something, fur maybe. He looked around to see if there were any stuffed animals that might have gotten caught on it, but he had gotten rid of most of them last year at their garage sale. They were most definitely baby toys, not suitable for a mature young man such as himself. He wiped the fur off on the edge of his blanket, watching it drift down to the floor.

Tossing the last of the toys into the box, he looked around the room to make sure he had missed nothing. It looked okay, considering. If he were lucky, his mom wouldn't even look in here today, and he could finish fixing it tonight.

Shutting the door behind him, he hurried downstairs and into the kitchen to see what kind of reaction his mom would have upon seeing him. He could tell as soon as he walked in that he was back in his own dark, suffocating kitchen. It didn't have the life that the other kitchen had. His mom was sitting at the table with her checkbook, paying bills. She glanced up at him when he walked in, but didn't look too surprised and had already moved her tired gaze back to the papers on the table before talking to him.

"I thought you were playing outside today. I didn't even hear you come in."

That's because I didn't, thought Teddy.

"Yeah, I just got thirsty, so I came in for a drink. Is Dad home yet?"

"No, he called and he won't be making it home until dinner. Figures. Did you need something from him?" She sounded far away, as if she herself was dreaming, but she always sort of sounded that way. She sounded as if she would rather be somewhere else, anywhere else.

"No, I was just wondering. Can I have a juice box?"

She nodded distractedly, and he grabbed a box of apple juice out of the fridge to take with him. Thinking quickly, he reached back in and grabbed a second one just so he wouldn't have to come back in here again soon. He was almost out of the room when he had a thought.

"Have you seen Sprocket today?" She looked up at him only briefly before answering.

"No, I don't remember seeing him. I assumed he was with you."

Teddy managed to spend most of the afternoon outside and away from the sadness and anger that made his house feel so heavy. He fought imaginary wars in his tree house and rode his bike down to the corner and back, calling for Sprocket a few times. He wasn't allowed to go past the corner unless an adult was with him, and that didn't happen very often. There was no sign of the mischievous feline, but he sometimes disappeared for a day or two. Teddy always pretended he was off on a magic mouse hunt, conquering whole towns of little mice with a single swipe of his paw.

He managed to keep the curiosity about what had happened that morning in the back of his mind. He knew it was something very important, but it was a nice sunny day out and he had already had a good morning, even if he didn't know how or what had happened. He didn't want to ruin it. He didn't even notice it getting dark until his mom called him from the back porch for dinner.

He grabbed his coat and headed inside, where the lights in the kitchen made it seem warmer and cozier than it felt. His mom was just setting plates out on the table, and he could smell dinner coming from the oven. Even though she was unhappy and distant most of the time, she was an awesome cook.

He ran to the bathroom to wash his hands and came back just in time to hear his dad unlock the front door and kick his boots off in the mudroom. He met his dad in the kitchen and could tell immediately that something was wrong. His dad's normally rugged tan skin had gone pale, and he had a look on his face. Teddy couldn't tell what kind of look it was, but it wasn't a good one.

"Dad? What is it?" Teddy's anxious voice made his mother turn to look, and even she noticed the strange expression on his dad's face. It was both sad and disgusted.

"It's… Katherine, can I talk to you in private for a minute?" His mom must have heard she same seriousness in his voice that Teddy did, because for once she did as he asked without complaining.

"We'll be right back, Teddy-O. I just have to talk to your mom outside for a minute." He turned, and Teddy's mom followed him out of the kitchen and out the front door. Teddy tried to listen in, but after a few seconds, he heard the door to the garage open, and then they were too far away to hear very well. All he could make out were muffled noises, and maybe a gasp from his mom.

He gave up on spying and went to sit at the table, wondering what it could be that made his dad look so strange. After a few minutes, they walked back in. His mom was now wearing a similar look. Teddy waited with a sick feeling to hear what they had to say. His dad sat down next to him while his mom went over to the sink and picked up a hand towel to dab at her eyes with. Fear started to churn in Teddy's stomach.

"I don't even know how to tell you this," his dad started. "When I pulled the car into the garage, I found Sprocket. He was lying in the corner. I'm so sorry, it looks like something… another animal may have gotten in and had a fight with him. I tried to help him, but it was too late. I'm so sorry, buddy."

Teddy sat motionless for a minute. He had been a little worried when he couldn't find the cat earlier, but he had no idea something like that had happened. Sprocket had been pretty much his only friend for as long as he could remember. He felt the news settle like a weight in his chest. His mom came over and put her hand on his shoulder. The news seemed to have broken through the haze she walked around in and made her more human-like for once. She actually looked concerned. Teddy didn't know what to say. Nothing seemed right.

After a minute, his parents moved away from him and started serving dinner. Teddy picked listlessly at his food, wondering what could have happened in the garage. Sprocket was a pretty tough cat, so it must have been something big to hurt him that badly. It was right in the middle of a bite of chicken that he remembered the tuft of fur on the corner of his old fire truck.

It hit him like a lightning bolt, and he gasped involuntarily and then choked. While his dad jumped up and started pounding him on the back, the inner voice that had been banished to the far corner of his mind all day sprang back into action, shouting. It was him! Other Teddy! He trashed your room, and then for some sick reason he killed Sprocket. He smashed him right up with that fire truck!

Teddy's vision swam for a minute as his eyes filled with tears, partly from coughing but mostly in realization that this wasn't just an accident. What had happened this morning wasn't just a pleasant daydream in a dusty attic. He had gone somewhere, and someone else had come here in his place.

He finally got the food down and took a gulp of his water as his dad sat down with a relieved look on his face. As he sat watching his parents resume dinner and make idle conversation, his mind whirled with possibilities. Was the other Teddy evil? Maybe that's why his other parents had seemed so happy this morning when Teddy "visited". Maybe they were relieved to have a nice version of their son for a day. Or had they even noticed? Maybe the other him was pleasant on the outside and a serial killer in private.

Teddy excused himself from the table and went up to his room. It felt violated now that he knew what kind of person had been in here. He sat down next to the toy box and dug through for the alleged murder weapon. It made him sick to think that a gift from someone's grandma could be used for something so hideous. He had asked during dinner if he could go see Sprocket, but his dad said no. He said that he would put him in a box later, and they could bury him in the morning.

He found the fire truck and brought it over to the light to inspect it. A few hairs still stuck to it, and as Teddy looked closer, he noticed that the edge of the truck was a little darker red than the rest of it. He didn't know how he could have missed it this morning, but it was lined with blood. That bastard, no, that fucker has killed Sprocket. Some of the dried blood rubbed off on his thumb, and he suddenly felt the dinner that he had eaten coming back up in a rush. He sprinted for the bathroom and barely made it as he vomited forcefully into the toilet bowl.

He gagged and dry-heaved as the realization of the whole day hit him over and over. When the retching finally subsided, he sat back against the bathtub and wiped his mouth. He knew one thing for sure. This wasn't over.

He went back to his room to ponder what he could do about it. It felt lonely without his cat curled up on the bed, and he felt fresh tears stinging his eyes.

He scowled as he pulled his freshly wrinkled comic books out from under the bed and flipped through them without really looking at them. It was hard to concentrate. As usual, once his parents came up for bed, words and phrases found their way to his room through the vents. This time, however, they weren't fighting. Their voices were a little quieter, but worried.

Teddy wondered if they were talking about Sprocket and crawled out of bed and over to the vent cover to listen closer. *There's just no way… He's not that… smashed, looked like someone… I refuse to believe… to a pulp, Katherine… he's just so quiet… alone too much… what do we… No, don't say…*

Teddy jumped back from the vent like he had been burned. They thought he had done it. They actually thought that he had taken the fire truck and beaten his own cat to death and left him in the garage for his dad to find. They thought he was capable of something like that. *He framed me*, he thought. He thought about what evidence the other boy might have left around. Did anyone see him outside? A neighbor maybe? Teddy started to panic. They would never believe him. Who would believe a story like his?

He got into bed and pulled the covers up over himself. What options did he have? He could try telling his parents what had happened with the trunk, but they would reward his honesty with a one-way ticket to the loony bin. He could just deny everything, but what if someone had seen something? What if they found other evidence he didn't know about yet?

He thought about the parents in the other world. They seemed like the type who would believe him. They would try to understand, And help him out. If only… But they don't have to be his parents, Teddy-o. They could be yours, just as easily. Just a quick hop in the trunk, and they're all yours.

Just as Teddy started to fall asleep, he realized that maybe that little voice wasn't so crazy after all. Before he could consider it any further, sleep claimed him. Anything else that happened that night was the stuff of dreams.

Morning brought realization to Teddy Harrison. He sat up in bed, knowing what he would do that day. To borrow a phrase he had heard his mom say often enough, Other Teddy had made his bed and now he could sleep in it. Teddy wasn't going to be blamed for some identical psychopath from another dimension (and as weird as that sounded, he was pretty sure that's exactly what was going on) killing a cat, and in such a gruesome fashion at that. If he wanted to screw with this world, he could live in this one.

He looked around his room to see what he might want to take with him, if he could even take anything. He realized that pretty much everything was the same over there, so he wouldn't miss much. He thought about his parents. Would they miss him? Would they ever even notice that an imposter had taken his place? He guessed not. If the nice version of his parents didn't even notice, how would his version?

Still, he felt like he was leaving them, and it felt like shit. He wanted to say goodbye to them, but he didn't know how to tell them he was ditching them for the alternate universe version of themselves. Teddy settled for going downstairs to at least see if his mom was up yet, and to see if his dad was home. It was Sunday morning, so there was a good chance he was still in the house.

The stairs creaked on his way down, and he felt a weird sense of pre-déjà vu. He knew he would hear that sound many times in the future, but down happier stairs. Both of his parents were sitting in the kitchen drinking coffee when he walked in. They looked up and smiled at him, but he could see the hushed conversation from last night in their eyes.

So they do blame me. He tried to act cool, but the thought that they could think so low of him bothered him. Why not blame the bully down the street, or a random drug addict breaking in, or aliens attacking? Blaming their own son? Unthinkable to most parents, and yet his had grabbed onto the conclusion like a life raft on a stormy ocean.

"Teddy? Are you okay? You look pale. I hope you're not coming down with something."

Sure, Mom, he thought, Now you're concerned about me.

"I'm fine. Just tired, I guess." He sat down in the chair at the other end of the table and watched his parents eat their breakfast silently and flip through the paper without chatting with each other. He wondered if it was wrong of him to leave them, but he wasn't leaving them, really. He was just choosing another path for himself.

Evil Teddy didn't deserve the parents he had, anyway. The looks on his parents' faces this morning had made up his mind for good. He was leaving, and he wasn't wasting any more time thinking about it.

Teddy pushed his chair back suddenly, startling his parents. He excused himself and just about ran for the attic before he changed his mind or lost his nerve. He didn't even bother being quiet as he went up the attic stairs and headed for the trunk.

He held his breath as he got in, praying that this would work and it hadn't all been in his mind. The trunk had the same smell and faint sounds coming from it as before. He closed the lid and tried to steady his breathing. The aromatic wood smell filled his nostrils, and he felt the same sleepy feeling as last time. He wasn't sure if anything was happening. After a few minutes, he figured it was now or never. He creaked the lid back open and peered through the dim attic, his hands damp with anticipation.

He sighed with relief when he saw the mannequin in the corner, still wearing the half-finished shirt it had last time. He had done it. It wasn't just a figment of his imagination after all. He really had changed places. He ran down the attic stairs into his new house, so much like the other and yet so different. The hallway had the same creaky spot in it. He poked his head into his new bedroom door to see if it, too, was the same. It was, for the most part. Most of the toys were the same. He went in and lifted the dust ruffle of the bed to check and see if the comics were even the same. Instead of superheroes, though, there were glossy horror comics, the gory kind with vampires and zombies. So Evil Teddy had slightly different tastes than he did. It was okay, he could work on rebuilding his collection.

Leaving his bedroom, he went down to check and see if his new parents were waiting in the kitchen for him, like in his old life. Sure enough, there was breakfast on the table, and his new, happier parents were sitting in the same seats. In this world, though, they were happily sharing the newspaper pages and laughing over the comics together. They looked up as he walked in, smiling at him.

"Good morning, sweetie. Are you hungry?"

He nodded in relief and sank down into his chair, ready to start his new life. He ate quietly, soaking up the vibes coming from this more cheerful version of his former kitchen. His dad hugged his mom as she was cleaning up the plates after breakfast and reached over to ruffle Teddy's hair as he walked by. Teddy knew then that he had made the right choice. He didn't know how they had missed what a psychopath their son was, but it didn't matter to him now. He had the parents he always wanted, and the other boy had the dull, unhappy life that he seemed to deserve.

"Hey Dad? Do you think we can do something today?" His dad looked mildly surprised, but in a happy way. Maybe Evil Teddy hadn't paid much attention to his dear old dad.

"Well sure! I'd like that. Maybe we should go down to the park again and throw a ball around for a bit. We can even walk down for ice cream after lunch. That is, if your mom approves." His dad looked up at her, smiling, and she gave a playful sigh.

"Gee, I suppose that's okay. Though it would be nice if you invited the boss of the family with you."

His dad laughed and kissed her on the forehead. "You're always invited, my love. What good would ice cream be without the prettiest girl in the world?"

She blushed, and Teddy smiled, glad to be where he belonged for once. This was going to be a good life.

Teddy sank into bed that night, feeling better than he had in a very long time. As long as he could remember, for that matter. He had spent a great day with his family. They even followed through with the suggested ice cream, getting an extra scoop and sprinkles too. They had spent the afternoon at home. His dad had let him help change the oil in the car while his mom made dinner. They even popped popcorn and watched movies after eating dinner. He couldn't imagine a better day.

He had thought about his other parents a few times during the day, but the feelings of happiness and love in this house overshadowed any lingering doubts he might have had. Remembering all the arguments and tense voices he was used to hearing at night, he slipped out of bed and crouched by the heating vent, just to see. He heard whispering voices from his parents' bedroom. As usual, it was only bits and pieces of the conversation floating through, but it was enough for him. So happy today… seemed like a new… like he used to… A new leaf…

They could tell the difference, and they were happy about it. They seemed like such good people, they deserved a son that loved and appreciated them, not some angry cat-killing weirdo. Teddy got back into bed and pulled the blankets up around himself. He drifted off to sleep, thinking about the great day with his family and looking forward to many more.

Teddy woke up suddenly, disoriented and confused. He had been in the middle of a dream where his new parents had taken him to Disneyland, and they got to go to the front of every line without waiting. The next thing he knew, he was waking up in the trunk.

It had never even occurred to him that this world-hopping could be initiated both ways. Teddy shuddered as he tried to imagine what the punishment for this would be. If Evil Teddy killed an innocent cat just for the fun of it, what would he do to someone who tried to steal his family and trap him in this cold, unhappy house?

His heart beat faster as he scrambled out of the trunk and saw the train set. It was true. Evil Teddy had initiated another switch. As much as he wanted to climb back into the trunk and find a way back out of this mess, he had to know what had happened in this world, if anything. His parents were going to kill him if the other Teddy had trashed the entire house the way he had trashed the bedroom before.

Teddy crept out of the attic, desperately trying not to wake his parents in the middle of the night. There's no way that could end well for him. He stepped around the creaky spot in the hallway and got almost to his bedroom doorway. He listened for his parents, but the house was silent. He took another step, and then without warning his foot slid in something wet on the floor, and he went flying.

He landed hard on his back and had to bite his tongue to keep from yelling from the surprise of it. He groaned, wondering what kind of evil trap the boy had set up, and whether he would be able to get it cleaned up or get out of here before his parents woke up and found it.

Evil Teddy's parents, that was. He had no intention of taking the blame for this, or coming back here at all after his wonderful day with his new family. He sighed and got back up, wiping his hands on his pajama pants. He ducked into the bathroom and flipped on the light to wash his hands. As Teddy looked down at his hands and the smear of liquid soaking through the legs of his pajamas, he choked back a scream and suddenly felt like the world was folding in on him.

It was deep red and sticky. Teddy knew blood, and this was definitely it. He knew he wasn't hurt, so thoughts raced through his head. He sat heavily on the closed toilet seat, starting to shake. His vision was blacking in and out. This was a lot of blood, and Teddy had a feeling he knew where it had come from. Thoughts of him stealing the other boy's parents and the possible punishments for that flashed through his head, and he leaned forward abruptly and vomited all over the rug in front of the sink. It couldn't be. No one was that sick. Of course, most kids didn't kill household pets either.

Teddy didn't even feel the tears coursing down his cheeks. This can't be happening. It must be something else. It's a prank, corn syrup and red dye. Maybe some of that fake blood they sell down at the corner store around Halloween.

He knew in his heart that wasn't true, though. He could smell the coppery tang of blood. It smelled like when his dad came back from hunting and hung a deer in the garage to drain the blood out. It smelled like life and death, not corn syrup.

Teddy scrambled to his feet without thinking and looked back into the hallway. Now that his eyes were adjusted, he could see the blood on the floor. There was a whole trail of drips and smears, ending at the attic doorway. The other end came out of his parents' bedroom. Teddy started to see stars flash in his vision before he realized he wasn't breathing.

He took in a long, ragged gasp of air, gagging again at the scent of blood, now so strong that he wondered how he had missed it in the first place. He crossed numbly over to his parents' room and pushed the door open. It was obvious right from the doorway. Teddy didn't even have to turn the light on to see the damage. His parents both lay in bed, drenched in blood. His dad looked peaceful if you ignored the giant gash in his throat. Evil Teddy must have gotten to him first. His mother's body was twisted in the sheets, her hands and arms slashed and still dripping blood on the carpet. Teddy wondered wildly if it would come out, or if there would always be stains there. Her body was pushed up against the headboard, a large silver knife handle still sticking out of her chest. Her head hung down, her long hair almost hiding the blade.

Teddy realized that he was on the floor, tears flooding his vision. He was struggling for breath, trying to sort this out in his mind. How could this happen? Who does this?

His gut knotted up as he realized that his mother must have thought it was him. She died thinking her own son was murdering her. How would she know any differently? In a way, he had. He had killed them by leaving them here with this monster, who had the same face as him. Oh my god. The knife. If we are the same, will our fingerprints match too?

The reality of the situation finally set in, and Teddy started to scream. He sat on the floor covered in his parents' blood and screamed until his throat was raw. He was going to be blamed for this. He would never be able to convince anyone that it wasn't really him. There was only one way out of this.

He had to get back through the trunk and lock it this time. Let that little fucker rot in jail in this world.

He stumbled to his feet, acting on instinct and shock, and gotten as far as the bedroom door when he heard sirens coming down the street. Someone must have heard him screaming.

Panicking, he ran down the hall to the attic door. He fell twice trying to race up the stairs, his feet slick from the blood he had trampled through. As he got to the top of the stairs, he heard the police force the front door open downstairs. He could hear them yelling, but he couldn't make out the words over the pounding in his head.

He threw himself across the room towards the trunk. He could hear the cops more clearly now, calling for backup and an ambulance. As if that will do any good now, he thought madly. He collapsed next to the trunk and grabbed the lid with both hands. It didn't move. He tugged harder, praying that the wood was just swollen with the summer humidity.

He pried and pulled, feeling one of his fingernails break against the unforgiving wood. Above the deafening roar of his pulse, and the shouting and stomping from the police below him, he heard the sound that threatened to drive him over the edge. He heard laughter from inside the trunk. It was fading, but he could still make it out clearly. He knew it because it was identical to his own. It sounded like he was belly-laughing at the funniest joke he had ever heard.

He realized he was screaming again. The footsteps of the cops were pounding up the attic stairs now. His hearing faded in and out now as his body threatened to lose consciousness in the horror of everything. The cops sounded so far away, like they were voices floating in through a heating vent.

Hey, I got someone... Oh my God... he's covered in... do you think he saw... found a note... Oh god, he couldn't... it was him... this kid killed ...

THE MIDNIGHT GARDEN

The road was nearly empty. Elena drove with both hands on the wheel, her eyes fixed ahead as the trees and houses slid by. The late afternoon light flickered through the branches and across the dashboard. The steady hum of the tires and the gentle snoring of her children filled the car.

She had left the house without thinking too much about it. Jacob, the baby, had fallen asleep after crying most of the morning. Isla had been restless and bored, trailing her from room to room. A drive had seemed like the easiest solution. Something to break the long stretch of hours that felt the same no matter what she did.

Now the baby slept soundly in the rear-facing seat behind her. Isla was slumped beside him, her head tipped toward the window, one hand still holding the ear of a stuffed rabbit. Her mouth hung open slightly, and her breathing was deep and even.

Elena checked the rearview mirror again. They were still breathing, still safe.

She had checked so many times that the motion had become automatic. Mirror, road, mirror again. She told herself she was just being careful. Mothers were supposed to be careful, after all.

The radio played, some talk show she was not really listening to. A man laughed too loudly at his own joke. She reached over and turned the volume down until his voice became an indistinct murmur. Silence felt better.

She had not brought her phone with her. She had realized it a few minutes after pulling out of the driveway. For a moment she had considered turning back, but then she kept going. She would be fine without it for a while, people were too attached to their phones anyway.

There was nowhere she needed to be, so she drove aimlessly. The gas gauge hovered just above half. The temperature outside was warm enough that she had cracked her window an inch. Air moved through the car in currents that smelled of cut grass and sun-warmed pavement. Everything felt ordinary. That was what made the tightness in her chest so hard to explain.

It had been there all morning. A pressure just beneath her ribs. Not pain, not fear, but more like the sense that she had forgotten something important and couldn't remember what.

She tightened her grip on the wheel and followed the road as it curved to the left. Behind her, the baby made a small sound in his sleep. Isla shifted, but did not wake. Elena kept driving. The road straightened for a while, then dipped between two low hills. The trees thinned enough for sunlight to spill across the asphalt in wide, pale bands. Elena narrowed her eyes against the brightness.

A rusted mailbox leaned at the end of a long dirt driveway. The sight of it tugged at something in her chest. She didn't know why at first. She drove past it, swallowing her rising feeling of unease. It was just a mailbox, she was being silly.

Her father used to take drives like this. Long stretches of empty road the windows down, the breeze blowing through the cab of his truck. He always said he liked the quiet out there, that it was the only place he could really think.

She could still remember how the vinyl seat stuck to the backs of her legs in the summer, and how the radio stations faded in and out between towns. How he would reach across the bench seat and drive with his hand on her knee. She had not thought about that in years.

Elena adjusted her hands on the wheel. The steering felt heavier, as if the car itself had grown tired.

She passed a field with tall grass rippling in waves. For a moment she thought she saw movement near the tree line. A dark shape, just far enough away that she couldn't quite make it out.

She blinked and squinted, but then there was nothing there. It was just her eyes playing tricks on her.

Her mouth had gone dry. She ran her tongue along the inside of her teeth and tasted something bitter she couldn't name.

"Just tired," she said under her breath.

In the back seat, Isla's shoe tapped against the plastic base of the car seat as the car rolled over a patch of rough pavement. It was a small, hollow sound.

Elena's eyes flicked to the mirror again. Still asleep, still safe.

She exhaled and focused on the road. The memory hovered at the edge of her mind, one she hadn't summoned and hadn't thought about in a very long time. It was a place behind her childhood home, a narrow path through weeds that grew taller than she was. She remembered a hand guiding her forward in the dark.

He had called it something, but she couldn't quite remember what. She thought she almost had it, then the road curved again, and the thought slipped away. Elena pressed a little harder on the gas without realizing it. The trees crowded closer to the road until their branches nearly touched overhead. Shadows fell across the pavement in uneven stripes, the sunlight flashing in her eyes.

The radio murmured beside her with a different voice now, a woman speaking in a calm, measured tone about traffic delays. Elena reached over and turned the volume knob down another notch, and the words became too soft to follow.

She shifted in her seat. The fabric of her shirt clung to her back. She had not noticed herself sweating until now. The air in the car felt thick, even with the window cracked. The sweat stung her eyes, and she blinked hard and focused on the white line at the edge of the road. She told herself to stay inside it, just stay inside the line and keep moving. Everything would be okay.

She had not slept more than an hour at a time for weeks. Every time she closed her eyes, she woke to the sound of crying. Sometimes it was the Jacob, sometimes it was only in her head. She had started leaving the monitor on even when she was in the same room, just to be sure she wasn't missing something.

She thought about the night she had fallen asleep sitting up on the couch. She had woken with her arms wrapped around nothing. For several seconds she had been certain she had dropped the baby, and would look down to find his broken body on the floor. She had jumped up in a panic before realizing he was still in his crib upstairs.

She tightened her grip on the wheel.

"Focus," she whispered. The word sounded strange in the quiet car. Too loud. Too sharp. Behind her, the baby made a soft hiccupping noise. Isla shifted and let out a small sigh, the kind children make when they are deep in dreams.

Elena watched them in the mirror until tears blurred at the edges of her vision. She forced herself to look forward again.

A road sign flashed past on the right. She did not catch the words, and for a moment she wondered if it had been there at all. Not everything she'd been seeing lately had been.

The sensation returned, the one she couldn't name or explain. It was as if she were already late for something she had not yet decided to do. She pressed her foot down, and the engine responded with a low, steady growl as it sped up.

A pickup truck appeared suddenly in her rearview mirror. It had not been there a moment ago, but now it filled the glass, close enough that she could see the outline of the driver's hands on the wheel. He was following too closely, and Elena felt her grip tighten on the wheel.

She eased her foot off the gas and moved toward the right side of the lane to encourage him to go around her. The truck stayed where it was, hovering right behind them. Her stomach twisted painfully, and the sight of it pulled her backward in time before she could stop herself.

Her husband used to drive a truck like that. It wasn't the same color of make, but he had the same way of sitting behind the wheel. Leaning forward, jaw set, eyes locked on whatever was in front of him with a focus she had always found intimidating.

She remembered the sound of his tires on the gravel. That was always the warning. The crunch as he pulled into the driveway long after dark, followed by the slam of the door and heavy steps in the entryway.

She had learned to read his mood in seconds by the angle of his shoulders, the way he dropped his keys, even whether he called her name or stayed silent. Some nights he kissed her before he even took off his boots. Those were the good nights, the ones that made her believe things might still change. Other nights he went straight to the kitchen and opened a beer.

She remembered standing at the sink, finishing some dishes when he came up behind her and grabbed her arm hard enough to leave a bruise, spinning her around.

"Why is the baby still awake?" he had demanded.

"He just ate," she had said. "He'll fall asleep soon."

He hadn't liked that answer. His fingers had tightened around her wrist until she felt the bones grind together. She had tried not to pull away. Pulling away only made it worse, she had learned that too.

"I work all day," he said. "You sit around the house all day and can't even bother to keep that kid quiet when I get home. You think that's what I want to come home to?"

She remembered apologizing, the words spilling out before she even thought about them. She always said she was sorry.

Later, after the baby slept and Isla had been put to bed, he had climbed into bed beside her and pulled her close. His hand had moved gently over the same wrist he had bruised hours earlier.

"I don't know what you do to me," he whispered. "You make me crazy."

She had stared at the ceiling and told herself this was what love looked like when it got tired. It was a normal part of a marriage, everyone went through rough patches like this.

The pickup behind her blared its horn, and Elena jerked back to the present. She realized she had slowed too much. The truck swerved into the other lane and roared past her, the driver not bothering to look at her as he went by. Within seconds, he was out of sight.

Elena forced her breathing to slow down. In the back seat, the children still slept. She checked the mirror again, and they were still breathing, still safe. She kept driving.

The road began to climb. Elena felt it in the engine first, the low strain as the car pushed uphill. Her ears popped, and she swallowed and kept her eyes fixed on the narrow ribbon of pavement ahead. A headache had started behind her right eye.

It pulsed in slow waves that made the trees seem to tilt when she glanced at them.

She remembered another night when the world had begun to tilt like that.

The baby had been home for less than three weeks. She knew that because the hospital bracelet was still lying on the bathroom counter, even though she had meant to throw it away. She had picked it up several times, turned it over in her fingers, then set it back down.

He would not stop crying. Nothing worked. Feeding him made him cry harder, and rocking him only seemed to make it worse. She walked the length of the living room again and again until her calves shook. The house felt too bright, then too dark, then bright again. She couldn't tell if hours were passing or only minutes.

She had tried to watch the clock. She told herself that if she could make it to morning, she would be fine. Morning always made things feel less dangerous.

At some point she must have sat down. She remembered closing her eyes just for a second, and then she was standing in the hallway. The lights were off, and the house was silent.

Her arms were wrapped tightly around something. She could feel the warmth and weight against her chest. There was a damp patch where a small mouth had been pressed into her shoulder.

She looked down, but there was nothing there. Her hands were clenched around an empty blanket. Her heart began to pound in her chest. She couldn't remember getting up. She couldn't remember walking. The last thing she remembered clearly was the sound of crying, but now that had stopped.

She turned toward the baby's room. The door was closed, but she didn't remember closing it. She didn't remember leaving him alone.

For one long, terrifying moment, she was certain she had hurt him. She had fallen asleep and smothered him, or she had dropped him. She had done something she could never undo. She opened the door and saw the nightlight casting a pale yellow glow across the crib.

He was there, sleeping soundly. His chest rose and fell in small, steady movements. Relief hit her so hard she had to grab the doorframe to stay upright. That was when she had noticed her hands.

They were dirty, dark streaks running across her palms and up her wrists. Thick grime was caked under her fingernails. She brought them closer to her face, and the smell made her stomach turn. She could taste something cold and metallic at the back of her throat.

She turned on the hallway light in a panic and saw that her hands were clean. Nothing was on them at all. The baby made a soft sound in his sleep, and she stepped closer to the crib and stared at him until her vision blurred. She was afraid that if she looked away, he would vanish. That night she did not go back to bed. She sat on the floor beside the crib until morning, listening for sounds that were not there.

In the present, Elena's fingers tightened around the steering wheel. The headache pulsed, and the trees seemed to lean toward the car as she passed them, reaching out to grab the car and drag it back.

Behind her, the baby let out a thin cry in his sleep, a warning that he would wake up soon. She checked the mirror, but his eyes were still closed. Isla was deep asleep beside him, she had always been a good sleeper. She could not shake the feeling that if she blinked too long, they would disappear.

She pressed harder on the gas without realizing it, and the car moved faster down the road. Sunlight spilled across the road in uneven patches that made Elena squint. She lifted a hand to shade her eyes and felt the faint tremor in her fingers. It was getting harder to tell whether the shaking was from the road or from her.

A narrow gravel lane appeared on the right. It was barely visible, half-hidden by tall weeds and a broken fence post leaning at an angle. She didn't slow down, but she knew that kind of road. Her mind slid backward again before she could stop it.

Behind the house where she grew up, there had been a path like that. It started just past the rusted swing set and wound through a patch of wild growth that her mother always said she would clear someday. The grass there grew taller than Elena's shoulders in summer. Burs and sharp thorns brushed against her arms when she pushed through.

Her father was the one who showed her the path.

"Come on," he had said one evening. "I want to show you something special."

The sun had already set, and the air was thick and warm. He carried a flashlight that cut a weak beam through the darkness. She had followed him because she always followed him. He was her father, and that was reason enough.

The path opened into a small clearing. There had once been a garden there. You could still see the low stone border half-buried in weeds. A few warped wooden stakes leaned in crooked rows. Something had been planted there long ago and left to die.

He had spread a blanket on the ground.

"This is our special Midnight Garden," he told her. "It's a place for us to come, but only at night. It can be our secret place. Gardens are where beautiful things can grow."

She remembered the way he smiled when he said it, like he was sharing a joke only they understood, like he was giving her a gift. The flashlight lay on its side, casting light across the weeds. Crickets chirped somewhere nearby. In the distance, a dog barked and then fell silent.

She sat because he told her to sit. He brushed her hair back from her face. His hand stayed there longer than it needed to. His voice dropped to a whisper as he explained that this place was theirs, that they could do special things here in the dark that they couldn't do at home. He said that she was old enough now to understand.

Her stomach had twisted in a way she could not name. She remembered looking down at her sneakers, at the dirt packed into the seams of the rubber soles. She focused on that because it was easier than looking at him. When he reached for her, she went still.

She didn't cry. She didn't struggle. She learned, in that moment, how to leave her own body while it was still breathing. Above her, the sky was black and wide. She fixed her eyes on one bright star and counted her breaths until the world went quiet.

In the car, Elena blinked hard, and the image shattered. Her chest felt hollow, as if something had been scooped out of it and never put back. Behind her, Jacob had begun to make a sound that wasn't quite crying yet, more of a whimper. Isla shifted in her sleep and murmured something Elena could not make out.

The road curved ahead, leading out of a stretch of forest she didn't quite remember driving through, and her foot pressed down on the accelerator without her thinking. She didn't realize she was crying until a tear slipped into the corner of her mouth.

Patches of open sky appeared between the trees. The road straightened and widened, the yellow center line bright against the gray pavement. She looked in the mirror once again and saw that Isla was awake now.

Her eyes were half-open, still heavy with sleep. She didn't look scared, not the way Elena would have been at that age. She had learned fear too early and had done her best to shield Isla from that.

"Mommy," she said softly. "Where are we going?"

Elena opened her mouth, but no answer came. She looked back at the road. The baby stirred and began to cry for real this time. The sound drilled straight into her skull, and her hands tightened on the wheel. She could see their futures as clearly as the road in front of her.

She saw Isla at sixteen, sitting on the edge of a bed in a room that smelled of stale beer and sweat. A boy stood over her with his jaw clenched and a hand raised. She had the stunned look that always came first, the one that went along with the disbelief that someone who said they loved you could hurt you so easily.

Isla at twenty-five, calling home with a trembling voice, saying she fell, saying it was an accident. Saying she didn't want to make a big deal out of it. Saying she had deserved it and that she was sorry.

Elena's vision blurred.

She saw Jacob grown tall and broad-shouldered. She saw anger simmering just behind a careful façade, like it had in his father, like it had in her own father. She saw him punching a wall hard enough to split his knuckles. She saw the way he would learn to blame everyone else for the fire inside him. She saw him calling some woman crazy, saw him gripping her arm too tightly, then smiling afterward like nothing had happened.

The cycle did not stop, it only changed faces. Her mother had believed survival was enough. Keep the peace, keep the secret, keep breathing. Elena had believed love would fix it. Now she understood neither of those things were true.

"You deserve better," she whispered, though she did not know if she meant herself or the children.

The baby's crying rose in pitch. Isla began to cry too, confused now, frightened by the sound and her mother's silence. The noise filled the car until there was no room left to think.

Elena pressed harder on the gas. If she did nothing, the darkness would find them. It always did. It waited in bloodlines, in quiet houses, in special gardens where no one ever came during the day. She could not change what had already happened, but she could stop what came next. Her breathing slowed, and her mind sharpened with terrible clarity. She could no longer hear the children in the back seat.

Ahead, through a gap in the trees, she saw the first hint of steel rising against the sky. The trees fell away in long stretches now, but Elena barely noticed.

Her hands were steady on the wheel. Her eyes were open, but she was no longer seeing the road. The present had begun to dissolve around the edges. Sound grew distant, and she felt like she was floating into the past, like time itself was becoming less fixed than it had always seemed.

The memory did not come all at once. It crept in slowly, like it always did, with a tightening in her throat and a sense of being watched. She felt detached, as if she were watching an old movie on a faraway screen.

She was eleven. Her mother was working the late shift again, so she was home alone with her father. The house felt too large when it was just the two of them, but her mother had been working late more and more lately.

Her father let her stay up to watch a movie. He made popcorn and poured soda into the tall glasses they only used for company. He seemed happy and relaxed on the surface, but Elena had felt something was wrong all evening. He laughed at parts that weren't funny, and he kept glancing at her instead of the television.

She sat curled in the corner of the couch with a blanket over her legs. The glow from the screen flickered across the room and made shadows that made her want to jump.

When the movie ended, she said she was tired. He told her she could sleep there on the couch, like a sleepover. He said he would stay up a little longer and go to bed when her mother came home.

She lay down and turned her face toward the back of the couch. She closed her eyes and tried to make herself small. She felt him sit beside her. The cushion dipped. The blanket shifted, and she felt his hand slip under it and reach for her.

She froze. Up until now, she had been able to leave the memories of what was happening in the Midnight Garden there when she left. This was the first time she realized that the danger wasn't isolated to any one space. There was nowhere she was safe.

"Shhh," he whispered. "You want this."

Her mind split in two. One part of her stayed on that couch, breathing shallowly, staring at the dark fabric inches from her face. The other part stepped outside herself and watched from somewhere near the ceiling.

She saw a small girl lying very still. She saw a man who should have protected her leaning over her like she were something he owned.

He told her that she was special. Told her that this was what happened when girls grew up. Told her she must never tell anyone, or they would both be in trouble. This was their secret, and that she was very lucky to have a father who loved her so much.

She nodded because nodding was easier than speaking. Afterward, she went to the bathroom and washed her hands until the skin turned raw. She did not know why she chose her hands. She only knew she needed something to hurt, something to feel other than what he had done to her.

She never told her mother. She never told anyone. She couldn't make herself believe that it wasn't her fault somehow.

In the car, Elena let out a broken sound. Her vision swam, and the road blurred in front of her. She tasted salt and didn't understand at first that she was crying.

Behind her, the children's voices rose and fell. They sounded so far away, as if they were calling to her from the bottom of a deep well.

She blinked hard, and the present snapped back into place. Ahead, the bridge stood fully revealed.

Gray steel, empty lanes, dark water waiting beneath. Her breath hitched. It was almost time.

Elena felt the subtle change in vibration as the tires moved from worn asphalt onto rough concrete. The sound beneath them deepened. A hollow, echoing rumble that seemed to rise from the structure itself. She slowed to a stop in the middle of the lane.

She blinked furiously, trying to clear the tears from her eyes. The bridge stretched ahead in a long, straight line. There were no other cars or pedestrians, just them. Elena looked at the rusted guardrails on either side and the slow, dark surface of the river far below.

For a moment she couldn't breathe.

The children were both crying now, confused sobs that filled her with an aching kind of fear.

"Mommy," Isla said tearfully. "Where are we?"

Elena's throat tightened, and she forced herself to look in the mirror. Isla's face was flushed from sleep and tears. Her hair stuck out in damp curls, and her stuffed rabbit lay forgotten at her feet. The baby's cries had grown hoarse, and his tiny hands were balled up into fists.

They were still breathing, still safe, still trusting her to protect them. The thought hit with a sharp, physical pain, a stabbing in her chest.

The sky had shifted while she was lost in memory. Clouds hung low and heavy now, turning the light a flat gray and draining the color from the world. Her heartbeat filled her ears, each pulse louder and more painful than the last. She could hear her own breathing, thin and ragged-sounding.

She had imagined this moment so many times in the past few days. Lying awake in the dark, standing at the kitchen sink, rocking the baby while the world outside the windows went on without her. She had imagined fear and chaos and overwhelming emotions, but now she felt only a quiet stillness.

The engine idled, and for a long time she did not move. She stared out over the guardrail at the water below. It looked deeper and darker than it should have, as if it could swallow anything that touched its surface and leave no trace behind.

The children's crying was fading into exhausted whimpers.

"Close your eyes," she said quietly. She did not know whether they had heard her. Her hands rested on the steering wheel, and for the first time in a very long time, she felt calm. The fear that had followed her for so long had finally gone quiet. No more racing thoughts, no more questions she couldn't answer. She knew this was the only way.

Behind her, Isla sniffled and wiped her face with the back of her hand. The baby had worn himself out. His cries had faded into small, hitching breaths.

"Mommy," Isla whispered. "Can we go home?"

Elena closed her eyes. She pictured the house as she had left it. Dishes drying in the rack next to the sink, a basket of clean laundry waiting to be folded, a few toys scattered across the living room. Nothing that looked dangerous, or that warned of what could grow there in time.

She had believed once that love was enough to keep darkness out. She had believed that if she tried harder than her mother had, if she stayed alert and careful and strong, she could build something different for her children.

Now she knew better. Violence didn't just show up one day out of the blue. It crept in slowly in a raised voice, a slammed door, a hand that gripped too tightly and then let go with an apology. It disguised itself in ordinary moments until no one could say exactly when things had gone wrong.

She saw Isla years from now, sitting in a kitchen much like her own. She saw her smiling through tears, making excuses, and trying to teach herself to endure.

She saw Jacob grown tall and angry, carrying something inside him he did not understand. Passing it on because no one had ever shown him how to set it down.

She couldn't let that happen to them.

"I'm sorry," she said softly. "I'm so sorry." For the first time, her apology felt right, not made in fear or shame, but in genuine remorse for the two tiny lives in the backseat that would never know why this had to happen.

She opened her eyes. Her hands felt light on the steering wheel, almost detached from the rest of her body. She glanced into the rearview mirror one last time.

Isla was watching her, looking confused and scared. Elena swallowed hard and forced herself to hold that gaze for a single, unbearable second.

"Close your eyes," she repeated, then shifted the car into reverse.

The engine growled as she pressed the gas. The car rolled backward across the bridge, tires crunching over loose grit and broken bits of asphalt.

She stopped and shifted the car into drive. Her foot hovered over the accelerator. There was no more doubt left in her. Elena took one slow breath, then she pressed her foot down.

The engine roared, and the car lurched forward, tires gripping hard against the rough concrete. The bridge rushed toward them in a gray blur. Wind whistled against the windows. Behind her, her daughter screamed, and the baby began to cry in alarm at the sound.

Elena did not look back. Her eyes stayed fixed on the guardrail ahead. Her grip tightened on the wheel, and she aimed the vehicle for a spot between the struts of the bridge. Her arms felt locked in place.

The car rattled as it gained speed. The steering column vibrated beneath her hands. The sound filled the cabin until there was no space left for thought.

For one brief moment, something flickered inside her. A flash of doubt, an image of her stopping the car, pulling her children into her arms, and driving anywhere but here. It passed. She was the only one who could end this now. She held the line, and the guardrail filled the windshield.

Metal screamed as the front of the car slammed into it. The force snapped her forward against the seatbelt. Glass cracked and steel buckled inward. For a split second, the car shuddered in place, then the barrier gave way and they burst through.

The ground vanished beneath the tires and the world dropped out from under them. The sky tilted, and the river surged upward in a dark rush.

Time seemed to stretch out. For the first time that she could remember, she wasn't afraid.

Elena looked at her children in the mirror one last time. They were still breathing, still safe, and now they always would be.

"I love you," she whispered.

The words were torn away by the wind. The car fell, the water rose to meet them, and everything went black.

THE LAST EPISODE

Evan Cole leaned back in his chair and rubbed his eyes. The glow of his laptop was the only light in the apartment. The rest of the room was dark except for the small numbers on the digital clock on his desk that read 11:38 PM. He had been editing this episode of his podcast for almost two hours.

On the screen, the audio waveform stretched across the editing timeline in blue peaks and valleys. Evan dragged the cursor back to the beginning and listened again.

"Welcome back to Midnight Archive," his voice said through the headphones. "I'm your host, Evan Cole. Tonight's story comes from a quiet town in northern Michigan, where a late-night phone call led to a disappearance that was never fully explained."

He stopped the playback and trimmed a pause between two sentences. He hated when the pacing felt off. It was hard enough in this industry to get listeners even with professionally produced podcasts, he had to make sure his indie one was as polished as possible.

His latest episode had just over forty thousand downloads. Not bad. It was one of the better weeks the show had had in months. The more people who listened, the better the stories seemed to land. That was the strange thing about it, a story could feel flat when he first recorded it, but once thousands of people heard it, something about it changed. The comments filled up with listeners agreeing how captivating it was.

Evan checked the time again and took off his headphones. The apartment was quiet. He could hear the refrigerator humming in the kitchen, and a car passing by somewhere outside. He reached for the coffee mug beside the laptop and realized it was empty.

"Great," he muttered. He set the mug back down and opened the project folder on his desktop. He liked to keep everything organized, and he had separate folders for raw audio, edits, and final cuts. The current episode was labeled "Episode_213_Edit2". He clicked the mouse to save a backup copy, knowing you can never be too careful.

That was when he noticed the other file. It sat just below the episode he was editing. "Episode_214_Final.wav". Evan frowned. He stared at the filename for a moment, trying to remember if he had created it earlier and forgotten. That happened sometimes when he was working too late and losing track of himself. Something about this felt wrong, though. The next episode didn't exist yet. He hadn't even chosen the story for it yet. Besides that, his files went through a very specific series of iterations, he would never jump right to a final version.

Evan clicked on the file name and checked the details in the sidebar. The creation time read 11:35 PM, just three minutes ago. He leaned back and looked around the room, as if someone might be standing behind him, secretly creating new files. No one was, obviously. The laptop had been open in front of him the whole time, and he was alone in his apartment. Evan shook his head and gave a short laugh.

"Probably a listener submission," he said to himself. People emailed him audio all the time. Some of them liked to record their own versions of stories or send voice messages they thought he might use for the show. Still, he did not remember downloading anything tonight. He double-clicked the file, and the audio editor opened the waveform. It filled the screen almost instantly. Evan stared at it. The file was only about 5 minutes long, not even close to the length of a typical episode. He hesitated for a moment, then slid his headphones back over his ears. He pressed play and his own voice came through the headphones.

"Welcome back to Midnight Archive. I'm your host, Evan Cole. Welcome to the last episode."

He froze. The tone was identical to the way he normally opened the show. Evan frowned at the screen.

"I definitely didn't record this," he said. The recording continued.

"Tonight's story comes from a quiet apartment where a man sat alone late at night editing audio for a podcast."

Evan leaned back in his chair. His voice continued to narrate in the calm, steady tone he used for every episode.

"The apartment was dark except for the glow of a laptop screen. The man had been working for hours. The rest of the building was quiet."

Evan glanced around the room. The only light in the apartment was still the laptop. On the recording, his voice went on.

"He paused the audio and rubbed his eyes. He checked the clock above the kitchen counter."

Evan looked up. 11:41 PM. A small knot formed in his stomach. He leaned forward and dragged the cursor back a few seconds. He listened again.

"The apartment was dark except for the glow of a laptop screen."

Evan exhaled through his nose and shook his head.

"Okay," he said quietly. "That's weird." He let the recording continue.

"The man had nearly finished editing the episode when he noticed something strange on his computer."

Evan sat perfectly still.

"The file appeared in his editing folder without warning."

He looked at the screen again. The waveform rolled steadily forward as the audio played.

"He did not remember creating it."

Evan paused the playback. The room was silent again. He removed one side of the headphones and listened for a moment. Nothing. Just the refrigerator humming in the kitchen. He put the headphones back on and hit play.

"The file was labeled Episode 214."

Evan let out a small laugh.

"Very funny," he said.

He scrolled through the waveform. The track stretched on for pages across the timeline. Whoever made this had spent time editing it. The audio looked clean and polished. If it was meant to prank him, it was certainly doing a good job. On the laptop, his voice continued.

"The man believed the file had been sent by a listener."

Evan rubbed the back of his neck.

"Okay, that's a little creepy."

The narration continued.

"But the man had been sitting in front of his computer the entire time. He would have seen an email come in."

Evan's eyes drifted to the file information panel again.

Created: 11:35 PM. Modified: 11:42 PM.

He blinked, and the modification time changed. 11:43 PM. Evan leaned closer to the screen, frowning. His hand moved the cursor toward the end of the timeline, and he watched the waveform extend a little farther. He felt a chill move through him. He stared at the timeline, then he opened the file properties again.

The length of the audio file now read just over 7 minutes. As he watched, it changed to 07:30 and then 07:31. Evan swallowed hard. The recording was growing somehow. He looked around the apartment again, then back at the screen.

"But I'm not recording anything," he said to himself. Evan kept staring at the numbers and saw the file length continue to increase one second at a time. He moved the cursor to the end of the waveform and dragged the timeline farther out. The last few seconds of audio had not fully rendered yet. The shape of the waveform appeared gradually as the seconds passed. Evan removed his headphones and listened to the room. Nothing. He looked down at the laptop again.

"I'm not recording anything," he said again, trying to unspook himself. The microphone icon in the editing software was dark. The record button was not active, and the input levels were flat. He put the headphones back on. The cursor still sat in the middle of the episode where he had paused it. Evan hesitated for a moment, then pressed play again. His voice returned immediately.

"The man checked the file information again."

Evan felt a tightening in his chest.

"He noticed the recording length was still increasing."

Evan let out a quiet breath. "Okay," he said. "That's not fucking funny." The narrator continued without reacting.

"The man realized something else was wrong. The file was still being recorded."

Evan swore and tore his headphones off. He sat back in the chair and stared at the screen.

"Alright," he said to himself. "Who are you, and how the fuck are you doing this?"

He opened the task manager and scanned the running programs. Nothing unusual appeared, just the editing software, his browser, and the podcast hosting dashboard. He refreshed the project folder. The file was still there, but the length had reached 08:42. Evan rubbed his face and let out a slow breath.

"Someone's got to be messing with me," he said. He clicked the file and pressed delete. A small message appeared on the screen stating that the file was in use and unable to be deleted at the moment. Evan frowned.

"In use by what?" He closed the editing software. The message stayed the same, file in use. He tried again, but had no luck. He opened the audio editor once more, and the waveform reappeared. The file length now read 09:07. He stared at it for several seconds before pressing play again. His voice continued the story without missing a beat.

"The man began to feel uneasy."

Evan leaned back in his chair. "Yeah," he said quietly. "No shit." The voice continued.

"He had told hundreds of stories about strange events. He had spent years describing the moment when ordinary people realized something was wrong. But the man had never expected to be inside one of those stories."

Evan felt a cold weight settle in his stomach. On the recording, his voice continued.

"He looked around the apartment again."

Evan turned his head, almost without thinking. The living room was dark, and the hallway beyond it was darker. Nothing moved. Evan turned back to the laptop as the audio continued.

"The man still believed he was alone."

Evan stared at the screen. "What do you mean still?" he said. For a moment the playback was quiet, and then his voice spoke again.

"But stories need listeners."

Evan frowned. "What?"

"A story with only one listener is weak, but a story heard by many becomes stronger."

Evan hesitated, a sick feeling growing in his stomach, and then clicked to open the browser tab with his podcast dashboard. He didn't know what he expected to find, but he had a sudden urge to check. The page loaded, and at the top of the screen was the scheduled episode list.

A new entry sat at the top. "Episode 214 – The Last Episode: Scheduled release: 12:00 AM" Evan felt his pulse begin to quicken.

"I didn't upload that," he said. He leaned closer to the screen. The episode sat at the top of the release schedule. He refreshed the page, but the listing stayed. Evan clicked it, and the episode page opened. The description box contained several lines of text. He read them slowly, his confusion starting to turn into fear. "Tonight's story comes from a quiet apartment where a man sat alone late at night editing a podcast episode." Evan felt his stomach tighten. He scrolled down to the audio file attached to the episode. It was the same one that had appeared on his laptop. The runtime was updating in real time, which it shouldn't have been able to do. 10:12, 10:13, 10:14. Evan stared at the number disbelievingly.

He clicked the scheduling option and switched it from Scheduled to Draft. He hit save, and the page refreshed. The status returned to Scheduled. Evan swore out loud and tried it again. Draft. Save. The page refreshed, and it was once again listed as scheduled for release at midnight. He looked up at the clock. 11:52 PM. Eight minutes. Evan felt the tension spreading through his chest. He switched back to the editing window to find that the episode was still playing. He had forgotten to pause it. He grabbed for his headphones and heard his voice continuing.

"The man discovered that the episode had been scheduled for release at midnight."

Evan stared at the screen.

"You've got to be fucking kidding me."

"The man attempted to stop the upload."

Even as he clicked the delete button, he knew it wouldn't work. The page refreshed, and the episode remained. Evan let out a short laugh that sounded more frightened than amused.

"Shit," he said quietly. He removed the headphones and stood up. The apartment was silent and dark. He walked to the front door and checked the lock, making sure the deadbolt was fully engaged. When he came back to the desk, the audio was still playing softly through the headphones. He picked them up again, and his voice continued the narration.

"The man began to realize something about this particular story. This story was not meant for him."

Evan frowned. "What does that mean?"

Almost as if he were answering himself, he heard his voice respond, "It was meant for the listeners."

Evan turned back to the hosting dashboard. The episode page was still open, and at the bottom of the screen sat the analytics panel. He stared at the download counter. For a moment he thought his eyes were playing tricks on him. The number read: Downloads: 3. Evan blinked. The episode hadn't even been released yet. He refreshed the page, and the number changed. Downloads: 7. As he watched, the number jumped to 12. He stared at the screen.

"That's not possible," he said. The release time still read 12:00 AM. He checked the clock again, but it was only 11:56 PM. Four more minutes until it was even scheduled to be released. Evan refreshed the page again.

Downloads: 19

Downloads: 31

Downloads: 46

Evan leaned back in his chair. "No," he said quietly. "That's not happening." The headphones were still on the desk beside him. The faint sound of his own voice continued to play through them. He picked them up and slipped them back over his ears.

"The man checked the download numbers. He saw that people were already listening. The episode had not been released yet."

Evan stared at the screen, a numb sort of fear coursing through him now. Whatever was happening was more than some weird prank by a listener.

"But the listeners were already there."

Evan rubbed his hands over his face. "This has to be a glitch." He checked the server status page for the hosting service. Everything was normal, there were no outages reported and no warnings about any known issues. Behind him, the apartment remained quiet. In the headphones, the narration continued.

"The man believed the numbers were a mistake."

Downloads: 52

"But stories have a way of finding their audience."

Evan's eyes drifted back to the clock. 11:58 PM. Two minutes. His voice continued in the recording.

"The man did not understand what the listeners were doing."

Evan felt a slow knot tightening in his stomach. "What do you mean doing?"

The narrator answered him. "They were helping."

Evan sat very still. "Helping what?" he asked. The recording continued.

"A story needs listeners."

Evan's eyes flicked back to the screen.

Downloads: 61

"The more listeners a story has…"

Downloads: 74

"…the stronger it becomes."

Evan felt his pulse begin to thump in his ears. He refreshed the page again, his nervousness now escalated to a feverish feeling of panic.

Downloads: 103

"At first, the changes are small."

Evan froze. He hadn't moved, but something in the apartment had. A soft sound came from somewhere behind him. A faint creak, like a floorboard shifting under weight. Evan turned in his chair. The living room was dark, but there was enough light from his computer to see that the room was empty. He turned back to the desk. In the headphones, the words continued.

"But once enough people are listening…"

Downloads: 148

"…the story begins to take shape."

Another sound came from the apartment. A quiet movement from the hallway. Evan held his breath.

"What the hell was that?" he whispered.

"At this point in the story the man thinks that he hears something behind him."

He stared at the laptop screen for a moment longer, then turned his head. Nothing stood there. He exhaled quietly and turned back to the desk.

"I'm losing my fucking mind," he muttered.

Downloads: 192

Evan rubbed his temples. "This is not real."

"The man checks the room again, but sees nothing. He tells himself the sounds are just the building settling."

Evan glanced around again. The apartment building was old. The floors creaked sometimes, pipes knocked in the walls, that was all it was. He leaned forward and refreshed the page again.

Downloads: 247

"But the listeners are still arriving. The story is becoming clearer."

Evan felt his pulse pounding harder now. The clock on his desk changed to 11:59 PM. One minute until midnight, whatever that would mean. Evan stared at the screen.

"I'm shutting this off," he said. "This is insane." He reached for the power button on the laptop.

"The man decides to stop listening."

Evan froze. His hand hovered over the keyboard.

"He believes the story will end if he turns it off."

Evan slowly pulled his hand back.

"But the story does not belong to him anymore."

Downloads: 317

Downloads: 339

"Too many people are listening now."

Evan felt the room around him grow strangely quiet. The faint traffic outside faded. The apartment seemed to hold its breath.

"At this point in the story, the listeners are ready. They want to know why we're all here, what this story will be."

Evan looked up at the clock. 12:00 AM. The episode status on the dashboard changed to "Published" The download number jumped.

Downloads: 421

Evan felt a chill run through him. "Stop," he whispered.

"They are here to listen to a story about a man who valued success and a paycheck over truth. A man who twisted stories to entertain people."

"This was a man who didn't consider who he might hurt in the process, as long as people listened.

Evan heard a soft sound from the hallway. A slow step. Something moving closer. His throat tightened.

"Finally, the man realizes he is not alone."

Evan was frozen, unable to turn around. He kept staring at the laptop screen. The download number climbed steadily.

Downloads: 517

"The man can hear it coming from behind him."

Evan swallowed. Behind him, the floor creaked again. It sounded deliberate, as if someone wanted him to hear it. He closed his eyes.

"This isn't real," he said to himself.

"He tells himself that it's not real, that he's imagining things."

Another creak sounded in the hallway, accompanied by what sounded like the soft thump of a footstep. Evan opened his eyes and stared at the screen again.

Downloads: 579

"But the listeners know better."

Evan felt a cold tightening in his chest. "Who are you? How are you doing this?"

"The ones who are hearing the story. The ones who are helping it happen."

There was a slow step just outside the living room. Evan forced himself to turn his head. The hallway stood empty and dark. Nothing moved. He turned back to the laptop.

Downloads: 648

Evan leaned closer to the screen.

"Stop downloading it," he whispered desperately, clicking on the cancel and delete buttons to no avail.

"The man still believes the story can be stopped. He believes that if the listeners leave…"

Downloads: 745

"…the ending will not come, but the listeners are curious. The man had trained them to expect the unexpected, to revel in the scare."

Another step sounded behind him, this one closer. It sounded like it came from inside the living room. Evan's breath caught. He stared at the laptop screen.

Downloads: 803

"They want to know how the story ends."

Evan felt the air in the room change. Something stood behind him now. He could feel it, just behind his chair.

"At this moment in the story…"

Evan lifted his eyes toward the dark laptop screen's reflection.

"…the man finally understands."

In the reflection, something moved behind him.

"This story was never meant for him. This was his turn to BE the story instead of just profiting off of telling it."

Downloads: 902

Downloads: 941

Downloads: 1,003

"This one was meant for the listeners."

Evan stared at the laptop screen, unable to move or look away.

Downloads: 1,064

His reflection trembled slightly in the dark glass of the screen. Behind him, the shape in the reflection did not move. Evan kept his eyes on it.

"The man sees something behind him."

Evan's hands gripped the edges of the desk.

"He does not turn around."

The reflection seemed to move closer, a tall, dark outline standing just behind the chair. Evan felt his heart beating wildly in his chest.

"Go away," he whispered, almost inaudibly.

"He believes that if he does not look at it..."

Downloads: 1,203

"...it will not be real."

Evan shook his head. "No," he pled. "No, please stop already."

"But the story is already too strong."

Evan felt something move behind him, a faint shift in the air. The reflection changed as the shape leaned closer. Evan's heart pounded. The voice continued.

"The listeners are still arriving."

Downloads: 1,441

"The ending is becoming inevitable."

Evan squeezed his eyes shut. "This is not happening," he whispered.

"The listeners will not be denied…"

Evan opened his eyes. The reflection on the laptop screen had changed again. The shape stood directly behind him now. It was close enough that its outline filled the space over his shoulders. Evan's breath froze in his lungs, and his voice in the recording continued.

"…and the man finally understands that the story is still being recorded."

Evan looked at the audio editor. The timeline was still growing. The waveform continued to stretch farther across the screen.

"And the listeners are waiting for the ending."

Downloads: 1,902

Downloads: 2,041

Downloads: 2,276

Evan felt a hand touch the back of the chair. He jumped and began to turn.

"So the story finally gives them one."

The laptop speakers suddenly filled with noise. A chair scraping across the floor. A sharp breath. Evan's own voice shouting in panic. The recording continued, capturing every sound in the room. The desk slammed against the wall. Something heavy crashed to the floor. Screaming, loud and raw. The waveform spiked across the screen. The download counter kept climbing.

Downloads: 2,500

Downloads: 3,000

The sounds of the struggle continued for several minutes, agonizing shrieks and horrible tearing sounds. Then they stopped, and the waveform graphic on the screen flattened. Silence filled the recording. For a moment nothing happened, then Evan's voice returned. It was calm and steady, exactly the way it sounded at the end of every episode.

"And that concludes the last episode."

Downloads: 5,482

"Thank you for listening."

To my readers,

You're here! I'm so glad you decided to give this book a chance, and made it through to the end. These stories were written over many years, so this has been a long time coming.

I hope you enjoyed them, and I'd love to know what you thought, good or bad. Please stop by my website and let me know! There are links to all my social media accounts there.

I'm really excited about the next project I'm working on, and I can't wait to start sharing that with the world as well. Stay tuned!

Until next time,
Shannon Hatch

www.shannonhatch.com

ABOUT THE AUTHOR

Shannon Hatch is an independent author from Syracuse, NY, where she lives with her husband, two sons, two cats, and the most spoiled pitbull imaginable, Rubble. She is always hard at work on her next unsettling tale.